Sybelia Drive

Sybelia Drive

A NOVEL

KARIN CECILE DAVIDSON

BRADDOCK AVENUE BOOKS

UNCOMMON BOOKS · UNCOMMON READERS

Printed in the United States of America
10 9 8 7 6 5 4 3 2 1

FIRST EDITION, October 2020

ISBN 10: 1-7328956-8-3
ISBN 13: 978-1-7328956-8-3

Cover and chapter illustrations by Annie Russell
Book design by Savannah Adams

Braddock Avenue Books
P.O. Box 502
Braddock, PA 15104

www.braddockavenuebooks.com

Braddock Avenue Books is distributed by Small Press Distribution.

For Mary Mason and Cecile
—my Florida

For Hannah, Zak, and John
—my World

The evening's first fireflies
dance in the air like distant tracers.
– Yusef Komunyakaa

CONTENTS

Sybelia Drive

A NOVEL

GIRL

OCTOBER 1967

Rainey paraded down on us the year my daddy left. It was the year when Daddy traded in our family car for the red-and-white VW bus, Mama took to watching *Peyton Place* on Tuesday evenings, and I attached the gold stars for spelling around my dresser mirror. The Beatles asked us to sit back and enjoy the show from the stereo speakers in Saul's room, and the central Florida sun lit up the house like it was on fire. It wasn't like we didn't all know change was coming, what with Vietnam breathing down my daddy's neck.

On that October morning in 1967, Daddy put on his gray-green uniform and went to war. Mama put on her zigzag mini dress and went grocery shopping at Hull's Marketessen, one of the smallest storefronts on one of the busiest streets in Anna Clara. That was where she met Rainey's mother, Eva. Right in the middle of the produce section, mulling over avocados and melons, they had that dumb conversation about how to choose one. Mama chose Eva instead, dragged her past the checkout registers right out of the door and into our lives. It wasn't like she was a replacement for my daddy; it was just one of those things Mama did, like marrying more than once, or bringing home a stray cat just because it had pretty eyes and then realizing the cat belonged to the Lingstrums around the bend. Not that Eva was a stray or anything.

Of course, Rainey came with her. Straight blond hair and these freckles that coursed across her nose like fine sand. She caught me on the upside of down. Now here was a girl I'd seen before. On the school playground. The girl with the pretty dresses and the charm bracelet that jangled when she moved. She wasn't in my grade, but the one above. She'd shied away from me at school, but now I had her right in my own living room. "You know how to play jacks?" I asked her. She cupped her hands and shook them, then lowered one in a pretend toss. "What about board games?" I pulled her into my room and showed her the boxes piled in one corner—*Life*, *Mystery Date*, an old *Chutes and Ladders*. She only shrugged her shoulders. "You know how to play any cards?" I figured she did. Of course, her answer was, "Go Fish," but she said it more to the shag rug on my bedroom floor than to me.

Pretty soon, Rainey practically lived with us; Eva, too, when she wasn't lounging on a beach somewhere, luring in the GIs on leave. I was thrilled. A friend, all my own. One who'd follow my every step, fasten her arm in mine, and stick to the rules. The way she said my name—"LuLu"—the *L*'s looping around inside her mouth, soft and undecided, made me want her as my friend even more. Right away, I just loved her to death.

Once, as Rainey slept, I scissored her long hair in half, and she woke up with the shoulder-length cut she should have had. Sure, she was surprised, looked at all the blond on her pillow and cried. My mama evened it up where it fell crooked, and then punished me for good measure. And Rainey got used to it. She got used to a lot of things around here. Like getting in on the action, even when there was no action and we had to make some. Spying on Mrs. Laurent next door, knocking over the Callahans' garbage cans and blaming it on the Walbrights' dog, promising to meet my brother Saul at the lake and then stealing his hidden stash of cigarettes and sitting up in the orange trees and smoking.

The road we lived on, Sybelia Drive, circled the lake and curved around big yards and driveways and houses that were mostly one-story. My daddy had built our house, so it was one of the newest in our neighborhood, all one floor with the citrus grove in back and a yard of live oaks out front. We lived on a corner, with lots of windows and sliding glass doors, and I told Rainey if she paid attention, she could see everything that went on.

At the bottom of the road, there was a park with walking paths and scrubby azaleas, a strip of sand beach, and a splintered dock where Saul liked to fish. From there, the lake stretched out, green with hyacinths and warm for the end of October, still perfect for swimming. Rainey and Saul were back at the house getting their suits on, and I waited on the dock, dangling my feet in the water, making the reflection of gray-blue sky and shoreline birches disappear. A blue heron sat on the tallest branch of a cypress at the center of the lake, and I yelled at it to fly away. When it didn't, I thought of other ways to make it move. I wanted to see it take off, wings wide and skimming the clouds.

"LuLu, what are you shrieking about?" Saul called. He came down the path, Rainey and Alan, the Walbrights' only son, following. "We can hear you clear back at the house."

I glanced at the cypress tree. The heron had stayed put.

"No reason," I said. "Just yelling." I jumped up and joined them on the beach. "Besides, y'all take too long. I've been here forever."

"We were waiting for Alan," Rainey said.

"All right then," I said.

Lyman, Alan's yellow Lab, raced onto the beach and, after bumping our legs and barking at the water's edge, jumped in and started paddling.

We followed him, stepping across the sandy bottom and pushing off where the water was deep enough, where the grasses grew up and brushed against our legs. Here, in the cooler currents, we tread water for a few moments, Lyman circling, all of us staring at one other, eventually splashing. I was nine, pretty small for my age, and wore my bright red swimsuit stitched with YMCA swim patches, the one I had on almost every afternoon, even when we weren't swimming. Rainey had a two-piece she'd gotten that summer for her tenth birthday, white with an apron top, decorated with blue and green bows, and a bikini bottom with matching blue and green stripes.

"C'mon," I yelled, then started swimming to the floating dock anchored offshore, at least an Olympic-sized pool's length away from the beach. I raced forward, my arms windmilling, water flying. By the time I touched the dock's edge, Rainey was just beginning to make her way with careful strokes. She kept her head above water and then finally gave in to the glassy lake and slid under. I practiced my backstroke, thinking of my daddy and the way he'd cross the lake in a crawl and then return, always on his back, staring up, taking his time, his arms reaching up and over and back, up and over and back. I thought of how slow he went and how fast I wanted to go, how one day I might just break a world record.

Rainey surfaced, and we floated facedown and then on our backs. Alan swam past us and kept going, like my daddy, in search of another shore, but then circled back and climbed the dock's ladder. He paused there, seventeen and tall, nearly a grown-up, and motioned for us to come up too. Lyman, with a tug from Alan, clambered onto the smooth boards and planted himself, barking and barking. Saul, older than me by three years, stood in the center and shouted at us. "Move out of the way!" The show-off in his cutoffs. He jumped high with his legs tucked to his chest in a dumb-boy cannonball, water everywhere, Rainey squealing even though she was already wet. Then I climbed the ladder and tried flips off the diving board and smacked the lake's surface, all crooked and sideways. Alan pointed to me and said, "Watch," then took three steps, vaulted off the dock's diving board, and disappeared without a splash. Rainey asked him to teach her the same and, in just a few tries, her long arms and legs sliced the surface, just a tail of water coming off her arched feet.

Alan wasn't as quiet as Rainey, but almost. He stood straight in his faded madras shorts, Rainey balanced on his shoulders, her toes curled next to his collarbone, both at attention, the day turning white and drawn. Later, I'd remember this. How Alan hadn't yet decided to enlist in the U.S. Army. How Rainey would eventually practice her diving alone. But then, at that moment, before the clouds moved in, before the wind and sheets of rain broke the lake's mirror into whitecaps, Rainey touched her toes and grazed the top of Alan's head and dove as if in search of an answer, as if breaking the water would tell us why the world would soon fly into pieces.

For all that we knew, one day leading into another, all the days adding up from the seconds we were living, no idea of what might come, that day wasn't so different from others. Another Sunday, the weekend more than half over, another week of school before us. We stretched out on the dock in the sun. Saul, nearest the ladder, on his side, whistling. Rainey with her knees under her chin next to Alan, who leaned back on his arms and looked into the distance. I sat on the diving board, above the others, the rough surface of the platform under my crossed legs. I considered breaking the quiet and telling the others of the latest world record for cliff diving, for the 100-meter backstroke. I imagined how many gold stars it would take to make a gold medal. Alan might be impressed, but Saul would just tell me to shut up. And Rainey would listen, because she always did. Instead, Alan started talking.

"What's the earliest you've ever gone swimming in this lake?"

"We've got to go to school in the mornings," I said. "And on weekends we're lazy and don't come down until the afternoon."

"What about you?" Rainey asked Alan.

"Sometimes at daybreak, before the sun's even up. It's peaceful then. No motorboats, no water-skiers." He reached for Lyman's head, the flat of his palm pressing against the wet, blond coat. "It's like the times when my dad and I go out hunting. At first there's the sound of the outboard, until we choose a spot and land. Then we sit and wait, wait and sit. Mostly the waiting and the quiet are unnerving. I just want to lay my gun down and walk away. But I don't. The marsh around us buzzes with insects, and the reeds are so tall they hide everything. Then finally the blue teal show up. We raise our shotguns and ruin the quiet. Lyman here pushes through the reeds and finds the birds, their feathers damp and their bodies still warm. Then we get back in the boat and head home. That's all I think about the entire time we sit and wait. Heading home."

"How can you stand that?" Saul gripped one side of the dock's ladder and pulled himself up.

"How can I stand what?" Alan said. "The waiting? Or bringing down the birds?"

Saul didn't answer, just stared.

"I've done both for as long as I can remember. I'm good at both." He smiled at Saul, who balanced on the ladder's top rung. "Try it sometime."

"No way," Saul answered and jumped backwards into the lake.

"You like hunting?" Rainey tugged on the ends of her hair and looked sidelong at Alan.

"Like I said, I'm good at it."

The afternoon went on from there with Saul swimming back to the beach, throwing a towel around his shoulders, and walking barefoot up the path to our house. Rainey and I sat alone, watching Alan swim across the lake to his own yard, the one with the glass walls that faced the water. Lyman lay between us, the autumn sun warming his side and making him pant a little. Soon enough, the rain clouds shifted the day from open to closed, the sun gone, a sharp breeze in its place. Coaxing the Lab to follow us, we swam to shore, the rain already coming down. We grabbed our dripping wet towels from the sand, and ran up the path shouting to Lyman, "Go on home!" I didn't like the way the day had turned, dark and uncertain, and the knotted-up, bothered way it made me feel. My daddy always said if you don't like something, then figure out a way to change it. Just like he said to hightail it out of the lake if we ever heard thunder, and running as fast as we could, we were almost home before the first rumbles shook the ground.

My daddy, Charles Royal Blackwood III, was ranked a sergeant in the U.S. Marine Corps, his uniform sleeve decorated with three chevrons and a pair of crossed rifles. Mama had long since dubbed him Royal Three, which then became R3, nicknames Saul and I agreed were not only dumb but embarrassing, especially when she'd call out to him at the lake, at church, even at the bowling alley. "R3, come on out of that water and sit by me," she'd call from her lawn chair, "I'm missing you." And settling into the fifth pew on the right, "Royal Three, honey, hold my gloves just a sec." And then, squinting through her cigarette smoke, "R3, pick out a ball for me. One that's gonna get me some strikes."

Saul knew him as more of a father than his own, a handsome, hot-tempered Marine by the name of Isaac Finch Edwards, our mama's first husband, whom she'd divorced long before he met his demise on a beach in Qui Nhơn. I was sure he'd been dead to Saul long before he was killed in action. Until he left for Vietnam, my daddy had always been there, for Saul as much as for Mama and me. And as if to prove that point, Mama called her oldest "Saul B," subtracting from the Edwardses and adding to the Blackwoods, reworking family history and family names so that it suited her. She did like to keep things simple.

◊ ◊ ◊

Though it had only been weeks since my daddy left, that day kept flying back to me. Like I said, I was pretty small, more like a six-year-old really. Daddy touched the crown of my head, and his hand rested a moment, something he'd done since I could remember. Like a shared whisper between just the two of us, it always calmed me. He swung me up in his arms and hugged me hard, kissed me even, but in a way that seemed lost and faraway, then landed me lightly on the ground. His black hair was shaved so closely I could see his tanned scalp.

"You mind your mama," he said. "Don't sass her. When you feel a sass coming on, recite to yourself: romeo, sierra, tango. Then you'll be good to go."

"Yes, sir," I told him, pulling hard on the grommets of his duty bag, where they were cinched tight.

The night before I had emptied the duffel, hiding all his things under my bed—his pressed uniform shirts and trousers, coiled leather belts, white undershirts and socks the color of black coffee. Except for the one pair of socks I'd pushed to the back of my own sock drawer, he'd found and repacked everything without even taking me to task. I hated that he was leaving, and he knew it. Before he lifted his gear and turned to go, he held my chin for a long second. I looked up, convincing myself not to cry, and stared hard into his face. His eyes were my eyes almost, dark brown with gold flecks. Sad, uncertain eyes. He dropped his gaze and pushed through the screen door, calling back over his shoulder, heading toward the VW bus where Mama waited in the driver's seat. Through the engine's thrum, I swear he said he'd be right back.

And then practically three weeks went by, so I gave up on his coming right back. But that promise kept pushing in on me, making me mean. No military alphabet could save me. One minute I'd be yelling, "November, oscar, papa!" and then slamming on some other fourth grader at recess, and the next I'd be in the principal's office. Rainey watched me waling on other kids and maybe wondered if I'd do the same to her. But that wasn't how I imagined things. All I knew was, while I missed my daddy, I did have my friend. But Rainey couldn't promise me anything either. A good girl, she always tried her best to stay out of trouble—in my mind, a terrible waste of time. Who needed to be good? But Rainey leaned that way. Her memories were muted scraps of show tunes her father once sang; mine were of my daddy whistling, swinging me into the air, and if he had to, whipping the mess out of me and Saul with his leather belt.

Instead of a father, Rainey had a bracelet that she kept in a little round box. Unlike the rose-gold wristlet her mother had given her, this one was silver, engraved with her father's name and military rank, and marked with a little blue star inside a white circle, a symbol that I knew from Saul meant *missing in action*. Sometimes I'd catch her holding it, running her fingers over the grooved letters. "I want to see," I'd say, but she always put it away once she realized I was there. Secret with her things, even her feelings, Rainey knew to hide that cloth-covered box. Her father, a captain, had vanished, and in his place was this silver band.

From the beginning, there were things Rainey knew that I had no idea of. Like how to wish away a father's good-bye, how to hold the sadness like a pillow instead of a stone, how to keep hoping for a chance to glimpse him again even though the chance grew smaller and smaller every day.

And then there were things I knew that Rainey didn't. Like how to sneak into houses when everyone slept. How to slide open doors, step around dogs, slip little things into a pants pocket, and leave no trace. She didn't know how many times I'd been in Alan's house, how I'd walked barefoot down the hallway past the entry table, run my fingertips over the keys nestled in a shallow tray, eyed the leash hanging by the front door. In his mother's kitchen, the drawers were full of unsharpened pencils, string, seed packets. I'd taken the crumpled ones, marigolds and daisies, and planted them in our front yard, where eventually they sprouted, then crowded the walkway. I'd stood in the Walbrights' living room and stared into the dining room through a glass cabinet filled with crystal and colored glass and china cups. The little glass bird I'd taken—a present for my mama on her birthday—sat now on the windowsill above our kitchen sink, the sun bending through it every morning, a glimmering blue-green line across the floor.

And so, that night, after we'd run back from the lake and had our supper and gone to bed, I woke Rainey and said, "Let's go." She sat up and rubbed her eyes, seeming confused. But then she slid out of the covers and followed along, whispering, "Where are we going?" and "LuLu, wait up." Still in our pajamas, we ran barefoot through backyards, past puddles and swimming pools, stepping over garden hoses and around swing sets. Just in front of us, a lone firefly lit up, like a tiny bare bulb in all the darkness. Cricket song rattled the air, and tree frogs chirped in loops and bounces. Most of the houses were dark, but the blue light of a television set or the warm yellow of a lone reading lamp reminded us that some neighbors were still awake.

The Walbrights' glass windows gleamed against the night. The evening storm had moved on, the nearly round moon dull behind the remaining clouds. Alan's bedroom was at one end of the hall, facing the road. He'd see the glare of headlights all night long, his windows high and horizontal, unlike the floor-to-ceiling windows in the rest of the house. I hesitated for a second by the front door, and Rainey bumped up against me.

"Watch it," I said. My whisper sounded sharp, and she looked a little hurt.

Nobody in the neighborhood locked their doors, and Lyman lifted his head as we moved over the parquet floors. I leaned down to stroke his ears and he settled. Shadows landed here and there, and Rainey took hold of my hand. The door to Alan's room was closed, and I pushed it open quickly so the hinges wouldn't sigh. The room was like velvet, black and thick with quiet. Duck calls, like wooden tops, lined the back of his dresser. And I wanted one. A piece of Alan.

Rainey tripped and fell against me, and from across the room a light clicked on. Sitting up, Alan squinted at us.

"What?" My voice ricocheted, too loud.

"You're in my room," Alan said. "You tell me what."

"We came to steal something."

Alan had on pajamas with long sleeves and a pocket just above his heart. Uncreased and perfect, they were nothing like the boxers Saul slept in, no shirt at all. Rainey and I stood there in our baby doll PJs—all polka dots and puffed sleeves—so what did it matter? Rainey looked down, the top of her head blond and shy. She was embarrassed, and I didn't care.

"Really?" Alan said. He laughed and sat up straighter. "Well, go right ahead. I'd love to see what you take."

I reached for the smallest duck call, black with white letters on one side – P.S. OLT.

"That one? But it's so boring. Not even pretty."

The rest of the calls were wooden, polished, bright. I took the small black Olt and stared at Alan.

"Come over here," he said.

I padded over the cool floorboards and stood beside his bed. Rainey didn't follow at first and then came halfway, stopping under the windows, a row of patterned curtains above her head. Alan held out his hand, motioning to the little call in mine. I held it tight, afraid he'd take it away and not give it back.

"I want to show you something," he said.

I leaned toward him, opened my hand, the Olt in my palm. His fingers grazed mine. He touched the call to his lips, and then held it away. "Not like this." He puffed his cheeks and pretended to blow. "Like this, see?" He coughed softly, the air pushing up from his chest and through his mouth, the call inches away. "I'm not really going to demonstrate." He flipped the call around between his thumb and index finger, then smiled and added, "Too loud."

I nodded and noticed his breath, how it was somewhere between sweet and musky.

"This is a good one." He placed the slim call back in my hand and let his fingers stay around it a minute. "I'm not giving it to you, though. You're outright stealing it. Understood?"

Alan winked at me and surveyed Rainey, and I grabbed the Olt just as Rainey found my wrist and pulled.

The bedside lamp went out before we'd even found the doorway, and in the dark we felt for the bedroom door.

Patterns crisscrossed the hall floor from the outside porch light. Carefully, we stepped around Lyman through the front entry and into the night.

At home, Rainey already asleep in the bed we shared, I fingered the little call, thought of biting the mouthpiece, leaving my own teeth marks where Alan had once left his. I touched the letters – O L T – and knew I was bad. And I felt right for being bad. I always did.

Sunlight, creeping from the windows to the bed, woke me the next morning. Rainey's side of the bed was empty, a crumpled mess of covers. I sat up. I was always the first one awake, so her absence bothered me. She was probably sitting in the kitchen with a bowl of cereal and a book.

I pulled my pajamas off and a school dress on, sliding the Olt into a front pocket, and padded down the hallway. Saul's bedroom door was closed and so was Mama's. Mama was always the first one stirring, so it had to be earlier than early.

The starburst wall clock in the kitchen wasn't even hitting seven yet. And Rainey wasn't sitting at the table. I searched the living room, the porch, then slipped on sneakers and went outside into the backyard. The grove was loud with birdsong, and in the next yard Mrs. Laurent was standing over her camellias like she sometimes did. Mama said she was French or something, which is why she had an accent and wore her hair in a twist. She glanced over and then went back inside her house.

I had an awful feeling that Rainey had called Eva in the middle of the night to come and get her. That dragging Rainey out to steal from Alan had been a dumb idea. I patted the duck call in my pocket and felt right away the little knot of badness that made me feel safe and real and ready to go on. By this time I'd circled the house and stood in the front yard facing Sybelia Drive. Down aways was the lake and I began to run, certain Rainey was there, hopefully sitting on the fishing dock with her feet in the water and not drowned in the grasses between shores.

I flew down the path, only tripping once on tree roots. Just past a stand of birches, where Lyman lay, I stopped and stared. Out on the floating dock were two figures, tall, reaching, and quiet. Flat feet, then tiptoes, arms overhead, stretching, then springing together into the lake, the barest of splashes. Rainey and Alan diving. He was teaching her simple forward dives from the edge, jackknifes from the board, and then he held her waist as she arched into a back dive, pulling up at the last minute and shaking her head.

"Hey!" I yelled.

Rainey and Alan turned toward me, and Lyman raised his head.

"What are you doing?" I said, knowing full well what they were doing.

"Practicing diving," Rainey called.

Alan waved to me to join them. But I had on my school dress, and it was Monday morning. A day filled with teachers, rows of desks, chalk dust. Not a swimming day.

"Come on in," Alan said, his voice unmistakably clear, carrying across the water.

"Can't." I pointed to my sneakers, pulled on my pockets.

"Run get your suit on," Rainey said. She leaned down and touched the lake surface. "The water's still so warm."

I considered missing breakfast, the pledge of allegiance, arithmetic problems at the blackboard, morning recess. Rainey was asking me to be bad, and she didn't even know it.

"Okay," I said and ran back home to change.

Of course, when I got there, Mama was setting the table for breakfast.

"Well, look who's up already." She tried to hand me a little stack of plates. "Make yourself useful, please."

I thought a quick second, then said, "No," and skirted around her, knowing she wouldn't break the breakfast plates just to catch me.

I raced down the hall, snatched my damp swimsuit from the bathroom doorknob, and took off out the back door. I could hear Mama calling me. "LuLu!" I huddled behind the azaleas, kicked off my shoes, and pulled my dress off and my suit on. In minutes I'd crossed over the road and neared the end of the path, barely out of breath. The lake glinted with sunlight and the movements of swimmers, Rainey and Alan already swimming to shore. Now I'd be in trouble twice-times without even having gotten wet. I splashed my feet in the shallows and kicked at a school of minnows.

"You missed out," Alan said. He picked up a striped towel lying on the beach.

I couldn't figure his friendly tone. I had run home and all the way back and they hadn't even waited. Then again, I had the Olt from right off his dresser. The one in my—and then I remembered my dress under the azaleas, the wide pockets that didn't hold much. I hoped the duck call hadn't fallen out.

"You have to come with us next time." Rainey twisted her hair, no longer quite long enough to reach over one shoulder, teasing out the lake water.

Suddenly I felt forced into a place I didn't want to be. Early mornings, and another kind of lesson. I already had school and swim club at the Y. I had the "alpha, bravo, charlie" moments of learning and listening and being good.

"I don't have to do anything," I said.

Alan cinched his towel around his waist, and it ended just above his knees. He shook his head and smiled. "Why are you always fighting so hard? The world's not so mean."

I stared up at him. His smile was infuriating. Even the pattern of stripes on his towel made me mad.

"It is so." My voice caught and made me sound smaller than I already was.

Lyman stretched and padded over to us. Alan palmed the dog's head, all the while watching me. Rainey drew her toes through the sand and sighed.

"It is so, Rainey," I said.

"It's not really." Alan touched me lightly on the arm. "You just have to let things be. Not get so angry all the time."

"I'm allowed. I can be mad if I want. Who says I can't be?"

"See? There you go again. You'll figure it out, though. Someday you won't have to have your fists up. In fact," Alan said, as he turned and started walking away, "I'll bet on it."

I didn't know what to do or say and desperately wanted the last word. And so I called, "You don't know anything, Alan Walbright! You don't know anything at all!"

He didn't turn around, just threw out a wave, and then whistled for Lyman to follow. I guessed he was smiling to himself, because he always was.

Back at the house, Rainey and I threw on our dresses, ate cold scrambled eggs, and let Mama's scolding bounce around the kitchen. I hid the duck call under my pillow, and we weren't even late to school.

The weeks had thrown us straight into a dry November, with long spelling lists and longer grammar lessons. Every day

I stared at the clock above the world map and watched it tick down the minutes, which seemed to stretch out into forever as the long hand approached twelve, the short hand three. Making sure my teacher wouldn't see, I closed up my notebook and took hold of my things so that when the bell finally rang, I could fly out the door and down the hall and onto the playground for one last climb on the monkey bars. Rainey always waited for me, standing by the swings with her red plaid book bag in her hand. I could tell if she felt in a good mood by the way she'd swing the bag from its handle, her charm bracelet singing. Today she was standing still, her head tilted back and her eyes blinking at the sky, pale blue and cloudless.

Rainey and I set out for home, our school bags dragging in the dirt, and the dirt billowing around our bare legs. The path was dusty and the afternoon sun was too hot, and I longed for a glass of iced water, or better yet, something sticky and bright like a grape Nehi. Rainey hummed a song that Saul played on his stereo. I knew it by heart. I knew the whole album by heart—*Rubber Soul*. In class, instead of working on my long division, I'd written down the words to all of the songs inside the pages of my math book. The lines of "Girl," the song I associated with Rainey, edged the lessons on fractions and rational numbers, and surrounded the homework sections on probability, a unit we hadn't gotten to yet. Saul was certain it wasn't the lovesick lack of regret recorded in ink, but the way the first song brought girls and love and cars together that upset my teacher and steered Mrs. Esther Wild, the principal, to the usual consequences. I had to stay after school for weeks—cleaning blackboards, sharpening pencils, and learning my long and short division—but staying after was something I was used to.

We'd taken the shortcut and made our way over the spindly grass in the backyard. I shoved the kitchen door open and saw right away that Eva was back. Her long weekends away were more frequent now, and her weekday arrivals unpredictable and surprising. Even though it was hot, she and Mama were in the middle of making pies. Eva had her hair up and light blond tendrils fell around her face, which was flushed from the preheated oven and the labor of combining flour with butter. Rainey studied her mother, then the rolling pin, moving back and forth over the pale sheets of dough. I noticed how she didn't say hey or lean forward to kiss Eva's flour-dusted cheek, how she set down her satchel and backed herself against the counter farthest away from the kitchen table. Eva looked up and smiled, then laughed out loud, like seeing us was the best thing in the world. She even stretched out her long, tanned arms and threw us kisses. Pretty, pretty Eva, who laughed so easily. Rainey didn't laugh like that. She was careful and quiet and only sometimes smiled. Getting her to laugh was harder.

"Hey, baby," Eva said to Rainey. "Hey, Miss LuLu. Come over and give me a squeeze."

I let Eva hug me and kiss me on the top of my head, and I breathed in the spicy, sweet *Shalimar* she dabbed on the insides of her wrists and elbows and at the back of her neck. My mama stood at the sink washing up mixing bowls, whisks, and wooden spoons. She wore perfume, too, but not every day like Eva.

Rainey edged along the counter and avoided her mother's reach and sweet-pitched cries of "Oh, come on now, baby!" Rainey's red plaid bag, its buckles unfastened, leaned heavily to one side and fell over, spilling a neat pile of workbooks and colored pencils and school library books. Eva wiped her hands on her apron and picked up the pencils and books to put them back in the bag. She held a copy of *Beezus and Ramona* in one hand and fingered the torn jacket.

"What a funny title," she said softly, more to herself than to me or my mother and her dishwater or to Rainey now in the other room. "Have you read this, LuLu? Looks like it might be funny."

I stooped to scratch an itch on my leg and examined the floor, a good way not to answer a question I had no answer to. I didn't have a bag full of books like Rainey. I had YMCA swim patches, shortcuts through neighbors' yards, and things I'd stolen. But not library books or any other books, not hiding under the sheet with a flashlight reading, not bookmarks cut from old postcards and discarded recipes.

And then as if reading my mind, Eva widened her ocean-colored eyes and went on. "We're kind of the same, aren't we?" She returned to dusting the disks of flour and rolling them even thinner than they already were. "All that reading is saved for girls like my Rainey. All those words. Why, some stories sweep you out of this world into another, but others...Well, others go on and on and make no sense."

Still unsure of how to respond, I said, "I guess so."

"Well, sure." Eva spun a layer of light dough around the rolling pin and let it uncurl over a pie pan. "We have better things to do. Making pies, watching movies, waiting for whatever happens next in this crazy world. Your mama and I know a thing or two about crazy, now don't we, Minnie?"

There was my chance and I took it. Attention had turned back where it belonged, between grown-ups. I slipped past Eva, opened the fridge, and grabbed two bottles of grape Nehi before my mama could catch me and tell me to put them back.

In the living room, Rainey and I stood in front of the oscillating fan and sipped our cold purple drinks, and in the kitchen our mothers were laughing again.

In my room, Rainey and I sat facing each other in the woven hoop chairs my mama had moved in from the porch. Mama liked to think the porch was too chilly to sit on now that it was November, even though the stifling days still lingered. Patchwork throws and hand-stitched pillows were supposed to make the wicker chairs seem like indoor pieces, but they still smelled of summer dust and mildew.

With my feet up on the seat, I held Alan's little black Olt between my thumb and forefinger, like he had, and wagged it back and forth. Rainey stared at me over her book. Impatient, I kicked at the side of her chair.

"Why do you always have to read?" I asked.

"Why do you always have to steal things?" She stared back down at her book.

"Old *Beezus-and-Ramona* face," I said, in a taunting sing-song voice.

Rainey ignored me. I kicked at the book and missed, hitting her squarely in the chin. She threw the book down and held her hands over her mouth. I felt the meanness welling up in me, making me warm and giddy and glad. She didn't say anything for a minute and her eyes watered.

"You are mean," she finally said. "And you take things from people like Alan, who never even did anything to you. You are mean, mean, mean."

I'd gotten Rainey all riled up. I just couldn't keep myself from fussing with her. Getting Rainey to see me straight on and wide-eyed was a thrill, just like seeing the wrinkle and smart in her usually quiet face. And so I grinned at her and stood up on the chair, bouncing slightly, singing "Rainey likes Alan, Rainey likes Alan, Rainey wants to kiss and hug A—" The chair made a cracking sound and I fell right through, my feet on the floor and my hands flying forward, the duck call spinning to the ground. I landed right on top of Rainey.

"LuLu! Get off me!" she yelled, slapping her hands at my face and shoulders.

We were face-to-face, me laughing and her nearly crying.

"Girls?" my mama called from across the house.

"Rain, baby, you okay?" Eva asked, her voice coming closer.

I pushed myself back and stepped out of the gaping seat of the hoop chair, which looked like a broken basket with black iron legs. Eva peeked into the room, and Rainey immediately sat up straight, her expression like stone. And then Mama was there, taking stock, examining the broken chair, unaware of Rainey's bruised, slightly swollen lower lip.

"LuLu Blackwood," my mama said.

"Yes, Mama."

"You know better."

Though most times I wouldn't, I shook my head in agreement. Easier right then to agree, than take on my mama's wrath. I would have to behave, she said, her words at first stern, but then filled with breath, floating up to the ceiling. I would have to calm down and think about acting the fool before I started acting the fool. I would have to clean up my mess. I nodded my head and mumbled "Yes, ma'am" again and again. Then Saul was in the hallway, silently mouthing ugly words at me from behind Mama's and Eva's backs. I knew how to ignore him and looked down, as if I were miserable and sorry, in truth searching the floorboards for the duck call.

Soon we would have supper and the bad tempers would flatten, like the paper napkins unfolded into our laps. Rainey would crease her forehead and hold her water glass to her mouth, a cool, even surface for her anger. Saul's loud comments would bring on Mama's shushing and Eva's sighs. And I would think of Alan and his madras shorts, his slicked hair, his laughter and the way he leaned back on the dock. I'd wonder if he missed the tiny Olt, found that evening in a corner of my bedroom beside the stack of board games, and tucked again between my pillowcase and pillow.

Blackberry and cherry pies sat on the counter. Supper had gone on too long with too much talking and Eva and my mama drinking wine out of a pale green bottle. We'd eaten plates of creamed chicken and biscuits, sliced tomatoes, and iced tea, and the cooled pies were next. Saul glanced at them, at the lit cigarette in Mama's hand, and then kept on going out the door. Mama didn't even call after him, just let him go. Rainey twisted a strand of hair around her fingers over and over and over. Our mothers laughed over nothing, over the dumbest things. How the palm trees at West Palm Beach leaned east, not west. How that Walbright boy—"What's his name again, Rainey?"—had grown so tall. How ever since Mia Farrow had left *Peyton Place*, the show had gone downhill.

"Oh, but you have to love Gena Rowlands," my mama said.

"That kiss on the beach," Eva replied, which sent them off again, slapping the table top and then each other, breathless with fits of laughter.

Eventually, Eva pushed her chair back and stood up, pausing to down her last sip of wine. She brought both pies to the kitchen table, then put a fork into the center of the blackberry pie and raked out a bite.

"Lord, Eva. Help yourself," my mama said. "Don't be shy."

I remembered the rhyme about blackbirds in a pie, four and twenty, how loudly they'd have sung. Rainey frowned at her mother. Maybe Rainey wished for kings and queens and pattycake babies, for pie wedges on china plates, but I knew better. We were expected to behave, go out and play, stay out of our parents' hair, mind our manners, finish our suppers. But we didn't have any right to expect anything at all, not from grown-ups, not from life. That's why I took things. I knew if I didn't, I'd miss out. And there was no sense in that.

Eva had the fork in her mouth, and then a berry stain across her lips. I figured she was exactly who she'd always been. Rainey probably wanted a mother who stayed around, who did more than show up to bake pies, or drink wine, or whatever she felt like. But instead she got Eva. Eva, who came and went. Who mostly went.

Soon, Eva would stop showing up and Rainey would live with us on Sybelia Drive all the time. Eva might come by on a Monday and stay through Tuesday, but that was rare. When she did, though, she'd sleep the days away as if she hadn't slept in a long, long time, and Rainey would sit on the edge of the bed, waiting for her mother to wake up. I'd stand in the hall, waiting too, the door to the bedroom halfway open. Eva on her side, her cheek upturned, her face made up like she had someplace to go, and Rainey leaning over her, whispering and stroking the slim wrist that lay outside the covers. The rose-gold daisies, dogs, roller skates, seashells and stars of her bracelet fell apart and together as Rainey moved, and a soft bejeweled jingle fell too brightly against the quiet and against the waiting. Later, she'd tell me how her mother had given her the circlet of charms and how she only wore it because she felt she had to. The ruckus that I once raised with Rainey by then would seem old and used, and so I would leave her alone.

But at that moment I followed the leader and ate the pie from the pan, grinning at Eva, staring at Rainey, who sat in a straight-backed chair with her knees touching her chin and wouldn't even taste the tart berry filling. For the first time, being bad, eating straight out of the pan, and laughing out loud felt wrong. Rainey's look told me all this. She was a girl who'd come out of nowhere, from a moment in the grocery, after my daddy in his uniform left for Vietnam, when my mama was losing her mind and lonely and grabbing on to anyone she could, even a complete stranger named Eva who seemed to have fallen from the crazy blue sky. Something right then in Rainey's expression caught me and told me to stop and quit acting dumb and pay attention. She asked me with her eyes, and our mothers meanwhile shrieked and laughed and opened another bottle of sweet wine.

The next morning was a Saturday. I'd slept late and threw off the covers and quickly pulled on my red swimsuit, thinking of how I'd wasted most of the morning, how I'd be ready to race to the lake before anyone else. The hoop chairs were covered in yesterday's clothes, the one with its gaping hole. It would be so easy to stomp a hole in the good one, to wreck it into sisterhood with the ruined one.

I stopped in the hallway outside my parents' room. When Eva came, she slept in the big bed with my mama. "What with R3 gone, what difference does it make?" Mama'd said more than once, answering Saul's scowls, and my tugging at her, saying how we were like twins now that Rainey was sharing my bed. The big, windowed room was neat, the bed made up, and Eva's light brown suitcase and turquoise makeup case with compartments and pockets and inside mirror already gone. Most of the time I wanted Mama to leave me be, but I always checked on those days Eva left to make sure Mama was in the house and hadn't gone off with her.

I tramped through the living room into the kitchen, where sunlight spilled from the windows and the open back door. On the little dinette table, small plates edged in a rose petal design, Mama's china, and the uncovered cherry pie sat facing each other. A good fraction of the pie gone, a knife lay to one side. Saul sat on the back steps with his back to the doorway. He laughed, and I called to him.

"Saul! You ate nearly all the pie. And on Mama's rose petal plates. She's gonna—"

And then I saw Rainey and Alan beyond him, sitting in lawn chairs with plates on their laps. I stood in my red swimsuit, tracing the YMCA patches sewn near my hip, and felt dumb. Alan smiled, one foot resting on Lyman's blond back, and Rainey barely blinked at me, then kept eating, tiny bits of cherry on her fork.

"She's gonna what?" Saul turned to me, then slid his plate across the kitchen floor toward my feet. The porcelain met the polished linoleum, and the plate went flying. It slammed into my ankle, but didn't break. And then the surprising pinch of pain, the plate's fine edge leaving a mark, within minutes a welt. I heard a fork settle on a plate, and inside the tiny twist of pain I felt distinct, set off from Rainey and Alan, and especially Saul.

"Nothing," I said, embarrassed and unsettled and finally riled. "Nothing!"

The day would go on from there, the dishes washed and dried before Mama got back from the grocery, the still lake shrouded in late morning mist until we tested its temperature, one hoop chair put out by the trash. As the weeks stretched out into winter, bright blue and endless, too cold for swimming, Alan's visits grew scarce and then stopped. Saul and Rainey read together on the couch in the afternoons before supper, and I considered homework before boredom. I subtracted five and carried two, the same Beatles song moving around inside my mind, the one that had been there for a while. The one about the girl who came and stayed. Rainey then became the idea of Rainey, the girl I'd fastened into my heart, the girl I'd taken for more rides than she could stand, until she'd had enough and needed to catch her breath and back away from my careening, reckless world. And eventually, though I never stopped thinking about it, I stopped leaving the house after dark in search of things to take, things I imagined made me happy.

THREE WINDOWS

OCTOBER 1968

Behind my desk in the principal's office at Anna Clara Elementary are three long windows that face east. I like to think of beginnings when the morning light pours over my shoulders and the ten o'clock recess bell rings. The children whose mothers are beginning to look for office jobs, whose fathers are fighting in far-off places where the sun rises a day earlier, whose brothers are older and given more responsibility than they should already have, whose sisters are younger and may not remember the way their parents once carried them on their shoulders. The sound of children yelling, the swipe of jump ropes hitting the ground, the repeating squeak of the swings as they rise higher and higher, level with the sun.

Eventually, I stand up and observe the multicolored corduroyed boys, the polka-dotted girls, the page-boy trimmed teachers. Running, jumping, standing still. Leaning in and laughing, racing round and yelling. Primary patterns, primary colors, numbered primers. I think of the artist, Jasper John. Something modern for the tired curriculum, for the two girls standing together and staring up at me. I wave at them and they wave back and then shout, "Morning, Mrs. Wild."

"Good morning, Rainey, LuLu," I say to them, but they can't really hear me.

The second-grade teacher swings the handbell that announces the time to line up. Avocado boys and persimmon girls frown a bit, their shoulders lowering, and fall in behind their teachers. Twelve lines for our little elementary school. Slowly, they disappear into the building to wind through the hallways back to their chalk-scented classrooms. Numbers and letters and construction paper await them.

Outside, the swings are still. Only their shadows move across the playground.

THE PETERSON FIELD GUIDE TO BIRDS

APRIL 1970

Alan was a good boy. He grew up when things were easy in the world, and he kept up his end of that easiness. Good grades, chores done, friends that stayed friends. Up to the very end. Up until the day he died.

He wasn't so different from most boys back in the '50s. Tall, lanky, with dark brown hair like his father's and light brown eyes like mine, and a grin that lit him up. Like the Walbright men before him, he liked to follow the rules, not for lack of curiosity, but out of respect for those who had already paved the way. He didn't cheat; he didn't lie; he didn't steal. He laughed at his father's jokes when I didn't; he kept his elbows at his sides and off the table at dinner; he rested against me when we watched *My Three Sons*, once surprising me, asking why he had no brothers. I didn't answer, not wanting the truth to sit like a wedge between us, the simple fact that I couldn't have any more children, and as if he knew, he never asked again.

Back straight and head angled, he listened to his father tell stories about his side of the family. Jack, ignoring my sighs, would go on about rifles and heroics and medals of honor. Tales of those who fought in wars—Germany, France, Korea—fell around our supper table like the shotgun casings, duck feathers, and debris from Jack and Alan's hunting trips. Jack explained that learning to aim and shoot was not just for sport; it would lead to duty.

A few days after his high school graduation, Alan took stock of all he'd learned and enlisted in the army. In May 1969 he boarded a Greyhound for infantry training just one northerly state away, but Georgia may as well have been a nation away. The diesel fumes of the bus station, the springtime heat, and the initial goodbyes crowded against the memory of Alan's departure from the airbase in Orlando that September, when he received his orders for Vietnam.

Six months later, the world leaned hard to one side. 1970, not even half spent, became a new decade going straight to hell. There was a rift in the days, an opening I fell through, Jack peering down, not reaching to catch me, the wide expanse of silver lake below. I fell for days and somehow, once I landed, the splash was gentle. I floated, suspended between what was real and imagined, wanting another drink, wanting to swim out into the middle, surrounded by flat water, and lie on my back looking up at nothing but the white, blank April sky. No heaven, no clouds, only an unfinished canvas, a wash of drifting thoughts.

I knew that I wanted not to feel anything, not to remember anything, for inside the remembering was the fear that instead of drawing nearer, I might fall farther away from the memory of Alan's newborn head, the way he laughed over small things before he could even speak, how he walked away from me on his first day of school and turned at the door to wave, as if reassuring me when I should have been doing just that for him. Mornings became afternoons became evenings and the thoughts came anyway, tumbling, tinted with color, fading, bright, fading. I thought about what had been, back when my son was small, learning not to be timid, a mere boy.

At night, age eight, he slept lying on his back, his knees raised and the covers tenting over them. He'd turn to one side and the covers would collapse, eventually kicked off, the close Florida air enough. Above his headboard, the curtains I'd made, the ones he'd asked for the summer after first grade, lay flat against the window. The pattern of ducks, dogs, and canoes seemed odd and pointless to me—strange symbols of boyhood. Alan always slept soundly and, standing there in his doorway, I realized he was almost too good. There was comfort in this, and a puzzlement that all this happiness might come at the expense of a sorrow not yet known.

When he was twelve, his father went out and bought a Labrador. The two of them taught the dog to hunt. They brought home ducks and muddy boots and on one occasion, after a day at Ponce Inlet, a seagull they'd shot by accident.

"Lyman retrieved him any old way," Alan said. "He didn't care we made a mistake."

"I see that," I said, holding the gull over the kitchen counter. "Take this thing outside. There's nothing I can do with it."

"Soup?" Jack pointed to my saucepans. He knew better. "Come on, Lil. Surrounded with onions and thyme from your garden. A good dousing of wine. Delicious."

"Outside, please. Now." The white breast rose up as I laid the bird back on the counter. I could work with dead ducks, but somehow that gull seemed wrong. The black beak and feet made me nervous, and the bird had a peculiar smell. I wanted it out of the house.

Lyman lay in the corner, not even raising his head. White and gray feathers littered the floor, and I gestured again. First at my husband, then at the bird.

Alan brought in the Peterson field guide from the porch, where Jack kept field glasses and a log. He pointed to an open page. "Look, it's a laughing gull."

Jack carried the bird to the back door. "Not anymore," he said.

The Peterson guide had a lot more in it than gulls. The insides of the threaded green cover were lined with avian silhouettes, the first fifty pages dedicated to wood ducks, mergansers, shovellers, herons, cormorants, kingfishers and kites, harriers and skimmers. The water birds. From our lakeside porch we saw an occasional heron overhead, loud blue kingfishers, a rare black cormorant. But the rest were the ones Alan sighted on hunting trips, the ones he told me about later. Without making a fuss, I recorded the list, separate from Jack's infrequent inventories, in the back of the log. Date, time of day, place and weather sat alongside each entry, and anything Alan had noted about the markings—the tufted green-black crest on a merganser, the one Jack swore was a Bufflehead; the despairing cry of the wood duck; the soft, low bark of the black skimmer over Wilbur Bay that had made Lyman look skyward. Years of scribbled entries marked our years as a family.

When Alan left for Vietnam, the book stayed on the glass table on the porch, like a reminder, open at the last entry. It was late September, and several weeks had passed since his departure, 1969 slowly stretching out, the days thinner, more diminished. I sat on the porch, looking past the rain and waiting for something to come along so that I could record the date, time, wingspan, markings, the shrillness of the call, the lonely glide down into our yard. But only jays and blackbirds came, and dusty little tree sparrows. Nothing that Alan would have bothered to mention, and so I didn't write them down.

Instead, over the weeks and months, I wrote letters which I sealed in envelopes and at first didn't send, afraid to acknowledge the APO, the enormous distance between central Florida and the central highlands of Vietnam.

Alan wrote us, his letters on weightless blue paper. They came out of order in bundled groups of four or five. He wrote about his buddies, where they came from and how they handled their rifles. He wrote of mountains, their sheer slopes crowded with trees he couldn't identify, limbs heavy with black monkeys and dotted with blood-red sunbirds that shined in the dark. Sometimes there was just a single page with a line or two, the ink smeared, with promises to love us always. I took my time opening the envelopes, sometimes leaving them on the entry table for several days, as if time would season the words inside. I awaited midmorning when the postal truck pulled up, the mailbox's metal latch swinging open, the sound of the mail nesting together, magazines against leaflets against bills. I dreaded this time of day, too. I considered the deliveries in the same way I considered Alan's decision to enlist, the decision that Jack agreed with, the one that divided us into three parts, none of them equal, all out of balance.

I knew how the news might come, on a perfect day when I least expected it. And so I remained unquiet and on edge. Waiting for the doorbell to sound, and answering it to find a boy Alan's age, his head down, holding the uncommon, unwelcome telegram on yellow paper, its lines besieged and betrayed over and over by one word—STOP. I listened for the car coming up the drive or, perhaps out of respect, parked on the road. The doors of the black sedan opening wide, and men in Army green walking down the drive, their shoes hitting the pavement like shockwaves, their hats in hand, the news exiting their dark mouths like misunderstanding, like news that was meant for someone else's mother. The bright ribbons they wore above their hearts would not offer solace, their promises of honor and medals and arrangements already broken. And as they left, the day reflecting from the sedan's windshield would leave with them, taking away everything, including the sun.

Drinking helped. I thought of recording all the drinks I'd had since Alan left, setting them in columns the way I had with bird calls, mating rituals, time spent nesting and brooding and feeding young chicks. More pages for gin than scotch.

Jack, the good husband and the head pharmacist at Rexall, continued bringing home his samples. He searched his supplies for a happy marriage and found how easy it was to help that along. Back when the other pregnancies didn't take, when it was clear that Alan would be an only child, Jack placed vials of Miltown into the corners of the medicine cabinet, next to the book on my bedside table, into my drink before dinner. Later came the Librium and, when Alan entered high school and then the Army, the Valium. Capsules of pink and yellow, small tablets of baby blue—innocent pastel shades that tasted bitter and bent the world into an easier shape, one I could understand. Chicken casseroles and steaks on the grill. Martinis. And then slipping into something more comfortable. Something bright and small, against the tongue, followed by another drink, a 2:00 a.m. swim in the lake. I became the waterfowl, common and American, fascinating to observe, so different from the ones my Alan loved.

Disconnected, I moved through the days slowly. In October we celebrated the birthday without the boy. I wished the year already spent, I wished for another autumn, for Alan to be home and heading to college on the GI Bill. I separated thoughts from actions as if they could be categorized—getting in the car and driving across town, seeing a neighbor wave, yet unable to raise my hand and wave back; differentiating the Florida landscape from Alan's descriptions of Vietnam, one pocked with lakes, the other veined with rivers; studying the way the mail moved across the Pacific and then a sea of states, back and forth, slowly. I tried to write another letter and instead took out the last one Alan had sent.

20 October 1969
Chu Lai

Dear Mom and Dad,

I hope you're both fine. Dad, I suppose you and Ly have been checking out the marshes. Bring home some mergansers for me, okay? And Mom, are you still planning on making new curtains for my room? You know you shouldn't bother.

36

The birthday package with all the cards and presents was really great. Tell everyone thank you. Funny, I'm one of the oldest in my platoon now, but then I was always one of the oldest in my class.

We're moving out tomorrow. I can't tell you where exactly. Out there, somewhere in the boonies. I'm sure it will be as green and jungled as all the other places we've already been. Everyone is geared up and ready to go. Thanks to the CO, who's a decent guy, we all feel good about this mission.

All my love,
Alan

The words flew off the page along with Alan's name. I folded the letter back into its envelope. Whether I sat, unmoving, trying to read my son's handwriting, or washed every window in our modern house, the thoughts still crowded in. I considered making the new curtains I'd promised for Alan's room but only held the car keys in my hand, unable to walk through the foyer or find my way to the fabric store. Instead, I stood in the bathroom before the mirrored medicine cabinet, looking at my reflection and daring myself to leave the door closed, thinking of the little pills, neatly windowed into their foil pages.

November pushed in with clearer skies and colder weather. I recalled an earlier November, years before. The day had been crystalline, cloudless, and not yet cold. Jack had allowed Alan to miss school so they could hunt blue-winged teal. Lyman was young and still learning, but they brought down fifteen birds that day. Out on the water they didn't know that four states away, on the same afternoon, another man named Jack had been shot dead in Dallas. At twilight the evening news repeated the story, the same story I'd heard all day: "President Kennedy has been killed." My husband's car pulled into the driveway, but I didn't go out to meet them and congratulate Alan on his first successful hunt. Jack cleaned and dressed the birds and put them into the Deepfreeze. Alan watched the reports, then sat down and rested his head on my shoulder. He smelled of ocean, wet sand, dank water from the boat's floor, and the light from the television shone in his eyes. He saw that I was looking at him and smiled. Even then, only thirteen, he'd been the strongest one in the family. I recognized how cheated he must have felt.

In my mind, Alan had always been too willing to do things for others. Raking leaves, taking out the trash, walking Lyman, getting his homework done. I wondered where the bad was buried in my boy. I suppose I hoped for a little bad, something to taint him just slightly, to make him less vulnerable.

When life got complicated, he always took it in stride. The broken arm he'd gotten but blamed on no one in his fifth-grade Phys Ed class; the wooden canoe he and Jack had worked on one summer, that sank the first time it was launched; the lead role in the school musical that should have been his, but was handed to the Callahans' youngest boy, the one who couldn't even carry a tune; the girls who turned him down, though he was one of the better-looking kids in his high school class.

"What's wrong with those girls?" Jack said. "They don't know charming when they meet it?" He kneeled next to the shotguns that were stripped down and laid across the porch floor, along with gun oil, brushes, and stained cleaning cloths.

"They don't want charming, Dad." Alan held his Remington an arm's length away and, one eye shut, peered through the barrel.

From my place on the rattan sofa, a month of mending in my lap, I envisioned the narrow cylinder revealing the future: long and sure, with more girlfriends than hunting trips.

"What do they want?" I asked.

"Hey, breech to muzzle," Jack said. "What the hell are you thinking?"

Alan set down the gun and didn't respond to his father. Instead, he stood up and opened the back door, letting it slam as he walked into the backyard and around the house out of sight.

"What the hell is wrong with that boy?"

I stopped stitching the loose collar of my husband's shirt, thinking Alan had finally found a thread of impatience for his father's usual gruffness, and then I responded. "What the hell is wrong with you, Jack?"

Outside, in the sycamore tree, a chirring started up. A mockingbird making it clear, the terms abrasive and hard until a succession of sweeter remarks began. Farther away, Alan whistled and the bird stopped and then mimicked him.

Another bundle of thin blue letters arrived, stained and thick with pages. I held them for a few minutes and then tore open each envelope. I read them straight through and out of order, only understanding that they were all sent from base camp and had been written in the same week. Between Christmas and New Year's. I had to concentrate to make out the lines, as most were smudged with red dirt and something like oil, black and smelling of a place far-off and unknown.

Christmas had come and gone and we were well into 1970, March moving into April, and here was Alan telling me about Bob Hope performing for the soldiers in Chu Lai, officers dressed up as Santas and dancing girls dressed up as elves. An elf named Margaret had kissed him and she'd smelled of peppermint. I thought of all our Christmas mornings, candy canes poking from the top of Alan's red felt stocking, and now of women's stockings, of how finally a girl had taken notice of a boy who had always been good.

I read the date he'd printed at the top of one letter: December 27, 1969. And then at the others—Christmas Eve, the 26th, the 30th—and here, one from the 29th.

29 December 1969
Chu Lai

Dear Mom and Dad,

Nearly New Year's! I wish both of you a very happy one. The months are ticking by. Still though, we count the days till DEROS—you know, Date Eligible to Return from Overseas. I've got way too many to go, so I try not to count too often. One fellow in our platoon, Maurice from LaPlace, Louisiana, marks off the days on his helmet, a tick for every day he's been in-country. He's short now, only a few weeks left, but not too nervous about going out again. Says there's good duck hunting waiting for him back home. I imagine so.

Your loving son,
Alan

I thought of time, of tallies and counting the remaining days. I was afraid to try. There was a space on the kitchen wall where the calendar had been. I hadn't put one up for 1970. Tracking the months backwards and forwards in my mind, I had no idea where I was, where my son was. I wondered where he'd been since he'd written these letters, what he'd seen and done, and how he was now.

"Lyman!" My voice echoed across the lawn. The dog was gone again. He'd taken to wandering since Alan had left. At first I let him roam, but well-meaning neighbors had begun to call. "I worry about him, Lil," Jack had mentioned. "I worry that something will happen."

A routine began. Lyman taking off and Jack expecting me to track him down and bring him back home. And me, the dutiful wife, going out for a walk every morning, searching for the light yellow dog under light blue skies.

It was mid-April, the weather sunny, and the neighbors were out watering their flowers, raising their flags, sitting in their driveways in idling automobiles, watching me without making it known that they were watching me. Mr. Callahan stood in the center of his lawn and sprayed the hell out of his azaleas, and down the block, Margot Lingstrum tiptoed across her front walkway to collect the newspaper. Every morning she lingered at the curb in her pale purple bathrobe, just long enough for the automatic sprinklers to catch her and flatten the robe against her round thighs.

"Lyman," I yelled again.

Margot gave me a dull look and carried her damp *Orlando Sentinel* inside. I could see why she didn't open her shades. Those days, many of us didn't, the world outside assuring little. I wondered why she even bothered to get the paper at all. The news was always the same. Bombings, hijackings, political promises, body counts, and Westmoreland's "positive indicators" that the war was working, that we were winning.

"Dog run off again?" Mr. Callahan walked out to the edge of his yard to examine a pair of boxwoods. He kinked the hose and a tiresome hiss took over the quiet morning.

I nodded. "Every morning these days. Looking for something, I suppose."

Callahan examined my scuffed loafers. I gathered he'd retired: the early morning watering, the plaid shorts instead of the business suit. "Might try the Blackwoods." He pointed around the bend. "Seems he likes the boy down there."

"Thanks," I said, nodding again. I appreciated that a neighbor cared. Or seemed to care. "Thanks so much."

"Sure," he called as I walked away.

The Blackwoods' house was a low one-story like most in the neighborhood. It sat on a corner with a wide expanse of dry lawn and dying flowers out front and the remnants of the Sybelia citrus grove in back. From the branches of a live oak that shaded most of the house, colored glass bottles swung in the slight breeze. The morning sun reflected through them, geometric patterns shimmering, then shattering over the ground.

Lyman lay across the front steps in a cool, shady spot, Saul Blackwood at his side. Sometime before his senior year, Alan had stopped spending much time with the Blackwood kids. Still, I'd seen Saul around, mostly barefoot, in cut-off shorts, his hair in his eyes. I estimated by now he was fourteen or fifteen, his parents rarely keeping an eye on him. The Labrador hardly looked up as I approached.

"Is he camping out over here?" I asked, pointing to the dog.

"Sometimes," Saul said, his hand following the length of Lyman's blond back.

"You feeding him?"

"When he comes around." Saul stood up now, his head cocked, inspecting me through a tangle of dark hair.

I had my hands on my hips now, trying not to be mad, trying not to pity the dog who'd looked for a new boy, trying to understand the shape of things, as upended and disorienting as they felt. "Your parents okay with that?"

"Not really," he said. "I mean, my mama doesn't want him in the house. And my dad's not back yet."

"Yes, that seems to be the occasion. They're all not back yet."

Saul stared down at his feet. As usual, I'd said too much with so little. I settled my hands across the front of my thighs, patting them, calling to Lyman. Lyman wagged his tail and stayed where he was.

"All right then," I said and turned to go.

"Mrs. Walbright?"

I turned back, wondering what more needed saying. Even so, I held out my hand. "Don't you remember me? I'm not much for formalities. Keep it simple. Just Lillian, though I'd prefer Lil."

"Okay." He paused and then took my offered hand, resting his inside mine for mere seconds, the touch indecisive and damp. "You better take him home."

"It's okay," I said. "He'll only come back here." The tilt of the boy's head unnerved me. "Why don't we both take care of him until Alan comes home? I'll give you money for dog food. I certainly don't want to upset your mother, but Lyman seems to like you." And then I was sorry I'd rambled on.

"Should we write Alan and tell him?" Saul asked. "Do you think he'd like to know?"

"Sure," I said. "I think that would be fine." I considered how well the boys knew each other. Swims at the lake, the crossover of years at school, but what else?

"Do you know where he is now?"

"I don't. I only know where to send his mail." I crossed my arms. "I don't ever know exactly where he is."

Saul shifted his feet on the uneven stones of the front walk. "He used to come over, and we'd listen to albums. I set up speakers by my bedroom windows, so we could hear the stereo in the backyard, and we'd sit out there with Lyman. Sometimes with Rainey and my sister, too."

He looked away, down the road toward the lake, the gray asphalt rising up to meet the bright morning.

"Alan liked to put on *Buffalo Springfield*," Saul said, looking back at me. "I never did get that. That he liked that kind of music. I mean, it didn't make any sense."

To me, it made sense, Alan always agreeable to all sides of a story, without judgment, without disdain. And yet, I didn't want to cloud a boy's memory, so I left it alone.

"Yes," I said. "I know what you mean."

My letter to Alan that day explained Lyman's latest antics, how he'd come out on top instead of in trouble. How tying him up in the yard wasn't an option, so we let him roam through neighbors' rosebushes and into the grove and around the Blackwoods' house. I thought about the bottles swinging from the tree out front and decided not to mention them. I knew Alan had been inside the house, that he knew the color of the carpet, the sort of art they'd put on the walls. I wrote in blue ink, sent my love, sealed the envelope, attached the stamps and placed the letter on the silver tray atop my desk. The lone white envelope sat on its side, next to the letters we'd received, ready to mail the next morning.

"Did you find the dog?" Jack stood across the kitchen, peering into the cabinet where we kept the liquor. Behind him, outside the windows, a blue evening settled over the lake.

"Yes," I answered, not offering more. On the cutting board in front of me was a head of lettuce and two tomatoes. In the oven a chicken roasted. I wished for better things. Silver corn and sage, duck dressed with figs and red wine, a son safe at home.

Jack held a bottle of scotch, single malt, rare. The bottle I'd bought for guests we no longer invited, who no longer invited us, my behavior in the past months too quiet or too sudden for social gatherings.

"You didn't bother to bring him home?"

"No." I felt the apron at my waist and adjusted it, tying it tighter.

"Why the hell not?"

"Why the hell don't you just have a drink?"

"You sit around here all day—"

"No, I don't sit around."

In the laundry room, I'd spent three hours ironing Jack's shirts; at Hull's Marketessen, I'd gathered items into the shopping cart for Jack's favorite meals—simple, basic, unadorned; the beds were made, floors were swept, furniture dusted. All Jack's. And then I dressed a bird and put it into a slow oven. Only then did I sit for a moment with an iced glass of gin and lime and re-read three of Alan's letters, the ones that were written last year, the last ones we'd received. The ones in which he joked that "home for the holidays" had a different meaning now, home being the base in Chu Lai. That the South China Sea had taken the place of the Atlantic, and that he finally understood that brothers don't have to be family. The shape of his handwriting, the sheer blue paper still in hand, I swallowed the last of my drink and wondered why Jack had never read a single page of Alan's letters. And why I had never asked him.

I looked at Jack now, his eyes uneven and sad, the bottle like a weight in his hand.

"Just what do you do then?" He slammed the bottle of scotch onto the counter and tore the thick, shiny paper from its neck.

"Today? Yesterday? Obviously nothing I needed to." I watched as Jack poured the scotch against the side of a glass, how he added cubes of ice from the insulated ice bucket I'd prepared, how he didn't bother with soda or a splash of water and simply downed the drink all at once. He poured another and drank it more slowly, glaring at me.

"This isn't about Lyman, is it?" I ventured, looking for peace, expecting none.

"Goddammit, Lil. What do you think?"

The space between us widened every day. It pushed us apart and threatened to leave us that way, on opposite sides of the house, no dog to walk, no reason to keep on going, to wait it out as others did, quietly and bravely, in church, at business meetings, in line at the bank when the teller asked, "And how is Alan doing, Mrs. Walbright? Such a handsome, brave boy. You must be so proud."

"I think the chicken is done." I opened the oven door and the kitchen was filled with the scent of sweet poultry. It was then that Jack started to cry.

Sometimes morning came too suddenly, the twist of light through the blinds, the day already worn. This was one of those mornings. Jack had already left for work. He'd slept on the sofa, and a blanket lay across one upholstered arm, throw pillows scattered across the floor. In the glass cabinet that divided our living and dining rooms, the sun canted over intricate glass figures, vases, and china that Jack had given me over the years, things I'd never asked for, and a myriad of colored reflections flew across the hardwood floors, the path shaped by the brilliant springtime sun.

Not intent anymore on being the good wife, I left the room alone and fixed coffee and walked down to our dock. A mist hung over the lake, and I thought of the thin glass shelves of the mirrored bathroom cabinet, how a pink capsule might fit into the day. Something to lighten the already sharp sky to a paler shade.

I heard a pair of oars, someone sculling, heading across the lake to a different shore. And then a small movement, a slight separation in the low-lying clouds, a lone seagull diving. I considered my own selfishness and it cut deeply, like the gull before me, piercing the surface of the lake. After a few moments, the bird didn't resurface. I understood that it didn't matter anymore, not what I felt, not what Jack felt. What mattered could be measured in the number of times Lyman had roamed the neighborhood, in the months Alan had been gone and how many more lined up until his return, and in the hours I spent waiting for yet another water bird to record in the log and lingering over Alan's handwritten entries, his words slanting sideways, each one leading into the next. In his letters he'd rarely recorded the artillery fire, the helos coming and going, the heat and dust, the rain and mud, the boredom and the chaos. Details that the morning paper and the evening news supplied. Instead, he'd protected us, trying to account for the good, rather than the terrible.

The letter I'd written the night before was still in the tray on my desk, waiting to be sent. I left my coffee mug on the wooden boards of the dock and ran inside, hoping I had added enough postage, that the post office wasn't closed for a government holiday. With my wallet and the single-paged letter, addressed to PFC Alan Bonner Walbright, I searched for the car keys and couldn't find them. So I walked. Down the drive and down the road past Mr. Callahan and his drenched azaleas, just in time to see Mrs. Lingstrum shut her front door, the sprinklers going around, whipping water across the lawn and out into the street. Mr. Callahan motioned to me, but I kept walking.

The gray strip of road stretched out ahead. I could hear Callahan calling me. I turned to look back for a second, and a flint of fear, deep and weighted and centered, the very same that I'd once numbed with pills sent me forward. I gripped the envelope, the San Francisco APO written neatly across its center, and lengthened my stride. I rounded the bend at the Blackwoods', where the yard was empty and a group of blighted daisies leaned out from the house. Off Lakeshore Drive a stiff wind was coming out of the west.

Across the intersection the small post office was empty, other than the lone woman in blue who stood behind the counter, and the full-length windows reflected the sunshine, which grew brighter and warmer by the minute. A flagpole was centered in front of the building, with palmettos and a swarm of red and orange lilies around it. Long shadows fell across the road, the sidewalk, the path up to the door. The glaring brilliance of the lilies and the flag's moving shadow made me stand still. I didn't look up to see the stars in their block of blue, the thirteen bold stripes. Instead I saw the silhouette—dark, definite, and ribboning in the wind. It moved and changed and promised nothing. It was a ghost, a dark gray memory of movement, of what once truly was. The way Alan ran, laughing, on another morning, the sun behind him and his shadow lengthening, pulling him into places I would never know, mysterious and miserable, and even now, magnified beyond belief.

MERGANSERS

NOVEMBER 1963

The outboard gave us trouble, but eventually it opened up. The sky widened, the coastline hazy and horizontal. The bright scarlet flush of sunrise made me think the weather might close in, but the day ended up fine. Alan hunched over Lyman, our Labrador Retriever, in the jacket his mother had lined with flannel, trying to stay warm and out of the wind, and we rode across the waterway to Ponce, the little inlet where I knew the mergansers might head. It was their time of year. Heading down from New England past the Carolinas and Georgia to the tidal basins of Florida, where they'd winter.

Lyman bounced around in the bottom of the skiff, and Alan held him by the collar and told him to stay still. Lyman was young. He'd learn. And Alan would learn along with him. I had plans for the both of them. And I had plans for the day. Lessons would be doled out, and ducks would be brought down.

Lyman settled and his pale coat flattened in the wind. Alan looked back at me and tried to smile. I knew he didn't like missing school, but he needed a well-rounded education, not just one of classrooms and manicured playing fields. He needed rough-cut days to balance out the careful ones. And I needed some rough around the edges, too. Counting out capsules and filling prescriptions under the pharmacy's fluorescent lights wore on me. Customers waiting at the counter wore on me. My assistants in their light blue lab coats wore on me. Days off, surrounded by gray-green water and wind, marsh grasses, the mission of searching and waiting, sighting the black and rusty heads, the quick switch of wings, the direction of the V, then raising the Remington and firing. Days where objective and attention broadened and counted for something more than blood pressure, low iron, and over-the-counter offerings.

We swung along the shoreline, and I let up on the outboard's throttle. The skiff eased across the water, its nose now level. Alan was the first to see them. He pointed. Even from the distance, the white marks of the wings and hoods were clear. I stilled the motor and stared up at the formation. Brown and black and white. I gauged the pattern, the intent, and the reach of their long, stiff necks. There would be more. By midmorning we would have let three more groups cross over. Lyman would then be ready, and we'd have our day, father and son and dog, out in the marshes, mergansers flying and falling around us.

FOREVER AND A DAY

APRIL 1970

That morning, when we woke up, the air was still and warm and filled with our breath. Spring was creeping toward summer, and our days were thick with what we wanted, but what we probably wouldn't have. LuLu had her face half buried in a pillow and stared at me with one eye. Her sandy brown hair was scattered in all directions and her pajama top bunched up.

"Boo," she said without blinking.

I knew she'd been awake for a while already, just by the brightness in her cheek. The light in the room began to change, and Lu rolled over and waved her hands in the sifting flecks of dust. She pulled at my charm bracelet, and I took it off and put it around her wrist, knowing how loud it was, how I'd hear her coming. Outside, the wine bottles that hung from the branches of the live oak drifted in the breeze, and we could hear them clinking together. Lulu's mama, who insisted I call her Minnie, though I always thought of as Mrs. B, once invited me to help her twist lengths of knotted brown twine around their glass necks. She'd reached up into the thick leaves and tied off each bottle, humming under her breath. Even this morning they glanced together like wind chimes.

LuLu and I sat beneath the curtain of Indian tapestry, swirls of red and gold thrown around us, as the sun fell through the windows. Lu gave me a look like a silent scream and then started jabbing at the air with her fists, eventually mock-punching me. I held up my hands to block her swipes and then had to clutch her hands to stop her.

"What?" I asked.

"Rainey," she said, her teeth clenched to sound tough. "Don't be stupid, okay?"

She gave me that cross-eyed look, the one that made me feel dim and small, even though I was smarter and at least a head taller. It was just that my thoughts circled around while hers flew forward. She never hesitated, but dove straight into situations. When neighbors called the police, it was all because of LuLu. She was the one who set their dogs free and lit their trashcans on fire.

"Come on, slowpoke," she said. "When you were still sleeping, I heard Mama talking on the phone, saying, 'The druggist's wife is out in broad daylight, making another scene.' And we need to see that."

I hesitated.

"You know," LuLu pressed. "Alan's mama."

LuLu was in one of her moods. She'd insist on making the best of this moment, this opportunity to spy, to make sure that another's bad luck was worse than her own. By then we knew that Mrs. Walbright drank a lot, but I wasn't sure if we needed to see her embarrassing herself. Sometimes in the early morning when I practiced diving from the floating dock, I saw her white bathing cap from a distance, as she crossed the lake from one end to the other, her strokes long and graceful.

I thought about Alan, how I'd never see him again. How he'd taught me to dive, how I remembered this every time I stood at the end of a diving board. The way to balance, spring, arch, tuck, or twist. The moment before I entered the water was a moment back in time, Alan's voice calling out, clear and promising. And then there was the quick, cold slice of water over my wrists all the way down to my ankles, the barest splash. I could never quite find the crisp, quiet entry, the way Alan could.

LuLu jumped off the canopied bed and landed on the thick carpet. The bracelet jingled and the air shined around her. She smiled a sharp little smile and said, "Here," throwing me a pair of pink shorts. "Put those on. Hurry up!"

"All right, all right." I followed her off the bed, my nightie sliding up, almost to my waist. I knew she thought I was slow, but I was just longer-legged. My toes caught in the shorts' hem, and it took a minute to get my legs through. I looked down and realized there was a dark stain on my underwear. It wasn't the first time and I knew what was happening, but I didn't want Lu to know, so I pulled on the shorts, knotted up a pair of panties from the top dresser drawer, and slipped into the bathroom. The hamper lid clapped shut, and the bikini with the bows at the front corners disappeared under my shorts. I walked across the hall back to the bedroom, moving slowly, feeling a slight twinge, and remembering the bruise on the inside of my thigh. I tried to push away the reason. It was complicated and new and I didn't understand it myself.

◊ ◊ ◊

There were times that Saul found me alone, coming from the bathroom late at night or that one morning in the grove behind the house when we should have been collecting oranges. At first, he only watched me. Later, maybe because he was older, just a shade over fifteen, I let him touch me and whisper things I shouldn't have heard, that he swore he'd never told anyone else. He threaded the fine gold of my necklace through his fingers. He knew I was nearly thirteen. Old enough, he'd said, not to get caught.

But I was catching it a lot, living with the Blackwoods out on Sybelia Drive, ever since my mama had left for the coast. West Palm Beach. To find herself, she'd said. To find a new husband more likely. She did things like that since my daddy had gone missing in Vietnam nearly three years before. I still waited for him to come home, pictured how he'd tell us all about the places he'd been, but my mama wasn't keen on waiting. She was, folks said, like a tall blonde drink of water, and men probably needed to quench their thirst on the likes of her.

Instead of being mad, I collected the rumors, each one like a small stone, and I wore the necklace my mama had sent, comparing its weight to each of those stones. *For Rainey on her 13th Birthday*, the card had read. Mama knew how to plan ahead, how to account for her absence. When the little parcel came First Class, the necklace inside a box wrapped with pink ribbon, arriving several months before my birthday, I wasn't surprised. I opened it, by myself, in the bedroom I shared with LuLu. When I held it up to the light, tiny red sparkles hit the wall, and for some reason I thought of lies and promises, reminders of how my mama's return was always delayed. Letters and phone calls explaining her need to stay longer, how she'd come and get me when the time was right.

I didn't expect much from Mama though, especially since she'd named me after a mountain clear across the world from Florida.

"Rainier?" LuLu had asked, her hands on her hips, that day in the schoolyard during recess. The autumn sun lit up her face, and I wished to be back in the shade and away from this girl who played rough and whom I'd been so careful to avoid the first weeks of school. "What kind of a name is that?" She looked me up and down, squinting.

"Folks call me Rainey," I answered, wishing for the bell to ring, hoping she wouldn't punch me like she did the quiet kids.

It was too late though. She whacked me right there in front of Mrs. Esther Wild, the school principal. Right smack in the arm, just like she was swatting at me now, years later, in her bedroom.

"Come on!" LuLu yelled.

We ran down the hall, Lu pulling her shirt over her head. It had little yellow pom-pom balls stitched all over it, and they jiggled as she ran. At the entrance to his bedroom, Saul caught his sister by the arm. I skidded up behind, but not too close. From the stereo in his room, the same Elton John album played over and over again. I remembered how we used to listen to albums together—Saul, Alan, LuLu, and me. How we'd never do that again, the news of Alan's death marking us, dividing us unevenly. And then I thought of Alan's dog Lyman, how he'd taken to following Saul around. How he showed up again and again, claiming his place on the front steps, his pale coat dirty and unbrushed.

Saul glanced at me, and I felt at the back of my neck for the clasp of the necklace. He'd tried to take it a few days before, as though it were a prize. He smiled and then snatched a section of LuLu's shirt, all the while watching me.

"Let go, Saul," LuLu said.

"I won't until you give it up." Saul pulled her closer, and the shirt began to rip.

"Who are you talking to anyway?" She stuck her chest out and glared at her big brother. "Me or Rainey?"

Saul, shirtless, his body tanned from all those afternoons at the lake, held on to Lu. Rumor had it, at the lake there was a snapping turtle that now and again went for swimmers. Snake-necked and vengeful and hissing. And that's what Lu looked like, standing there in the hallway. One mad, hissing turtle.

"Damn you," LuLu said. She scratched Saul's arm.

"Why, you little—"

Saul barely winced, but his eyes teared up. I skimmed past, the rough surface of the wall catching at my blouse. I had seen Saul cry before, but I never told anyone. He'd talked to me about being afraid, about how confusing the world seemed. And his life seemed even more confusing than mine—Mrs. B's son by her first husband, half brother to LuLu, his stepfather not even around. Sometimes he stared into space or crouched with his head in his hands. Unlike him, I knew what it was like to be angry instead of sad.

Still in her slip, there was Mrs. B in the hallway, barreling down after us.

"And just where do y'all think you're going so early in the a.m.?" she asked.

"Nowhere, Mama," LuLu lied. She took backward steps into the kitchen until she bumped against the counter. Her shirt had a whorl of twisted wrinkles in the middle of it where Saul had grabbed. "We're just getting some Frosted Flakes.

That's all." She looked up at her mama and smiled a sugary, Tony-the-Tiger smile.

"You don't fool me, Miss LuLu," Mrs. B said. "Y'all stay away from that Walbright woman. She's out there again, carrying on and whimpering like baby Jesus on a bad day, making another one of her messes. She's been tossing her fine china out the front door and all over the carport, and praise be to G, young girls don't need to be seeing that."

Her jay-blue eyes looked right through us. Minnie Blackwood was beautiful, but she seemed slightly unfastened, with her long, crazy black hair and her strange way of seeing things. Like the time she told us she'd had a dream about giant birds that became helicopters, grass that grew so long it towered over your head, how her second husband would come home from Vietnam, flying low over the elephant grass, reeling sideways, his wing clipped.

"Now just stay right here and watch cartoons. *Merry Melodies* is coming on."

The sun flew in through the kitchen window, and the little glass bird on the sill threw all kinds of color around the room. Blues and greens, colors I linked to LuLu and the lake and this life in Florida. I knew LuLu had stolen the bird from the Walbrights' house, just like she'd stolen other things. We never talked about it, but in the center of that summer, bright against all the diving lessons and sunning sessions out on the lake, there was the place of secrets, of LuLu's stash, of all the things missing from the Walbrights' tabletops and drawers and glass-fronted cabinets.

LuLu poured two bowls of cereal, most of the flakes landing on the gold-flecked countertop. And then she spilled the milk and didn't even bother to clean it up. Saul sulked around in back of us, burning toast.

We ate on the couch in the den. The couch with the daisy-flower bedspread thrown over it because, like Mrs. B said, "Y'all children can be so messy." LuLu turned up the TV volume so loud there was no way we'd hear any of Mrs. Walbright's cries. I was sure Lu had never seen Mrs. Walbright in action, her episodes saved for the evening cocktail hour.

Originally, I knew about drinks before dinner from my mama and daddy. Before Mama and I moved to Florida, before Daddy left for Vietnam, before I knew anything about palm trees and tangerines. The sound of ice shifting in a glass, the jars of olives and tiny onions Mama kept in the fridge, the colored toothpicks standing in a glass jigger near the short and tall and stemmed glasses reserved just for their special drinks. And back when Mrs. B and my mama first met, they'd make drinks that were pink and fizzy, bright cherries or paper umbrellas crowding their glasses and eventually given to LuLu and me.

Months before, around Christmas, I'd gone walking with Saul after dark and we'd stared into neighbors' windows at flocked evergreens bright with colored lights and TVs flickering with the evening news and, where the street was crowded with parked cars, people jammed together inside a living room, laughing and drinking. Mrs. Wild's living room. Who would have thought the elementary school principal had parties? We pushed past the boxwood and camellias to the front window and peered in from one side, so no one would see us.

In one corner a large woman laughing, and a man with a foot up on the arm of a turquoise sofa, holding a glass etched with blue and gold, gesturing, nearly spilling his drink, and a thin woman sitting near him, smoking and nodding, and someone at the stereo cabinet, changing an album, turning up the volume, the bass line coming through the closed windows. We knew some of the people—the Lingstrums, the French lady who lived next door, and there was Mrs. Walbright, looking aloof. And suddenly an engraved glass flew against a wall. Guests backed away and stared. At the mark on the wall and the broken glass at their feet. At their hostess, whose hands turned upright, whose eyes searched the room. The man with his foot on the sofa stopped gesturing and the woman near him exhaled, her mouth a wide-open O. Our French neighbor smiled like she knew something she'd never tell, and Saul pulled me away from the window.

How could we just sit here? How could LuLu be so calm? But there she was, sitting and eating cereal, like it was any old morning.

On the television, gray mice with long eyelashes tried to blow up a black-and-white cat. The cat survived, his whiskers a little crooked after the explosion. The mice laughed squeaky, high mice laughs, and the cat looked worn out and miserable.

LuLu plunked her bowl on the couch-side table, the one with the lamp that had three settings—bright, brighter, and blinding. The crimson lampshade shook as the bowl came down beside it. Lu had a wild look on her face, her eyes shining, and I thought maybe she might start waling on me again. I flinched a little in anticipation of the first swipe. Instead though, she stood up and stamped her feet and shouted over the TV noise.

"Whoo-eee!"

"Lu, cut out that yipping!" Mrs. B called from down the hall.

LuLu stomped over to the television. I expected she would turn the dial, the mice would disappear into a tiny dot of light, and once the screen went black, only our watery reflections would stare back. But instead she turned the volume up even louder, leaned toward me, and whispered, "Come on. We're going to see what all that woman is doing."

She grinned so hard that I thought the space between her two front teeth might bust wide open. We walked barefoot to the side door. It was amazing how sneaky we were. Still hunched over his toast in the kitchen, not even Saul heard us leave.

Outside, the only sounds were the warm, unhurried wind through the trees and the buzz of cicadas. Another hot, humid day. We'd have to cool off in the lake again, snapping turtle or no. On the sandy path in back of LuLu's house, everything was overgrown. We pushed through cream-colored Ligustrum flowers, thick with scent, and past the bright red trumpet vine, then stopped under a tall pine, the shade cooler, the ground littered with green needles. Lyman lay there with his paws crossed, panting, taking a break from the heat, and I thought maybe that meant Saul was around. I didn't wait to see.

Further on, palmetto leaves caught at my sleeves and one snagged. I stopped to untangle myself and pulled away a loose thread, which floated to the ground like a damselfly wing. LuLu had gone on ahead.

I stood for a moment, listening, but there was nothing and so I walked on. As I rounded the azaleas at the end of the path, Saul grabbed me and pulled me back behind another untended Ligustrum. Dark green with perfumed blooms and a maze of thin, reaching branches. Saul stood too close and his breath was all over me.

"Saul?" I said. I knew LuLu was making her way through the grove, probably wondering where I'd gone, and my usual curiosity about her brother dimmed. I didn't want to be found out, to have my friendship with LuLu turn sideways and spill.

Saul said nothing, just stood over me and breathed. I stepped back. He blinked and mumbled a word. Maybe my name. Then he squeezed my elbow, drawing me closer.

"Ow," I said, trying to wrench away from his grasp. He twisted my arm harder, and his other hand reached inside my blouse. Everything seemed to slow down. The shallow breath of wind, the scent of flowers and the surrounding orange grove, the shafts of sunlight coming down around us. I tried to push Saul's hand away, but he just groped around even more, his fingers traveling to my throat, tangling in my necklace.

"Darn it, Saul," I said, still pushing at him. "Quit."

I forced him back, thinking I must look the picture of fierce and brave despite his hands up my shirt. Suddenly, his face closed over mine and his mouth parted my own, his tongue searching. The smell of pennies, sharp and coppery, collided with that familiar taste, the roof of Saul's mouth. And then I was kissing him back. I remembered lake water, snail eggs on the sides of the dock, the hard, damp floor of the canoe.

One afternoon, only a few weeks earlier, LuLu had gone shopping with her mama, and I'd made up an excuse about needing to stay at the house to finish a book for school. Saul and I stood inside the front door, watching them drive off, and he mumbled something about his canoe and going down to the lake. His shoulder-length brown hair fell over his eyes. He had a habit of brushing his hair away from his face, then holding it there, uncovering his forehead. I noticed the way he stared straight out into the day and then sideways at me. And so I said yes, I would go. I shouldn't have, but I did.

I sat in the bow and tried to paddle without banging the side of the canoe. I could feel Saul's eyes on my back, his strokes long and sure, guiding the canoe through slim canals. That same song under his breath. A snatch of lyrics, so quietly mouthed. The light gold chain of my necklace felt enormous and heavy.

Spanish moss hung down around us as we drifted through a shaded passageway that led from one lake to another. Soon we weren't moving at all. I turned in my seat, the red boat cushion slipping beneath me, my oar raised. Saul reached for my paddle, and I let it go too quickly. It clattered against the bottom of the boat. I started to apologize and realized Saul's hand was still outstretched, reaching for mine. I gave it to him.

By then it was late afternoon. Above us, a bare breeze, cypresses, a slant of sky. Beyond us, the distant sound of a motorboat, a dog barking. Below us, the curve of the canoe, its metal struts pressing into my back. No words, only breaths, small sounds. An egret fishing nearby gathered itself and flew over, a flare of white against the dull blue.

I wasn't sorry. And it wasn't like I didn't help it happen. He'd made me curious. Before my mama left, she said, "You be nice to Saul, just not too nice." Now she was somewhere on a beach, and here I was in the orange grove behind the Blackwoods' house, trying not to be too nice. I was mad enough without a boy making it worse, and so as Saul pulled away, I bit down on his lower lip. He covered his mouth and cried out.

I heard a tinkling sound, tiny and golden, a warning. The branches parted, and LuLu stepped out. "I saw that!" she said. "I saw you, Saul. You had better cut that out and leave Rainey alone!" She was all over Saul, hitting him, shoving him away.

"Yeah, right," Saul said. "Or what?" He pulled at a privet blossom, and it fell apart.

"Or I'll tell Mama, that's what." LuLu's voice turned inward. I wondered what she'd seen, whether she'd really tell.

"I don't hear you at all, LuLu," said Saul. "All I hear is the wind."

"I can tell you've been crying, Saul. I'll tell all your friends that Saul cries like a baby in the bushes." LuLu raised her chin up high, like she was the chapel of I-know-how-to-get-to-you. "I will tell, too. I don't care what you do to me." She yanked on my hands in her mean, loving way.

Saul stared at me, and I looked away. I blinked against the mottled sunlight as it fell through the low branches. My mind tumbled. All the misunderstanding, all the touching. It grew too quiet, and a strange, desperate moment flew forward, something unspoken stepping to the side. Unable to look at Saul, all I saw were his feet, edging backward. He turned and pushed past palmettos and Ligustrum and disappeared into the grove. LuLu and I stood there in a circle of hot sun and silence.

◊ ◊ ◊

In the distance there was the sound of wreckage, of breaking glass. The sharp, close shattering of glass on a hard surface. And cries, shrill and loud. Sounds a woman might make if her baby were stolen, or if her husband had left her for good.

"Do you hear that?" I asked.

"Don't be stupid, Rainey," LuLu said. "'Course I do."

At one moment the screams sounded near, and then they wavered and seemed terribly distant. One word hung in the air, calling to someone and yet to no one.

"No!"

LuLu tugged again on my hands, harder this time. It seemed as if she needed to leave the moments I wanted to linger inside. I stared at Saul's footprints, outlined so perfectly in the soft, ashy sand. Trapped in the shifting sunlight, I didn't know if I could move from the spot, the fascination of something dangerous—like the lit window of Mrs. Wild's house last December, the thrown glass and the mark it left against the wall—until LuLu's fingers closed around my wrist, tight and insistent.

Mrs. Walbright's moans, naked and unashamed, drifted with the breeze. Another word. "Why?" she called out. Her weeping sounded so sad, so unbearable. My mama never cried. The day the letter arrived, my daddy officially MIA, she was too quiet. She stared out of a window at the noon sun and then went to an afternoon matinee.

"Come on, Rainey," Lu said. "Damn, you are so slow!" And then through her teeth, "We are missing everything."

A lone bottle smashed into something hard. Like metal. A quick crack followed by a smattering of shards and more cries. And then there was an explosion of things breaking, splitting, crashing—an entire world flying apart.

Lu dragged me by the elbow out into the open and up the hot, glaring asphalt of the road alongside the houses and gardens. The screams echoed, bottomless and depleted, around each bend. Already the morning sun had heated up the pavement, so we stayed in the yards where the grass was cool.

Ahead, at the edge of a driveway, a woman stood in a nightgown. Sunlight sifted through the thin material, turning it sheer, and everything underneath was revealed, giving way to all those curves that LuLu and I wished for. And her hair, in the brightness a fiery auburn, swept over her brow, the waves around her face so knotted we couldn't see her tears. Her wails had softened, now more like sighs.

We'd come all this way to see Mrs. Walbright, and now we had no idea what we saw. Others had gathered, some pretending to walk dogs, staying by the curb. A couple of the Callahan boys rode up on their bikes, their father close behind, telling them quietly to get back home. Mrs. Lingstrum looked like she might walk around all the glass, maybe find a broom or help in some way. And in the middle of all our staring and disbelief, Mrs. Walbright wept, her shoulders rounded and shaking, a pale pink remnant of china held limply in one hand.

"It's a wonder nobody's called the police yet," LuLu said a little too loudly.

"Shush, LuLu," I said. "Can't you see how sad she is?" A fierce tendril of fear wrapped around me. I didn't want to believe in Mrs. Walbright's misery, in what it might mean, how it might connect to me.

A pathway lined with thick green ferns led from the front door of the Walbrights' modern, multi-windowed house to the carport. A sea-green Impala was parked there,

66

surrounded by scattered shards of broken glass. Bits that seemed cruel, amazingly sharp, and others oddly curved in an almost inviting way.

"There must be a hundred thousand pieces of glass," I said, my breath caught in the back of my throat. "How will they ever clean it all up? It'll take forever."

"Forever and a day," LuLu said, nodding her head, hushed for a half-second.

Layers of glass colored the pale gray walkway. Clear bottle necks, wavering pieces of silver pier glass, smoky indigo and topaz goblet stems, milky lavender vase rims, china cup handles painted with lilacs, perfect and tiny. LuLu moved closer to me and held my hand, this time gently.

Cradling her own arms, Mrs. Walbright noticed us. She seemed to trace us with her wandering eyes, as though she knew we were there and yet realized the impossibility of two girls so bold, so curious. And then she looked directly at me. Her eyes were swollen, red-rimmed, and I tried to look away but couldn't. She fastened on to me with her disbelief and despair. LuLu started to cry then, and I held on to her. I wondered if she finally knew what was happening, why we were all here. Mrs. Walbright's eyes searched mine and, while I should have answered her look with something kind, a gesture—a smile, a wave, something generous— instead, I frowned. And in my look Mrs. Walbright must have seen something, something we shared, opaque and indefinable and unspoken.

I remembered Alan, how he talked sometimes about his father, but never once about his mother. I'd done the same. And now I tried to push past my own confusion and fear and anger and understand Mrs. Walbright's bitterness, bright with the memory of Alan, how she would never hear him laugh again, or kiss his cheek, or wave another good-bye. She held herself even more closely, grasping the bit of plate in her hand, perhaps fearful that if she let go, if she once more heard the fragile sound of fallen china, she'd stop remembering.

For a moment, the glass-covered drive fell away, and the day felt dizzy and undone. All my thoughts stumbled and became mistakes, and my attempts to understand adults foolish, because we didn't share anything. They drifted in the past, while all I wanted was the future, a life with my mama as crazy as she was. I knew that life with the Blackwoods was all I would get. Back in their kitchen sat the only piece of glass Mrs. Walbright hadn't broken, the little teal bird, once LuLu's pocketed treasure, safely perched with its folded wings intact.

LuLu took the corner of my blouse and tugged. The little yellow pom-poms on her shirt had become dirty, and she seemed dazed. The sun was higher now, and I realized she was pointing to the ground, the shadow of her extended arm so very small.

Jagged, brittle, luminescent rainbows shined up at us. Miraculous red edges shimmered, catching the sunlight and making us shade our eyes. Closest to the door, just below Mrs. Walbright's bare feet, a carmine sliver caught the sun and cast a reflection clear across the walkway and over her polished toenails. I felt for the thin line of gold at my throat, for the birthstone, the present from my mama. It was weeks and weeks away from my thirteenth birthday, but still I wore the necklace. A ruby for July. Saul had tried to take it that day at the dock and I hadn't let him. Then, I'd had no idea why. And now, here, at the edge of Mrs. Walbright's driveway, I held the faceted stone between my fingers, comparing it to all the red glass before us, all the red glass in the world.

THE LATE AFTERNOON LIGHT CRASHED ALL AROUND

MAY / JUNE 1970

By the time 1969 ended and a whole new decade began, Daddy had been gone nearly three years, and Mama said she'd never heard of a tour of duty that lasted so long. "Your daddy is just fooling with us," she said. "Goes off on a TWA jet halfway round the world, with thirty hours of pretty stewardesses and cloud-level views, like he's taking a vacation. And never once comes home. For all I know, he's probably lying about the war, taking his stateside leave over in Asia, shirking his family responsibilities."

And so, on that hot, breathless Monday, when my daddy finally did come home, we were just going on like usual, eating breakfast, slipping on sneakers, running to school, wishing hard for summer to come faster, thinking of the lake shallows already turning warm and how we'd have to swim farther out to find the cool spots. Then—no call, no warning—he just showed up.

I'd been kept after school again for talking out of turn and made to sharpen all the pencils in the principal's office before I could leave. Mrs. Esther Wild wore her glasses on a chain and, sitting straight in the hardback swivel chair at her desk, peered through them at the papers in front of her. She sighed and said I'd better watch myself. A girl like me, a sixth-grader with spirit and potential, needed to set a good example for the younger ones. And then she raised her glasses off her nose and excused me, calling in her thin, wavering, important voice, "Next year, Miss LuLu Blackwood, you'll start junior high. And, sweetheart, it's time to fly right."

The school steps, the boulevard, the quick dirt path between houses all seemed to trip me up that day. I skirted newly constructed red ant mounds, pushed against the low branches of the tangerine trees, and for some reason came around the house to the front door instead of the back. When I finally got inside, Rainey and Saul were watching reruns of some show they'd already seen a million times. I felt all distracted and hot, the Florida air pushing in on me, the wobbly sound of Mrs. Wild's pencil sharpener still in my head.

In the kitchen, I got a drink of water and listened to Mama singing "I'll Never Fall in Love Again." Like Saul, she sang off key. She scolded me for leaving the front door open, so I went back to close it. But someone was there, which seemed strange because, just minutes before, I hadn't noticed anybody out front. Through the screen door, he looked hazy and gray, like a memory right before you can't remember it any longer.

"LuLu?" he said softly.

"Daddy?"

For a minute I stayed in the hallway, and then I walked toward him, stumbling on the entrance rug, its red-flowered pattern rushing under my feet. He stood there as if he'd never left, with one arm resting against the doorframe. A slow smile came to his face as I stepped past the threshold. Then he leaned down and, with that same arm, hugged me with all of the might the past few years had prevented. Mama always said that absence cannot embrace, only presence can. And with his duffel bag across his back, the thick green strap wrapping his chest, my daddy had presence. He was home again and he swept me up and out of my dull state of mind. The late afternoon light crashed all around us in bright blues and yellows. Mama came to the door with a bag of trash and started screaming, "Royal! Praise be to G! Charles Royal Blackwood III! R3, you, Son of a B! Oh my lord, it's you." And then there was kitchen trash everywhere, all over the steps, and the neighbors looking out of their houses, wondering what was going on.

Saul and Rainey came running, but once they reached the door, they stood back and stared. Rainey hid behind Saul and tugged on his shirt. He ignored her, though, so she stopped. Their quiet didn't matter because Mama was still beside herself, draping her arms around Daddy's neck and kissing him, and yes, he kissed her back. I backed away a little, thinking something was wrong. Things slowed down, each motion taking on even more meaning. Daddy was thinner, his face drawn in lines, angled, not the round laughing face I remembered, and I didn't understand why he wasn't hugging like he usually did. He was doing it one-armed. His right sleeve fell to the side, empty and unneeded. From the shoulder down, his arm was completely gone.

"Daddy, your arm." I reached up to touch the sleeve, but Mama hushed me, and I tucked my own right arm behind my back.

That evening we sat in the backyard and ate barbequed shrimp and hush puppies with slaw, and Daddy drank beer from long-necked bottles. Saul pointed out that earlier in the day students had been killed at Kent State. Mama told him we didn't need to hear all that nonsense. Mama smiled a lot, and then cried and finally yelled, "R3, why the hell didn't you call?" Saul and I gave each other that "oh-my-god" look, and Rainey kept on peeling shrimp, for the table, not just for herself, her fingers stained with spices from the barbeque sauce.

Daddy laughed and said, "Now, Minnie, why should I spoil a good surprise?"

She tore around the table, her hands clenched tight, like she might beat him. She leaned against him and said, "We're all so glad you're back." And then, of course, she cried some more. I felt proud all over. Proud of my daddy for showing up, proud of my mama for putting on a good show, proud of Rainey for quietly sharing, even proud of Saul for stirring things up. That was how it was that spring. Then summer fell on us, low and rumbling.

Days melted by, May into June, and Daddy moved around the house like he had to memorize it all over again. He had come back, and we were all getting used to the new way he walked and talked. He still laughed, but rarely and with restraint. And in response, we were cautious, too quiet, holding our breath, waiting to slip back into the way things had been before.

By trade, my daddy had been a carpenter, and now he'd have to learn to live on GI benefits, to depend on others to offer their help because he wouldn't want to ask for it. The moment he'd stepped in front of his own home, the one he'd built, everything changed. Or maybe everything had changed once he'd walked away three years ago and boarded the flight to Vietnam.

Tired of being careful, I sidled up to the window seat in the living room where Daddy was sitting and having a smoke. A nearly full ashtray rested atop the seat cushion. I moved it to one side, and then perched on my knees next to him. I played with the hem of his shirt and touched the edge of the empty sleeve, and he smiled.

"Where'd you go?" I asked him.

"I've just been sitting right here, Lu." His eyes crinkled, cheerful and sad all at once.

"No, I mean where'd you go over there? In Vietnam."

"Oh, over there." He tucked me under his chin, my back against his chest, both of us looking out the window. "I've been to the other side. To emerald mountains and faraway fields of tall, waving elephant grass. Places that should have been beautiful, places that should have held shrines. But I lost men there. On days bright with sunshine, crossing rivers rough with rain, in the blackest of nights. Stepping on land mines, getting shot down at the top of a rise, just trying to have a smoke."

He spoke to me as though I weren't even there, as though he were talking to himself. And then he put out his cigarette, stubbing it three times into the glass ashtray by his knee.

I turned around to look at him, but he stared right past me, and from across the room Mama held a finger to her mouth. She'd been standing there listening and now she gave me a look, the one that meant, "Hush your mouth, or pay the price." And for weeks now, we'd all stayed quiet about the price Daddy had paid and would keep on paying the rest of his life.

I held Daddy's hand and sat with him, not asking any more questions, just letting things be. I puzzled over his words. How they sounded like they were right out of storybooks, how there was another side to the stories. At night Daddy woke up screaming sometimes, saying things that made no sense. He seemed not to be home yet, but somewhere else, a place that claimed him, a place he couldn't leave. It wasn't until later that I'd understand what war meant—why boys like Alan never came home, what had happened to my daddy in a faraway field of "tall, waving elephant grass," where day became night and everything could change in an instant.

"I can't take it anymore." Mama was slamming things around in the kitchen. "I wait all these years for you to come back."

I was listening from my room. The summer morning pressed in and I kicked off my covers. Rainey was in the bathroom again, doing something, and I was waiting to get in.

"I just can't." A sharp, startling sound echoed through the house, like metal on metal. "I just can't!"

I heard my daddy's voice, low and gentle. Maybe he was trying to calm Mama down. Maybe he was agreeing with her—that a man with one arm, who couldn't even hug his wife properly anymore, wasn't fit to be had. Maybe he was shushing her, leaning up against her, the way she liked, the way she always quieted down best after a fight.

I wandered down the hallway from my bedroom into the living room, just shy of the kitchen. I sat on the sofa and shrank down real low so I could barely see over the back of it. Under the fluorescent ceiling light, the kitchen looked washed out and overly bright, and in all that light, Daddy seemed to disappear. He sat at the kitchen table and stared at Mama's straight back. From where I was, I had a sideward view of both of them. Mama stood still, a knife in one hand and a pile of onions chopped up in front of her, potatoes off to the side, not yet peeled for our weekend hash browns. The onions had a sharp scent, and I guessed that was why Mama was crying. Daddy touched the rim of his coffee mug but didn't drink from it. The more he stared at Mama, the more she didn't turn around. And the more I watched them, the more I tried to understand.

There wasn't any breakfast that morning. Mama went back to bed, and Daddy left the house. Eventually, I got up off the couch and threw the onions and potatoes in the garbage. I thought about how it all started with trash, and now, how it might end the same way.

Rainey finally came out of the bathroom, and we walked down to the 7-Eleven to get a package of doughnuts to share. In front of us the road curved around, and all of the houses sat back beyond their smooth, sunlit lawns, grand and still, their front doors facing out as if nothing ever happened inside.

"Was that your mama crying?" Rainey asked me. Her long blond braid slipped over one shoulder, and she pulled it taut.

"Yeah," I said. "And then Daddy went off."

The door chimes rang as we left the store, and I tore open the paper bag, its cellophane window promising better things. Rainey took a half-sized doughnut and then a half-sized bite.

"Daddies do that," she said and licked powdered sugar from her fingers. She stretched, reaching up, as if she could pluck a father or two out of thin air.

The sky that Saturday morning was a metallic blue, shining like some kind of big American car.

I stared up at the sky and her dancing fingers. "Do what?"

"Leave," she said.

THE PRETTY DAYS

NOVEMBER 1967

In Chu Lai the base spread out in a fan of tents, once white, turned a rusty color. Sand and wind. Wind and sand. South China Beach. That wasn't the first visual, though. The first was the mountains. The green of the hills. The vast flats of rice fields. And the river, like a long blue-black snake. All the places where we carried our guns, radios, half-empty canteens. All the places where we expected to die.

We had enlisted, willing to serve our country. We had not dodged the draft, knowing what duty meant. Sergeant, Lance Corporal, Private First Class. We became Blackwood, Shields, Franklin, rank understood. Names we were called at home—Royal, Titus, Walt—were traded in for ammunition, for cigarettes. We threw familiarity to the side, the collective now vital. Only later, in Vĩnh An, would we fall back to first names, their pronunciation easier, more immediate among the Vietnamese soldiers in our squad. But Vĩnh An was to come. In this month of moments we were still getting our bearings, Chu Lai like a sleepaway camp with artillery fire.

The best part about Chu Lai was the beach. The sun, the crabs caught and cooked, the bottles of tepid beer drunk, the hours slept. Until we woke up to the blasts. And to the bright flares overhead, gold and red waves of light against the sky, as we beat our way past the weight of sleep into the long, insistent sound of sirens and shouts from the bunkers, into the sand littered with the corpses of the crabs, their shells cracking under our boots, our massive black boots.

And eventually the morning would come, more gold for our faces, our eyes like gashes against the early cloth of daylight. And the fighting would dismiss itself like something only the dark was allowed to know and discuss. Somehow there was breakfast and then more sleep, for some of us sooner than others. An eventual swim in the dark waters beside darker fishing nets. Another day, another blue sky. We didn't ask our purpose; we knew our purpose. And yet it wasn't that simple; it was clouded by the red dust of too many trails; it was complicated and out of control. Still, we cleaned our weapons, packed our gear, and got ready for the next camping trip. We knew we'd smell more than the sharp green scent of trees, we'd make our way through more than elephant grass, we'd flatten ourselves into the days and then the nights and make it through.

But for the moment, the view through the rip in the tent was the beach and the sky and a thin line of horizon. Those were the pretty days. The days in Chu Lai.

LAKE SYBELIA

JUNE 1970

Summer was finally here and the days were drenched in heat. The palm trees waved in the high breeze, so high we couldn't feel it in the yard or through the wide-open windows of the house. The tangerine trees kept dropping their fruit as if they'd had enough and just couldn't hold on any longer.

Royal had come home nearly two months before, in May, when the air was still calm and the days warm but not yet weighted with humidity. We were all getting used to each other again. A man in the house after so many years. Years of me and the three kids, LuLu and Saul and Rainey, getting along on our own. Ages it seemed.

And now here he was, like he'd never left, like someone else had come home in his place. Charles Royal Blackwood III. My husband, my Marine sergeant, my R3. Finally returned to the lakes of central Florida. He'd been gone for so long I thought he was on permanent R&R—but his rest and recreation had actually been rest and rehabilitation. Stateside without a word to me, he spent months at a west coast VA clinic getting used to the one thing he'd left behind in the village of Vĩnh An: his right arm.

I had to think about that arm, missing as if never before attached to Royal's muscled shoulder. The muscles still rose from his body, but he was thinner, sadder, quieter. And he smiled at me to hide these things, bits of gesture and attitude that riddled the air around us. The days and nights became overdone and endless, the unspoken space between us wider, and I knew they were leading up to something, something that littered my mind like gone pecans, something not worth keeping anymore.

The only man I'd ever loved, every night he wanted to hold me in bed. He slipped beneath the sheets beside me and outlined my body with his own, his chest against my back, his legs against mine, his breath in my hair. "My woman, my Minnie," he murmured, his voice soft and stricken. I'd spent the past three years alone in this same bed, used to its empty width where I could lie with outstretched arms, only sleep to keep me company. I took up the entire bed; there was no room for anyone else.

Now he whispered, "Come here," and patted the mattress like it was some kind of landing zone.

I stood at the dresser and put down my brush, looking at him past my own reflection in the mirror. He pulled his white undershirt off in one motion, all with his left hand, and sat there bare-chested, waiting. I felt my breath pull into me, at the sheer measure of his missing arm, the scars raised around the site marking the newness. The hush of the room, and then a lit cigarette—the click, the hiss, and the lick of flame from his lighter. When he first showed me how it was engraved, I'd stared at the lighter's details—on one side the word *VIETNAM* and a tiny map of the country, and on the other the Combined Action Patrol insignia, *USMC, 1967-1968-1969*, and his initials *CRB III*. A small dent marked the map side, somewhere in the South China Sea. The lighter snapped shut and smoke trailed like a gray ribbon toward the ceiling.

I crossed the room and took his cigarette and, without taking a drag, crushed it into the ashtray on the bedside table. I drew my nightgown over my head, then reached across his left shoulder and traced the tattoo that ran along its blade, a double-edged sword, like a length of bamboo, dark and cool. He followed the line of my chin to my center down to my inner thighs, to places slow and reeling and hidden. I searched for memory, for the body of the man I'd once known. There was no beginning or ending to him. He'd come back to me after too long, and the time he'd been gone seemed to disappear in his presence. He laid his hand across my back and pulled me to him, his touch flying up my spine. He breathed my name and then words I didn't understand. How Royal could lie next to me, his one arm keeping me close, and how the lonesomeness was still there. A feeling that I'd known too long, that he must have known as well.

"I love you," he said.

His expression somber, his body above mine, scars across his throat, his chest, his arm pressing down, the mattress giving in, and my hands traveling, mistrusting where to touch. The strange newness, the ravaged roots where arm had once met shoulder.

"I love you, too." I tried without knowing how to try, without a map.

"Minnie, baby."

It didn't matter. The past was gone, and remembering didn't help. His hand around the back of my neck, his mouth over mine, our breath tied as one.

"I can't believe you're leaving," I'd told him the day he left. "Please, Royal, don't you go and get hurt." The minute I'd said the words, I wished I could take them back. But it was too late. And Royal smiled at me then. The last thing he did was give me that smile—a smile like a promise.

I traced the hollowed space above his breastbone, and then along his throat to his shoulder and the emptiness where his arm had once been. Before, I'd been afraid, but now I longed to know all of Royal, and I ran my fingers over the emptiness. He opened his eyes and then shut them, moving from me, trying not to. From his closed mouth a sound of distress stretched over us, and I drew my hand away.

Outside, through the bedroom window, night and moon blanketed by clouds blurred through my tears.

"I'm sorry, baby," he said, his hand in my hair. "It's not fair to you. The way I am now."

I didn't say anything, feeling the layer of blame, knowing that he felt it, too. He held his side and fell asleep. The hush of the room, the clamor of insects outside in the grove, Royal's face unlit and lined. Nearly two years younger than me, he seemed older, the burden of all that he'd known and seen, what he wouldn't share, pressed between us.

"How is it you have such a wild mind?" Royal once asked me.

We'd been driving around to stay cool one summer evening, several summers before Vietnam crept into the nightly news, before Royal traded his work as a carpenter for that of the Marines.

"What on earth are you talking about?" I sat up straighter and turned toward him. He had one hand on the steering wheel, the other stretched across the top of the seat behind me.

"Just that, Min. You've got the wildest mind of anyone I've ever known." He glanced at me and then back at the road, his dark eyes bright with reflection. "You're willing to get in the car and go for a drive with no idea of where I'm taking you. You talk about things everyone else is afraid of, like how people can be cruel and crazed and then turn around and smile, as if meanness can just disappear. How the sun and the moon have nothing and everything in common. How the glimmer of a smile from Saul can do you in. You don't think in straight lines, none of that A to Z. Your mind is too tangled and untamed for that."

"Well then, it's up to you to calm it down," I said and leaned in to kiss his cheek.

"I'm willing," he said.

And he was willing. Willing to forget that I was barely divorced, that I had a three-year-old son, that I was just making it and nearly losing my mind with whatever folks expected me to do. I hated expectations and there they were, always waiting, always insistent. Do this, do that, do it right. Raise a boy with no father, keep your house neat as a pin, go to church, praise the Lord, forgive, but don't forget to honor the men who died for this country. Why didn't they ever talk about the ones who returned? The ones, like Isaac, my first husband, who carried war inside him, whom I'd let go, afraid of the direction he might take.

Like Royal said, I didn't know where we were going, but the breeze was as cool and unconditional as his promises. He said he'd take the load off me, and after nearly a year together, a year of finding I could laugh again, of understanding how devoted he was, I believed him. Heading east toward the ocean, we drove for more than an hour and crossed the waterway over to Cocoa Beach. In the distance, the Cape Canaveral lighthouse searched the night, its light swinging out toward the Atlantic. Royal parked the car and came around to open my door. When he took my hand, I felt a tug of uncertainty. I hoped I was ready to try this again—another man, another marriage.

Every night since Royal's return I'd slept without dreaming, eventually waking to his sudden, reckless movements, his screams, words I didn't understand, humming past and gone. There was grit in his voice, fierce like fire, like bad driving rain. And tonight there were names.

"Walt! Jimmy!" he shouted, tangling the sheets, kicking them loose.

Then something about pretty. Pretty little bastards. And then more yelling, without words. I sat up, again not knowing what I should do. Like they had on previous nights, his shouts, streaked with terror, with secrets and misery, would wake the kids.

"Wake up, Royal." I stroked his cheek, though I knew he might try to lash out if awakened in this state.

He lay there, quite still, his eyes wide and staring.

"Royal?"

The sheet spread white across his waist. There was a sadness to him I'd never known and didn't know if I could take. Hesitant, not knowing if I could help him or ease his pain, I reached out to touch him again. And then stopped. I lay awake, as alone as I'd been in the past three years, the silence stringing across the room and into the night.

The hands of the clock glowed, upright at two, then at a quarter after and half past. The house was hushed with sleep, and I climbed out of bed and wandered from one room to the next. In the living room, I pulled open the blinds. The moon, not quite full, was veiled in cloud lines, and the sky was washed a dark indigo.

Years before, I'd looked from another window to the car in the driveway and wondered if I should take seven-month-old Saul and leave. Isaac, my first Marine, knew I'd never loved him and turned mean. A marriage out of desperation, a divorce that didn't keep him away, a death on a distant beach, which I divined as the only peace he'd ever known. The last sky I hoped Isaac had seen, blue and spare. But the sky beyond this window. Like ink. Like the bottom of a well.

I pushed open the front door and walked out to the road. I could have walked into town in my nightgown, and no one would ever have known. My feet were bare, and the road, even now, held the day's heat. I moved onto the cooler grass of the Callahans' front garden, stepping over a hose and moving around the mounds of azaleas. An immense quiet had taken hold of the night, even the insects settling. Between yards, I cut down to the water's edge. A light was on in the Walbrights' glass lake house, and I thought of Lillian Walbright, how she swam every morning and evening. Late at night. How she might be out there, a silhouette on a long dock, a silent sidestroke alongside the shore. Two housewives shedding their nightgowns, well beyond midnight, only their slick, wet heads above the bright surface.

Lake Sybelia was calm, a mirror to the distant, cloud-swept moon. I stepped out of loose cotton into cool water, finding the sandy bottom, wading up to my thighs, and pushing off. Water hyacinths surrounded me—how simple it would be to sink beneath them. I thought of dogs that disappeared every now and then, and when they didn't turn up, the neighborhood laying blame on alligators.

I sank below the surface and opened my eyes to the green watery light above, the darkness beneath. Grasses from the lake floor brushed against my shoulders, my arms and legs, and wrapped around my wrists and ankles. I held my right arm against my side and tried to think of it as gone, how I might swim in circles without it. Like a minnow, flitting between the sharp tangled grass blades, looking for shadows, looking for excuses, looking for a place to hide.

I'd never been able to hold my breath for long and came up to tread water, my hands fanning back and forth. Swells of silver and black left me and moved toward the shore. And on the shore, a figure standing all alone. Only his broad shoulders and white T-shirt placed him in the dark yard, that and the firm click of his lighter, the cigarette he held at his side. I sank underneath the surface again, wishing the lake would swallow me right then and there.

I didn't know it then, but on the drive to Cocoa Beach all those years ago, I was already pregnant with LuLu. I'd begun losing things, just like I had the first time around with Saul. House keys, grocery lists, lipsticks. Royal noticed I seemed dazed, distracted. I thought it sweet he'd take me for a drive, like it was a way to channel my attention.

There at Cocoa, he slipped his hand out of mine, and we kicked off our shoes and carried them. Coquina shells speckled the sand, and undersized waves brushed the shore, leaving lines of foam. With each step, I could feel something slowly rising inside me, like salt water, caustic and cold.

"What is it?" Royal said.

He'd stopped walking, and I was slightly ahead of him. I turned around and looked past him into the dark. There were stars everywhere, and they were much too bright.

"I don't know," I said. "It's just that I never have been able to get through much alone." I pulled my foot back through the wet sand. "And I don't really want to. But even if I can count on you, then something will come up because something always does. And then, praise be to G, I'll be alone again. I don't know if I can take that."

Silent and watchful, he stepped closer and held me.

"You know I wouldn't be here if I didn't want to be, and I don't plan on going anywhere." Holding my shoulders, he turned me around so that I faced away from him. His arms surrounded me, and I relaxed into him. "That's what I know now, okay?"

"Okay," I said to the beach before me. I tried to turn around, but he wouldn't let me.

"Do something for me," he said.

"What, Royal?"

The sand disappeared into the darkness, and I felt his breath against my temple.

"Close your eyes."

In the distance, somewhere out there, was NASA but no moon.

"Are you some kind of crazy?"

"Yes, I'm crazy. About you."

Royal lay on the bed in his boxers, smoking, the covers pushed to one side. I thought of the night before, how little sleep I'd had. I didn't know what the day would bring, only that it was seven o'clock in the morning and already stifling.

"What's on your mind, Minnie?"

"Nothing, R3. Nothing at all." My hair was full of knots the brush wouldn't run through. "I'm just over here, trying to breathe." I thought about breakfast, getting three teenagers out the door and off to swimming lessons and summer jobs. "Why can't we get a breeze?"

"R3? You haven't called me that since the day I got home." From across the room Royal's face registered a new kind of amusement, but he barely smiled. "Come back to bed."

"The kids will be waking up." I thought of Saul and LuLu and Rainey the night before, supposedly asleep in their rooms, the hollow pine doors cracked open. You could hear everything in this house. A simple sigh, a wisp of laughter. It all carried through the hallways.

"Come on now, Minnie. We're just making up for lost time. They're teenagers; they know that."

"Well, not LuLu," I said, raking the brush over one ear. "She's still young."

"Oh, she's not all that naïve. She keeps her eyes wide open, does that Lu girl."

"Well, all the more reason for us to get dressed ASAP. Eyes wide open doesn't need to be seeing that."

I put the brush away and took my dress off the back of the chair, draped it over my head, and guided my arms through the short sleeves. Everything felt catawampus, like time was coming at us from the corners. The abbreviations were back, falling from my mouth, impatient and ready to escape when I least expected. I knew I only reeled in my words out of nervousness, saying things that made the kids laugh and made me look the fool. Royal never said the habit bothered him, but I knew it made him curious. Slippery little phrases I couldn't control, and then his hand over my mouth, uncovering it for a kiss and then silence.

"Damn," I said, trying to smooth down the pleats of my dress. I crossed the room and turned my back toward Royal. "Zip me up, okay?"

I felt his hand against my bare back, and the neat line he drew up to my neck. Like the way he measured wood for the cedar chest he'd started, straight lines, the boards balanced between chin and shoulder, hand and foot. A way to keep busy, to rethink his carpentry skills, to build something that might be filled with hope. It was amazing how much he could do with one arm. I turned around just as he took the cigarette from his mouth, wincing a little.

"You all right?"

"I'm always right with you around, Min." He grinned at me, and I waved away the smoke. If he could have had his way, he'd have kept me in bed an entire month, his painkillers and a carton of Lucky Strikes nearby.

"You're hurting, aren't you? I can tell you can't ignore it."

"Just like you can't ignore me." He put out the cigarette and pulled a clean undershirt over his head.

"That's right, baby," I said. "You are my one and only pain." I leaned down and kissed his unshaven cheek, the smells of cedar and tung oil mixing with ash and smoke. "My one and only R3."

Sunlight poured through the kitchen windows, reflecting colored prisms through the glass bird on the windowsill, and landed on the counters where Saul and Rainey sat, pennants of light across their bare legs. Saul watched Royal break eggs, one-handed, onto the rim of a widemouthed bowl, while Rainey took a sip from Saul's orange juice. The kids never questioned Royal's absence, all the months he'd spent in that rehabilitation hospital and then in the clinic way across the country with no word to us—but I still couldn't get over that. On the wall, the sunburst clock was just shy of eight, the second hand sorting through time, bit by bit. The morning was too loud and sudden, everybody talking at once, and I kept shushing.

"Now, R3, you are just talking the talk."

"Please, Mama," LuLu said. "Can't you let Daddy finish just one story?"

"How about it, Minnie?" Royal ran his fingers across the back of my neck as I passed by to put the egg carton back in the fridge. "Just one story."

"All right, all right. Tell your damn story then."

He leaned against the fridge and told us about the water buffalo.

"A dark hide and a thick attitude, horns from here to there, and a sad, hopeless stare. Moving through the Trà Bồng River, slow and massive, sometimes resting on the bank, her sturdy legs tucked underneath. And once, a lone egret next to her, leaning in, as if to whisper a secret."

Royal leaned in and whispered to LuLu, which sent her into a fit of laughter.

"And then what?" LuLu said.

"And there was the time I saw her in the distance, grazing, a small girl on her wide brown back. At first I was afraid, but then the girl waved to me and leaned forward to pat the beast's side."

I listened, but pretended not to—pulling a pan from the cupboard and setting it on the stove—thinking it was just a story, one that came from Royal's wandering mind, from another world. The years he'd been gone, on a round of tours he couldn't refuse, he'd collected stories. He didn't talk about his sense of duty; he only talked about the buffalo, the villagers, his squad.

Sure, now he could tell his stories. About where he'd been, what he'd seen—the elephant grass, mountains swallowed in mist, a girl named An who fought like a boy. But I knew, down under all the sweet flourishes and phrasings, these tales simply blocked the way to the real story. The story none of us asked him. How he'd survived.

Saul pulled at the leather bracelet on his wrist, then interrupted Royal. "You act as though it was all okay."

Rainey sat up straighter, and LuLu frowned at her brother. There was no more reason to shush anyone. The morning gave way to questions without answers.

"It wasn't all okay." Royal's expression didn't falter, but his voice did. "None of it was okay."

"Then I don't get it." Saul kicked the lower cabinet doors with his heels. "Why are we even over there?"

"You'll understand someday. Or maybe you won't." Royal looked at the kitchen floor and then back at Saul. "You know the hottest days of summer? Take away the shade. The worst of rainstorms? Add floodwaters. The tallest dune grass? Grow it high and deep enough to hide a herd of elephants. The best of friends? Complicate those friendships with death. And enemies? Don't even try to define them."

Rainey slid down off the counter and took a stack of plates to the dining room. Royal stopped talking, and the room became still.

Since his return, there'd been the succession of listless days and broken-down nights, the handfuls of pain meds—the yellows and blues—surely the reason for his blank, distracted stares and the thick quiet surrounding him. His stories seemed a way for him to force himself out of this state, though at times it seemed the colored pills did the talking. He shined more like the old Royal then, less inside himself, more animated.

He came home with military medals and that tattoo across his back, so different from the Marine Corps emblem just below his shirtsleeve. I knew he was capable; I knew he still loved me and could make love to me, but I also knew nothing would ever be the same. And somehow his smile was wider, his soul larger, and his body—strong and ravaged—unlike any I'd ever known. He came home with a kind of suffering so deep that at first we didn't know it was there, and once it did surface, we didn't know how to respond. But he came home.

When he was gone, he'd sent letters, which sometimes arrived in lots of three or more, after months of nothing at all. Sometimes the pages were stained with the clay-colored soil he said got into every crevice, from fingernails and flak jackets to M-16s and bandoliers and machine gun belts. At first the notes were long, but they grew shorter, and eventually stopped showing up.

I re-read his descriptions of Vietnamese girls with long dark hair, their staring eyes turned toward tall Americans, the men in his squad. I recognized how Royal might tell the girls a few jokes, how they'd lean in and laugh. And then in my mind, I identified him lying in a field hospital, crowded with other wounded men, and in the chaos, a handful of nurses, one sweet-faced, with curls falling from her cap. I thought up these women out of jealousy, but also with a trace of hope, that he was telling stories over there, stories that helped him remember where he came from and what he had to come back to.

For a while, I was convinced he was MIA. I refused to think he was dead but couldn't bring myself to pick up the phone to find out what was what. And then one afternoon, there he was, standing in the doorway.

It was nearly time for the kids to head into the day, and I circled around the kitchen. There were too many bodies and not enough room to think. I handed silverware to LuLu and napkins to Saul and sent them out into the dining room, where Rainey sat already, her back to us. Royal followed, his stories done with, quiet filling up the day.

At the counter, I turned the bacon and whisked the eggs and deposited them into the skillet. Their rich scent traveled straight out into the morning air, along with the words I mumbled under my breath. "What the hell?"

Even as I pulled biscuits from the oven, my mind folded in on itself. I leaned over the pan of light yellow eggs, then turned off the gas burner. The biscuits sat piled high on a white plate, and sun flooded the kitchen. Everyone was waiting in the dining room for me. I waved Royal into the kitchen, knowing he would take over and serve the eggs, seeing the understanding in the corners of his eyes. I padded down the hall and ran a bath, climbing into the tub as it filled, sinking under the tepid water, imagining the depth of the lake, the muddy bottom like a refuge.

November 1967. Letters every day. April 1968. Postcards for LuLu, packets for Saul. October 1968. The letter on thin white paper, each word weighted. Just in time for my birthday. Three pages, the last saved for the news that he'd been reassigned. August 1969. The one-paragraph note about An, a village girl, only eleven, who wore a necklace of bullets. How her grandmother invited him for a supper of spicy broth and vegetables. I followed his lines, where he'd put pen to paper, trying to fathom another family, all those families with daughters and sons, mothers and fathers, uncles, grandmothers, crowding my mind. December 1969. The last letter we received. Christmas greetings from the United States Marine Corps, 1st CAG, Vietnam.

For every letter that arrived from the San Francisco APO, I saved myself from counting the months by memorizing the words and phrases Royal wrote down. Words like *klicks* and *calling cards* and *cowboys*. I latched onto their hard sounds, their new meanings, and the ones that were completely new I said out loud. *Di di mau* for running the kids out the door and off to school. *Xin loi* for saying I was sorry when I really wasn't. *Beaucoup* surfaced only when I'd had more than enough of Saul's sullen looks or LuLu's backtalk.

Out in the front yard, I'd stand underneath the oak tree, tying another bottle to the twine looped through the lower branches. One bottle for every letter. Once, Rainey helped, threading the twine, handing me the bottles by their long necks, her pretty face lit by their colors as the sun reflected through. Sea, scarlet, cobalt, lilac. I reserved the word *dep* for Rainey, for her beauty and quiet kindness, the way she reached through the leaves, the way she smiled but didn't speak. She didn't ask where the bottles came from, and I imagined her months of waiting for her mother merging with my months of waiting for Royal, the oak strung with colored glass a reminder that they would return.

For every letter, a new word. For every letter, another bottle.

Down at the Marketessen, close to Christmas 1967, with barely two months gone since Royal's departure, Vita Hull invited me into the stockroom for a glass of wine. We stood and talked and drank almost the entire bottle. A slender green bottle from the region of Italy where Vita had been born.

"It's lovely, isn't it?" She didn't sip, but swallowed. The glass tipped and the swirl of vermillion disappeared.

Like me, she was alone. Before, she'd run the store with her husband. But for years she'd been in charge, ever since August Hull had put that sign on the front door. *GONE FISHING FOREVER*—written in grease pencil on the brown butcher paper from their meat counter. I think Vita wasn't a bit surprised. The sign was still on the door, faded and torn at the edges, the hours still eight to four, no one to remind her to fill the produce bins or wear an appropriate shade of lipstick for the customers or keep her little poodle off the checkout counter.

I had to wonder how she'd ended up with a plain little man like August Hull. And how a man could love fishing more than his shapely, low-voiced wife. Of course, fishing was the excuse. Real estate was his true ticket out of town. Plots of swampland, a series of rented sales offices, disappearing acts all over the state, and eventually prison. August Hull in the headlines, and the lines of gossiping women in the Marketessen.

Without him, Vita seemed more relaxed. Happier even. She'd kept up her smart dresses and her enormous hairdo, a pile of black twisted with gray, silver pins holding it all in place. Some said it was gambling, even men, that kept Vita Hull at ease, but I liked to think it was freedom. No one to answer to. For me, that seemed a lonesome, unhappy thing, but Vita seemed to thrive without a husband coming and going.

She had good words for all of her customers, especially the wives whose husbands had gone off to Vietnam. Wives like me. And those like Eva, already acting like a war widow when I met her, along with Rainey, inside the Marketessen. Wives, like Vita Hull herself, who might never see their husbands again. The monogrammed white handkerchiefs she kept tucked in her sleeve or in the pocket of her dress occasionally found their way into the hands of customers. I called to mind all of the distraught women of our town, each with a white cotton square in her pocketbook, each embroidered with the looping V, the hovering H, the mysterious L.

That December afternoon in the stockroom was not typical, and yet we talked of typical things. Recipes for meatloaf and hash, how LuLu and Saul were doing in school, and the little girl that lived with us.

"Rainey is her name?" Vita stroked her toy poodle's ears and asked me questions before I could manage to ask my own. And then offered opinions. "What was her mother thinking? Giving a child that name and then going off without her. Rainey? Like downpours and puddles and being caught without an umbrella."

Her voice reminded me of wind and cornhusks and gravel.

"You're missing that husband of yours, my dear?"

I glanced at Vita.

"It's okay, honey. You don't have to tell me."

"Oh, but I do miss him." I felt the flush in my face. "All the time."

"He's very handsome, that Royal Blackwood. I'll bet you miss him something fierce." She kept her eyes on me and clicked her fingernails against her wineglass. "I'd be very worried if I were you."

I hesitated. "Well, of course I worry."

"Oh, no!" she laughed. "That's not what I mean at all. You should be worried about other women. I'm telling you—those languorous looks over a shoulder, one drink too many, too much R&R. Heavens, war is war. But other women. No, no, no."

"Royal would never..."

She held one finger over my lips. "Never say never. That's exactly how things happen. You say *never*, and what you wish away will come true." She winked at me, looked up at the ceiling. "Did you hear?" she said, still looking up. "She said nothing at all."

Around us, bags of onions and potatoes leaned together, and shelves of canned pineapple and peaches lined the walls. Not once had the entry bell chimed, customers perhaps waiting until the end of the day to rush in for Martini olives and minute steaks. Along with Vita's humor, the gritty air of the room was somehow comforting, and I held the nearly empty wine bottle under the ceiling lamp. Its sea-green hue much like the little windowsill bird LuLu had given me one birthday, streaks of jade and tiny air bubbles caught inside the glass.

"It's such a pretty color," I said.

"You should have it then." She corked the remaining wine and handed it to me. "Besides, we've had our fill." She laughed and added, "For today, at least."

From then on, Vita slipped a wrapped bottle of Barolo or Dolcetto into my grocery bag. Tall bottles of red wine, their glass sleeves bright and unusual. Sometimes, though, I'd find a pale, opaque bottle of white wine, its color muted and its taste floral. And the next two Decembers, when the crates of oranges were sent north and tinsel decorated the cash register and her poodle wore red-and-green bows, we'd share a glass or two in the stockroom.

I dressed. My hair, barely wrung out since my bath, fell against the back of my blouse in damp strips. Royal came through the bedroom and motioned to me, then to the bed.

"Come here." He pulled me over, his hand down my back.

I thought yes, but said no, the word heavy and mean. "I have things to do."

"You can still do them." He smiled.

That smile. I kissed him, then pushed him away.

"Are you afraid of me?"

"What?" I said.

"Just what I said."

"Don't be ridiculous."

"You are all up in your head, Minnie. Thinking too much."

"Well, right now, I'm thinking about getting this house picked up. You want to help?"

His smile grew broader.

"Of course you don't." I gave in and laced my arms around his neck. I kissed his cheek and pushed him away again. "Later on."

"Sometimes later doesn't come."

"You going somewhere?"

"You tell me."

I surveyed Royal, his white T-shirt, the dark stubble across his jaw. The unmade bed needed making. The bedside ashtray needed emptying. His words spilled and spun inside my mind. *You tell me.*

In the stretch of silence, I groped for a way to understand him. Royal waited, not speaking. I thought he'd search for his lighter, his cigarettes, but he just stood there. His head angled slightly, he finally spoke.

"There's only one other girl who ever pushed me away."

At first, I looked for something to throw at him, all impulse and jealousy. *Only one other girl...* I grabbed the brush off my dresser. And then I paused and lowered the brush, bristles at my side.

"An," he said. "The girl I've told you about. Young and incredibly stubborn. Wouldn't listen. I tried to tell her. She wasn't much older than Lu. Just eleven when I met her; thirteen when she died." He blinked and knotted his fingers into a fist.

"Royal, hush. You don't have to tell me."

"No, I don't. But mostly, I don't know how."

I didn't know what else to say. Royal leaned in and kissed my forehead, marking the moment by stepping away from it. He walked across the pine floor and closed the bathroom door. I heard him start a shower and stood for a minute, listening. Running water, and some song he was singing—that Johnny Cash tune about walking the line. His mood had gone from open to shut and right back to open, just like that. His voice rang clear, not clenched, as it had been only moments before.

Sure, I thought, walk that line. Like he's doing that alone. Like I'm not trying, like I haven't been trying. The floorboards seemed to warp right under my feet, and I wondered how long I could keep this up. I was wearing thin. What would Royal and I be doing in another two months? The idea of running away came to mind—as if I were in combat and *di di* was the only way out.

Instead, I went through the kids' bedrooms, a plastic clothes basket under one arm, picking up socks and jeans, little bikini underwear, a paisley blouse, a halter top—things the kids should have thrown in the hamper. I straightened bedspreads and threw pillows into place and ignored the scattered record albums on Saul's floor and the mound of pennies, ponytail holders, and barrettes on LuLu's dresser. A little duck call, small enough to pinch between two fingers, lay at the center of the clutter. It was one of those things that seemed to have turned up out of nowhere, one that LuLu claimed, its sharp tone driving me to distraction. All the pretty pink hair things were Rainey's, and I realized how she had to share, how she probably would've liked a little space of her own.

I reached into a dresser drawer where LuLu's socks were balled against layers of underwear and little T-shirts. In the back were the drab pair, Army-issued, hidden in the drawer since Royal's departure. I'd found them only a few days after he'd left and realized the love LuLu had attached to her father. How these socks would keep him safe, because they'd never made it into his duffel. I pictured LuLu with them under her pillow at night, then tucking them back in the drawer, a dark, dull pair under her own frilly white and bright-colored ones. I closed the drawer and took up the basket of clothes.

Water poured into the washing machine, and I thought of Royal in his shower, the water pressure surely compromised. I had to get through this day, and he'd just have to make do. One load of wash begun, I worked on the kitchen. Breakfast cups and plates piled in the sink, more hot, sudsy water, my hands around a sponge, I looked out the window and beyond the oak strung with Vita's glass. White clouds filled the sky, and the road leading down to the lake was empty. Rainey and LuLu had planted daisies beside our walkway and they spilled over to one side, all leggy and lacy, like the girls. I loved that they cared enough to actually begin something, even if they'd given up once the weather had turned hot. I knew I'd probably do the same—give up on something that had started out tender and promising, the once-white petals taking on a sad yellow hue, the possibilities tipping to one side. And then my neglect, seeping through the days, killing off everything.

I imagined asking Royal to leave. He'd promised to come back and he had, and now all I could do was think of him not being here again. I hated the way I felt, and yet my heart finally stopped pitching around in my chest once I thought of him as gone. The scent of the dish soap, sweet and penetrating, filled the air, and the memory of my mother's white kitchen made an old fear rise inside me.

I remembered a morning with my mother, standing outside the Baptist church and holding her gloved hand. The silk ribbon that wound through the wrist of the glove, the warmth of her palm coming through to mine, the way she squeezed my hand a little as we entered the doors, the church interior rising above us. I was barely five years old.

And then later that day, when I'd asked for something to eat before dinner was ready, my mother said, no, I could wait. The scent of roast chicken and rolls rose as she lowered the oven door to check them, and I asked again. This time I felt my father's fingers around my wrist, yanking me out of the room, no words, just the pressure of his grip tighter and tighter around my arm, as if his forceful quiet would quiet me.

Now I held the edges of the sink, the porcelain solid, the morning makeshift. The sunburst clock swallowed every second. I thought of how it would be when I asked my husband, who loved me, to leave me alone. I imagined the quiet that would fill up the room, once he'd heard me. He'd breathe and stare straight ahead and nervously tap his top shirt pocket for his lighter. There would be no sound, just a hush like in the church so long ago. And how the calm would roar through the empty house, taking me around the wrist and pulling me. Because I knew Royal would leave; he would leave me alone. And then I'd hear his sighs at night, coming from across town in a place where he, too, would be alone.

Outside, the flowers tipped further, and a slight breeze felt its way across the windowsill, its warmth like a blow.

The bathroom door was open, and Royal had stopped singing. He stood before the mirror, drying his hair and neck. I took the towel and ran it over his back while he watched me. His eyes searched past his own reflection to mine. There were always the images of ourselves, the ones that crossed between us like barriers or boundaries, that kept us apart. And still we watched each other, carefully, unsure of what might come next. Now Royal's image was altered, obscured beyond belief. I tried to remember him the way he'd been before and felt ashamed.

The faded towel, once the color of daffodils, now the palest yellow possible, felt enormous and heavy in my hands. I moved it over his waist and hips and down, and then his hand was over mine, stopping me, not stopping me. I tried to speak and found nothing came, no words, the barest sound. Nearly a cry.

"I know, baby." And he held me, this rare and naked man. "It's too hard."

"You don't know. You don't know at all."

"I'm living in this body, aren't I?"

I expected anger, but he gave none. Where did this man come from? This man I didn't deserve. And before I knew that I would, I said it. "I need you to go. I can't breathe like this."

I felt his arm soften around me, his breath lighten and then stitch more tightly.

"Just for a while," I said, my words leaden and close. Then I backed away from him, trying to see his face.

In the years Royal had been gone, new lines had grown around his mouth and eyes, but they seemed undiscovered in this moment. His expression was blank, without the surprise I'd expected. His gaze was down, but then he looked straight at me and his eyes welled up.

I dropped the towel and faltered for a moment, then ran through the hallway. At the front door, I took the car keys from the table. I could only imagine what Royal thought when he heard the door close and the VW start up, its tinny motor trembling against the day.

In the parking lot of Hull's Marketessen, I sat, unable to get out of the bus. It was hot and the windows were rolled down. The sun beat against the VW roof, though the morning was only halfway to noon. I opened my door and a slight breeze whispered up through the gap. Without thinking it through, I'd driven to Hull's, where I could go inside and buy groceries, where I could find the thickest chops in town. Where the stockroom might offer cool metal shelves to lean against. Where someone like Vita might understand what I'd done.

I could hear what friends would say once they knew Royal was living elsewhere. The same friends who wondered why I bothered driving to the other side of town when the new shopping center had a bright Publix with wide aisles and handsome bag boys. The Marketessen was where I'd always done my shopping, ever since I first married Royal. Why, practically before that, back when we were dating and everything seemed possible.

I sat in the damned VW bus that burned a hole in Royal's military pay. Things had changed. I was no longer a wife with a husband "over there." If I went inside the store and saw Vita's open expression, her Chanel smile, I'd fall apart. I'd break down and cry and my black mascara would run all over. Vita would lend me her white cotton handkerchief and I'd ruin it. The heat inside the bus was unbearable, and I pushed the door wide and slid from my seat to the pavement.

Acacia trees were clustered in one corner of the parking lot, their shade falling short of the train tracks and Fairbanks Avenue, and I crossed the lot to stand under their low branches. Traffic hummed with the constant sound of tires on asphalt. The dwindling yellow of the acacia flowers littered the tracks and the pavement around me. I crouched down to pick up a spray of spent blooms and felt a rumbling rising from the ground. A train rushed along the tracks. There was no train whistle, no warning to the great heaving grayness before me, only movement.

Startled, unfastened from the moment, I stepped backward and watched the wall of cars speed past. I held the once-golden flowers and remembered what it was like to be going somewhere, traveling. The excitement of moving forward. Those times with Royal when we'd just get in the car and go. The train wheels wore against the track, pitching and sighing. The boxcars blurred before me, and I was relieved not to be moving, and instead, to be standing still.

Well cars, tank cars, hopper cars. I only knew the names from a book that Saul and LuLu had loved when they were little. The bright drawings, the simple words.

The train pushed on, heavier than before, loaded with something that seemed to slow it down. Grain of some sort. Enough to feed this entire town. The ground rumbled and quaked; the line of freight cars scudded past. And then the train was gone. The parking lot was still and nearly empty. A sedan had pulled up and a woman in high heels walked toward the Marketessen's front door. Her heels tapped along the pavement and the entry bells rang out, sharp and shrill. And then nothing, the sudden quiet filling me up with fear, sending me back in time, forcing me to look at things I didn't want to see.

The sky, a pale unreal blue, extended before me, taut and unremarkable, from my mother's death when I was twelve, and my father's disapproval, which certainly began the minute I was born, to all the unfortunate boyfriends—lining up and then leaving me. To the husbands who went off to war. And to the damned war itself. And now to a house full of teenagers.

I walked back to the bus and rested my hands on the top edge of the rolled-down window. The little grocery was nearly empty, peaceful, and I needed to go inside where it would be cool, only the one customer in her heels, coming and going. The glass of wine that might be offered. A shallow, unsettled breath caught inside me. I needed to buy sliced ham, tomatoes, a ribeye for supper, but instead I stood next to the VW, my hands fastened to the door, trying to understand what lay between coming and going.

I felt scattered and undone, and still there was that sky, large and wide and bleached. It seemed to be pinned up, curling at the corners, loosely draped over the morning. The moon was out, three-quartered and waning, a slightly diminished version of the one reflected in the lake the night before. An invisible line stretched toward this moon, first circling its surface and then plummeting back to earth to trace the contours of my mind.

◊ ◊ ◊

That night years before at Cocoa, there had been no moon. The sky reeled out like a black sequined evening dress. "Close your eyes." It was a command I couldn't seem to follow. I started to speak and Royal hushed me. Reluctant, I took a breath and closed my eyes. All went black. In my mind, I sketched the sky aslant, the stars falling into the sea. The fear I'd felt all along traveled up my spine. And then fingertips brushed the back of my neck down to my waist as Royal unbuttoned my dress, the folds of cotton falling around my ankles. The breeze moved over me in a different way, and Royal whispered, and I let him take my underclothes. The sound of a belt buckle and loose pocketed change hitting the sand, and then the touch of Royal's bare legs against mine. I had to resist opening my eyes as he guided me into the rising shallows. We walked slowly, water around our calves, our thighs. I invented the searchlight finding us, lighting us up, the surf carrying us out, a pair of drowned fools. And then we were swimming.

"Open your eyes," he said.

He held me against him, his body buoyant, holding mine adrift. There was a passion to his strokes, the way he held me, at the same time pulling us along, parallel to the shore. Out in the ocean, everything seemed softer and yet more defined, the surface skimmed by the wind, the depths dark, disguised. I lost all sense of myself—there was only the Atlantic spreading on and on, and our movement through the water. Arms, legs, scissoring along. There was only this night, this ocean, this man.

A wave crested farther out, and Royal motioned for me to swim by myself, to follow him. The wave reached us as we swam toward shore and carried us to the shallows. Our clothes were a ways up the beach, but the wind was warm.

"What if someone comes along?" I said.

"What if?" Royal laughed and took my hand, and we walked toward the pale heap lying just above the damp sand.

I twisted the salt water from my long rope of wet hair and stepped into my dress. Royal pulled on his shirt and trousers and sat down. I looked at him sitting there, his dark slicked hair, his bright white shirt, the most amazing man I'd ever known. He stretched out his legs, leaned onto his elbows, and observed me.

"Sit down, baby." He patted the spot next to him.

I sat and gathered my dress over my knees. Royal shifted then, taking something from his shirt pocket. Cigarettes and a matchbook most likely. But then something in his hand shimmered, and he held it out to me. A ring circled with tiny diamonds. And then, right there, in that soft white sand, he slid onto one knee.

"Will you marry me, Minnie?"

I couldn't believe that he could fool me like that. First, skinny-dipping in the dark, and then this. But there he was on one knee holding a jeweled band, like the stars overhead, bright and surprising. It was so different, so damned romantic. I hesitated, startled and happy, and then confused and crying. I made my way through the moment, not willing to question it, though I could see the result of my wavering in Royal's expression.

"No, it's all right," he said, interpreting my hesitation, the ring disappearing into his closing hand.

I reached for his hands, taking them, wanting him to slow down for me, to know that I was trying to answer. He brushed the fingertips of his open right hand across my cheeks and smiled. A smile twisted with unknowing. A smile that, when I finally answered, opened wide.

"Yes, Royal, I will. I will. But promise me one thing—"

And before I could tell him what, he stood and lifted me and promised me the world. He swung me around and kissed me. Then, back down on that one knee, he reached for my left hand and slid on that little ring. It felt right. It felt so right.

That morning outside Hull's, it felt all wrong. The hand that had slipped the ring onto my finger was gone. I should have felt a deep sadness for Royal, but anger came instead, dark and hollow and frightening. A pattern of shadows crossed the parking lot. The sedan had gone, and now another figure crossed the pavement.

I opened the door of the VW and climbed back into the driver's seat, thinking of escape, not wanting to speak to anyone. The sun-seared vinyl burned the back of my thighs. In the rearview mirror, I saw Vita approaching. Her hair appeared taller and darker than usual, and her lips a milder shade, something more like melon. She waved at me through the passenger window, then opened the door and climbed in.

"Hello there, Minnie." She faced me. Surprisingly, her hair cleared the ceiling.

"Good morning, Vita." I didn't know what else to say. There was Vita Hull, sitting right next to me in my VW bus.

"Look at this," she said of the radio. "That's nice. You can listen to Doris Day and Frank Sinatra while you drive around, can't you?"

I listened mostly to country stations—those that played Wanda Jackson, Johnny Cash, Loretta Lynn. But I nodded, knowing full well the tuning dial was nearly always set to the stations Saul and Rainey and LuLu liked, the ones with loud disc jockeys and louder music. One-syllable bands like the Doors and the Stones, but I wasn't about to tell that to Vita.

"It's a pleasant morning, isn't it?" she said.

"Well, yes, " I said. " A bit warm."

"And why would anyone be sitting in a car on such a hot day?" She smiled. "Why don't you come inside? We have the air conditioning going, and there's a sale on pork chops. You like chops, don't you? Or at least that husband of yours does."

I looked over at her and then down at the brake pedal.

"Is that why you're sitting out here?" She touched my arm gently. "Come now, you can tell Vita."

"What?" I said.

"Don't act so confused. I can't tell how my customers are doing? Of course I can. They wander around the produce and linger over the string beans, then pick up a tomato and put it back down. Of course I can tell. But you, dear girl, sitting out here, not coming in. What am I to think?"

I had no idea how to respond. In the lull, the moment settled, laden and expectant.

Vita ran her hand over the red vinyl seat. "I hear these seats come in some kind of scotch plaid. Did you know that? So fancy, cars these days."

"Yes," I said, thinking instead how simple the red seats with white trim seemed.

"How's LuLu doing? And Rainey, sweet child." Vita fingered the wide gold links of her necklace. "They must be getting to be young ladies."

"Yes, they are. LuLu's nearly ready for junior high. Hopefully, she'll straighten up and do some work there. She hasn't been so keen on school these past few years."

"What with her father gone, I suppose not. It's hard on children when their fathers are away, don't you think? Just as much as it is on the mothers." She sighed and pulled a handkerchief out of her dress pocket, and then she touched the white cotton to her throat. "Sometimes, I'm just as glad I didn't have children." She noted me, her glimpse cool and forgiving.

"Yes, children." I stared at her handkerchief. "Even my husband—all those needs."

"Oh, yes," she said, not laughing. "Men. So dependent. I wonder how they'd survive without us. Not that I have to worry about that anymore."

I thought of August Hull, in prison. I remembered my father and how he cursed under his breath when he came home each day from his mill job, whenever he had to pass me in the hallway. And Isaac, how he'd drink. How he'd malign me with words and lash Saul's small backside with his belt. I couldn't think of Royal as a link in this line of men. It was wrong of me to say unkind things about him. He had survived and then come home to us.

"I'm sorry." I tried not to, but started to cry. "I should be grateful. I mean, Royal is home, after all."

"But honey—"

"Oh, please. Don't be nice to me. I don't deserve it."

"Well, of course you're crying, my dear. Of course you are." She reached into a side pocket of her navy dress and pulled out another handkerchief. "Listen. I started out as little Vita Lucci, nearly twenty. Like my family name, full of light, full of hope. And then I went and married Augie—what did I do to deserve him? The man who gave me a name that contains nothing. Hull. No light, no hope, just a lot of emptiness." She waved the clean handkerchief at me. "But I always talk too much. Here, take."

"Thank you." I wiped my eyes and nose, relieved that my mascara didn't blacken the cotton. "I just feel so confused. And so damned mad."

I thought of Royal all those years ago, swooping in out of the blue and sweeping me off my feet. I liked my feet on the ground now. My life blurred before me, every edge crooked and broken. And what was broken I couldn't fathom trying to fix. I'd kept going all this time, but I hadn't bargained for this, this idea of a man.

The day Royal arrived home with his bags on one shoulder, he'd dropped them before he reached down to hug us all. At first, I didn't understand. He was as strong as ever, and there was a leanness to him I'd never known before.

I buried my face in my hands.

"That's right," Vita said. "You just raise a ruckus. We all deserve at least one good cry in this lifetime. When Augie left, I thought I could brave the world without looking back. But life doesn't work that way. Eventually, you just have to let it all go."

I swallowed and tried to breathe between sobs. And then I stared past Vita, past the parking lot and the railroad tracks. "I asked Royal to leave this morning."

Vita was silent, and then she said, "Did you now?"

An arc of white trails scarred the sky, reminders of departing jetliners.

"Go inside and buy your family's groceries. And then go home, look your husband in the eye and tell him everything you know, everything you feel. And you know what else?"

I dabbed my eyes with the handkerchief, afraid of what she'd say next.

"Be thankful. That Royal is back home, ready to keep on. Be thankful, even though everything has changed—and I know it has. Believe me, I know it has."

There was something like earth and grit in her tone, an insistence that dared me to go and do what she'd said. It was as though I'd been turned inside out and given a chance, a white phosphorous moment that lit up my mind. She'd never had another chance. And here was mine.

"I can't do that," I said.

Where there had been fear, where there should have been remorse, there was now a needle of anger. I was the forward observer, I was the listening post, I was the damned short-timer who didn't want to go out on any more missions. I was as done in as Royal seemed strung out. Military man. Military, ma'am. I knew I was unreasonable, demanding what couldn't be given. I folded the wrinkled handkerchief and held it tight. "I'll wash this and return it to you."

Vita shook her head at me. "Keep that one for yourself." She opened the passenger door and climbed down from the bus.

I turned the key in the ignition.

Vita closed the door and didn't wave as she usually did whenever we said our good-byes. She stood there for a minute and examined me through the open window, then turned and walked back inside the store. Her hairdo was taller than Wanda Jackson's, and her stare had gone right through me.

I listened to the rhythm of the VW's motor, then turned the steering wheel and swung out of the parking lot onto Fairbanks. Before me, the railway crossing lights began to flash and the gate swung down. I could hear the train whistle in the distance. At home, there'd be a packed duffel at the foot of the bed, a singular, one-armed man pulling it closed.

I'd get there in time to undo the straps and put everything back in the dresser drawers. But right now, there was a train coming and Royal was surely sitting and smoking one more cigarette, thinking of ways he could stay. In my mind, I heard the lighter click shut. The train ripped past and then was gone, the caboose a red smear against the day. The warning bells stopped their clamor and the railway gate raised slowly. Royal would tap his top pocket to make sure the lighter was there, just above his heart, and stand and walk out the door, closing it gently behind. I drove through town and around the lake. Above, the sky opened out like an old bedspread, and the distant moon lowered itself, as if ready to sink into someone's arms.

BOOKKEEPING

MARCH 1965

Three crates of oranges and grapefruit from Hollyanna Orchards. Two boxes of pimento-stuffed olives, twelve jars in each. One case of milk cartons, quart-sized, whole. Another of skim. A half case of butter, divided into slim two-stick boxes. Cartons of brown eggs.

I press the red subtotal and total keys, the small broken hearts of this adding machine. I pull down the red-handled lever each time. The math is always correct.

Some say I've been left alone, forsaken. But that is incorrect.

When I first met August Hull, he was one of the most sought-after men in town. Not so tall, but those Burton blue eyes, that bronzed face, those crisp white shirts. What with his thriving grocery business, a full head of black hair, the way he winked and smiled and chatted with his customers, believe you me, he was quite a catch. Sinatra played on the transistor radio by the checkout while I checked him

114

over, pausing by the packs of Wrigley's chewing gum, the household matches, the metal rack of cigarettes. With me, he'd step out from behind the register, twirl me around, and croon along with Frank.

"Vita!" he'd say, his voice always exclaiming, as if I was at the back of the store and not standing right next to him. "Vita Lucci! You are like sunlight in my day. Always brightening things up."

Young, just another girl in a pencil skirt in a row of girls in pencil skirts in a local college course that taught typing, filing, and basic office skills, I was silly enough to believe him. But someone named August who dances with you in the middle of his own grocery and breathes "Begin the Beguine" into your ear, how can you not get carried away?

He hired me as a bookkeeper, and I then fell into other roles—running the cash register, accepting deliveries, locking the Marketessen doors each evening, and eventually making his four-minute egg each morning. Sure he was romantic, right up until the time I said "I do," a plain platinum band for my left hand. "Simple, elegant, and durable," August said of the ring. "Like you, Vita!"

I wondered at simple, and then at durable. I held on to the idea of elegance and hoped for more. Much more.

What I got was shelves stocked with Pepperidge Farm thin white sandwich bread, and another of Bays English muffins, Arnold's Whole Wheat, and an assortment of packaged lady fingers, molasses cookies, and pound cake.

Only after we'd been married for a while did I realize August was only in this world for the big catch. And I don't mean love or money. I mean fish. He would rather spend an afternoon with a pole in his hand, baiting his hook with scraps from the meat counter, the still lake air surrounding him, than spend a precious second more with me.

The Lynn Dairy delivery boys came every other day, and always took off their caps at the back door. I could count on their pints of half-and-half and their giant grins, the same way I could count on August's trips to the lake every Thursday. Another way to add up the weeks and months and years. I'd slap another pair of perch into a pan, sizzling with Lynn's creamery butter, and think of cows and barns and all the milking and churning it had taken for one pat, and then I'd think of the underside of the rowboat August took out, how its oars had been touched more than I had.

One day he didn't come back. Left a note for his customers on the front door of his little Marketessen. Some say he left for bigger opportunities, for real estate, for fortunes found further south. That he searched too far and landed in prison. Let them have their rumors. To me, those tall tales, they smell like fish.

For me, he left the inventory, the lists, the curling register receipts. And I still have the platinum band. So generous, so impossible, don't you know. Like the man who bought it for me. I keep it in the cash register, in the coin slot that's meant for half-dollars, so that every time I make a sale, I see it from the corner of my eye. The register keys are black, except the single scarlet one. No Sale.

I ring up bottles of wine now—a way of brightening the books. "A bottle of Chianti to go with your sirloin, Mrs. Lingstrum?" The drawer opens and there are the small shining circles, half-promises. A single Kennedy profile surrounded by the word LIBERTY, and beneath it, a glimpse of memory, still alive and still elegant.

HOW CAREFULLY WE TOOK THE CORNERS

JULY 1970

Halfway into July, Rainey's thirteenth birthday came around. Eva wasn't there, as usual promising to make it up with a special visit someday soon. And even though Rainey didn't want a party, Mama made her a cake and Saul blew her air kisses.

Standing in the center of the dining room that day, Rainey seemed different. Her shy way of smiling had faded into something even more hidden. Where once there'd been a friend all my own—to fool with, to boss around, to lie to—now there was a girl who had discovered something without me. She'd taken all the ribbons off the gifts and, instead of putting them in her hair, she'd thrown them aside—loops of pink and yellow on the floor. As I stared down at our bare feet and the crushed ribbons, I realized Rainey would always be a year older than me. I'd always be the smaller and younger one—little LuLu.

Rainey leaned in toward the candles on her cake, holding her hair back with one hand and palming the tablecloth with the other, and closed her eyes. She had this way of standing so still, pretty and delicate, not quite perfect, like gathered-up flowers. "Make a wish," Mama said. Saul hummed "Happy Birthday," in his uneven, unbelievable pitch. Rainey smiled with her eyes still shut, then took a breath and in one slow moment blew out the tiny flames. Mama laughed and clapped her hands and said, "Just think, you've got your whole life in front of you!" We all looked at each other, the noonday sun slapping around us. Rainey pulled out a candle and licked off the icing. Mama went to the kitchen for plates, and Saul and I reached for the candles, too. Saul's clumsy fingers glanced over the sugar-pink roses and smeared Rainey's arm. I stared at him, then at the both of them, and wondered, What in the world? After all, Rainey was my friend.

"Saul, quit!" Rainey said.

Saul pushed his pinkie into the cake, at the place where the R in Rainey's name curved into the a. White icing caved in at the cake's center.

"You're gonna be in so much trouble," I said. "Mama will be furious."

He pulled his finger out of the cake, flicked it at me, called me "LuLu in the sky with crazy eyes." Mama came back in as I was brushing the stickiness off my cheek.

"Saul B," Mama said. There was a warning in her voice that disappeared as soon as she'd said it. "I just don't know what to make of you these days. Now quit that foolishness." She smiled through her words, then took up the knife to cut the cake.

"Happy Birthday, Rainey," I said.

"Thanks," she said, careful with her plate, making each bite last too long.

"Do you like your presents?"

She stopped eating and looked at me. Saul did the same, though his squint was mean, a half brother's half-look.

"Of course I do," she said.

"You like mine best, don't you?"

"I love yours, LuLu." She picked up the earrings, small silver sand dollars dangling from thin wires. "I'll put them on right now."

Rainey wasn't the only girl around that had pierced ears. But she was the only one I knew that had her mother's permission. Eva had shown up one day and taken Rainey out shopping, and when they came back, Rainey had little gold loops in her ears. Now that Eva had moved to the coast, several months gone by since we'd last seen her, she sent little gifts. The last one had arrived well before this birthday: a birthstone necklace. Rainey always got the precious things. When I asked for the same, Mama always gave the same answer: "Little girls don't wear jewelry. Just wait until you're older."

That's why I hid the charm bracelet Rainey had given me, the one Eva had given her when they'd moved to Florida. At night I played with the tiny roller skates, the starfish, the six-petal daisy. I loved the bright gold, the weave of links, the way it sang. If I heard Mama coming, I'd quick put it back in the drawer. I guess that's why I went ahead and got Rainey those earrings. I would have liked them myself.

Her head tilted slightly, she took out the gold loops one at a time and laid them in the small white box with my earrings. In seconds she had on the silver pair, and I realized how wrong they were. But I had to look at them and smile. She walked over to the mirror in the front hallway and held back her hair, admiring the earrings and herself.

"LuLu, eat your cake," Mama said. "It's nearly time for your daddy to pick you up, and you need to be waiting outside. Get a move on now. ASAP."

"All right," I said, no less impatiently, and carried my plate to the kitchen.

This afternoon would just be me on my own with Daddy, Saul getting out of it, lying that he had "things to do." Since Daddy had moved across the lake, he'd come by now and then and take us for A&W hamburgers or just for rides to catch a breeze. Sometimes, we'd head to his little house and sit on the porch with the busted-out screens and barely a roof. The house had been in the Blackwood family for a long time and wasn't far away, just a canoe ride or a long walk around the lake. Of course, since Mama had asked Daddy to leave, I wondered if for her it was far enough.

When I got to the narrow entry hall, Saul was there, too, lacing his fingers through Rainey's hair and on down past her shoulder blades. They looked at each other in the mirror, while I pushed past to open the front door and get outside. Saul jabbed me with his elbow and sang under his breath, "LuLu's got the stars in her eyes, yeah, she's gone," and Rainey followed me in the mirror. She seemed sorry, but I knew she really wasn't.

"Bye, LuLu," she said. "Have a nice time."

Rainey was always full of whatever she should say, anything polite that would cover up how much she didn't care. Or maybe it was that she didn't want to have to care. So sweet things budded from her mouth as substitutes. Saul liked sweet things, like Rainey. Right now, I hated them both. The way they touched and whispered, the way they sometimes lay together on the couch, all tangled up and laughing at the stupidest things. Rainey was supposed to be my friend, and instead she was becoming Saul's. But with Saul, she was more than a friend. The thought of it made me sad; the thought of it wrinkled inside my head, like a hard shiny knot that jangled and reminded me of how everything kept getting ruined.

I sat on the front steps and stared at the road. It was rough and gray and curved in two directions—around to the left was the rest of Sybelia Drive and to the right was the stretch down to the lake. It was hot, and the afternoon had a mean glare. Sun poured down and burned the top of my head. Behind me, the screen door swung open and hit me in the back.

"LuLu," Mama said, "why are you sitting so close to the door?" As if it was my fault that she'd banged me. "Where is your daddy? He's late again."

I turned my head and looked up at her. It was too much effort to say anything, so I didn't. Daddy pulled up in his sky-blue Corvair, and in back of me the door slammed.

Sometimes I wanted to drive off with my daddy and never come back.

From the driver's seat he smiled at me. I walked across the crinkled Bermuda grass and past the dried-up marigolds that were done begging for a good watering. Daddy rested his arm on the open window, and I could see the curved anchor and coiled rope of the Marine Corps tattoo under his shirtsleeve. The shirt was an old one that he wore for yard work or just for sitting outside. Once red, it was now a pale rust color. And like all his shirts, right above his heart it had a top pocket where he kept his cigarettes and lighter. He looked tanner than usual, and his dark eyes glinted as his smile got wider. Leaning sideways, he opened the passenger door, and I climbed in.

"Hey, girl," he said.

He reached around the steering wheel to give me a hug, and I tried not to bump up where his right arm used to be, where his sleeve was sewn to the side seam of his shirt. It was as though he'd never had that arm and had never even needed that sleeve.

"Hey," I said. And I smiled because I felt like it.

"You want to go fishing?" he asked.

"Not really." I thought for a minute while the car idled at the edge of the yard. The palmettos looked white in the midday sun, and the cluster of lemon trees seemed to droop. "It's too hot."

"Well, you could jump in the lake then."

"It's even too hot for that."

"It's July, Lu." He kept on smiling, his teeth white and even. "Let's go to town."

"All right."

Daddy pulled his sunglasses down over his eyes and put the altered, left-hand gearshift into drive. A breeze entered the car as we rounded the corner and drove past all of the level green lawns. Through the blue-tinted band at the top of the windshield, the white day changed. We took the lakeside route and passed under the tall moss-draped cypresses that edged the shore. Past the library and the Episcopal Church that Mama, having been brought up Baptist, called too high and mighty, we circled the brick avenues and ended up in front of the hardware store.

"Why are we stopping here?" I said.

"I need to pick up some things. Besides, it's always cool inside Arundsen's. Those smooth concrete floors and all that metal."

"But Daddy—"

"Come on. You can get me a bag of three-penny nails."

"What are you building now?"

"A hutch."

"A what?"

The glass doors swung open, and we stepped inside.

"A rabbit hutch."

Long rows of shelving cut the store into sections. Everything in Arundsen's was too angled and sharp. I followed the back of my daddy's sun-bleached shirt as he moved past rows of turpentine and sandpaper, and then between bins of screws, washers, and bolts. He pointed to the little paper bags that nested between bins. I tried to take one and ended up with several, linked together by their saw-edged openings.

"What are you going to do with rabbits?"

"Raise them."

"And then what?"

"Maybe you can help." He rested his hand on my head, let it stay there a second, a reminder from before. Before he left, and then left again.

I was still his little girl, the smallest twelve-year-old around. As small as the younger kids I'd given up thrashing in the schoolyard, all that "feeling mean" having gone once my daddy had come back. Since he'd returned from Vietnam, Daddy hadn't taken off his belt in anger; now there wasn't a reason to. Now I was acting my age, and he was making plans. I thought about rabbits and their dull little hops. I thought about helping.

"Maybe," I said.

"Well, you can think about it."

I pictured one rabbit, then two. The first lop-eared, the color of cocoa, its small flat nose lifted, its haunches round and sitting. The other like charcoal—a dwarf rabbit with soft gray eyes, a blur of lashes, upright ears and a desperate need to dig. I might stroke their velvet backs, their bunched shoulders, and the space above their eyes.

"They would bite," I said, running my hand along a pyramid of paint cans.

"They might," he answered.

We left the store with several pieces of lumber and wire mesh, along with crumpled bags of metal bits that would eventually hold the hutch together. I was surprised that nearly everything fit into the trunk of the car. Without saying so out loud, I knew I'd rather set a hammer to the nails we'd bought than spend any amount of time taking care of rabbits.

The sky had become overcast, but the afternoon wasn't any cooler. Daddy gave me a dollar to get two Dreamsicles at the corner store while he rearranged the contents of the trunk, probably intent on getting it all in there, neat and interlocked, like a jigsaw puzzle. By the time I came out again, it had begun to rain. The kind of rain that falls in enormous drops and soaks through summer clothes in seconds. We climbed into the car and rolled the windows almost to the top, since it was too hot to shut them all the way.

The rain fell onto the windshield, and we ate our orange-and-vanilla ice cream. People ran in and out of shops, as if they could avoid getting wet. Through the thick, rain-flecked glass, their shapes waved around, irregular, almost comic. We were quiet for a while, and then Daddy spoke, his voice far away even though he was sitting right next to me.

"Do you remember coming here when you were really little?"

I nodded a yes.

"One time when you were just three, you had on these little white overalls. Probably a pair you'd inherited from Saul. They were faded and covered with berry stains, in a kind of haphazard pattern, like some of that old china your mama likes so much." He stopped talking and folded his ice cream paper around the wooden stick. Deft, assured movements, given that he had only the five fingers of his left hand to work with.

"Do you miss her?" I asked.

"All the time."

The rain fell harder now, and we had to roll the windows all the way up.

"She's not very friendly these days." I bent my ice cream stick, and it cracked in half.

"Well, she doesn't like change, so I don't fit into her scheme of things." He turned to me. "Are you okay with that, though?"

I thought for a minute.

"Lu?"

"I remember something, too." I looked right at him now, and I felt like I was looking at him for the first time. "I remember when I was nine, after you'd left for Vietnam, Mama was talking to Eva about you. You know, Eva? Rainey's mama?"

"I don't know her." He laughed a little. "But I know of her. That whole men-in-uniform routine."

"Well, Mama told her about when she first met you, how you were so dreamy and handsome, like the astronauts down at Cape Canaveral. She called you her NASA man."

"She did not."

"She did so. I know, go ahead and laugh. It is funny. She said something like, 'God, I love that man—when I first met him, he sent me straight into space.' You know how she is."

"Lu-girl," he sighed, "I know how she was." He held the steering wheel, his wrist at an angle. "I only know how she was."

The rain had slowed a bit. We stared out the window at the street and at the lonesome spaces between the fat drops of rain.

"Mama thinks you've changed." I traced a line down the center of the fogged-up windshield. "I think she's wrong."

"She's right, Lu. Your mama's always right."

The front door shut with a click. I meant to be so careful, and still the door closing sounded abrupt and loud. Mama was asleep on the sofa, and Johnny Carson was talking to Charo on late night television. I turned all the lights off except for the one above Mama's head. Soft yellow lamplight rested on her cheek. I thought of fireflies and campfire—things that used to happen in July.

"LuLu?" Rainey came out of the hallway that led from the bedrooms into the living room.

"Cuchi, cuchi, cuchi," said Charo. In the blue television light, Charo shimmied, and Johnny tried not to smile too much.

Rainey held her hand over her mouth to keep from laughing, and Mama kept on sleeping. I held a finger to my lips and tried not to laugh as well. Something seemed to well up in both of us. Rainey—flushed with trying to stay soundless, but still shaking her shoulders in imitation of Charo, pointing at the television. And me—caught inside the moment, not knowing how I felt about Rainey and Saul, and my daddy, and my mama asleep on the couch, and I tried to let it all slip into something easier to feel. I waved my hands at Rainey, again signaling her to hush, but we ended up on the floor behind the couch, completely hysterical, loud, breathless laughter under our hands.

"Stop," I hissed.

"I can't," said Rainey, crying from laughing so hard.

"Come on," I said. And we crawled all the way to our room, stopping once, miserable with our own giggling.

I closed the door, and we doubled up, laughing and slapping at each other, calm for a second and then starting up again. Once we finally stopped, the room was filled with breath. We flattened ourselves against the shag carpet. Rainey's face was damp and rosy, and the fan of her sleeve spread like swamp hibiscus from her shoulder to her cheek. Her eyes were shining, full of colored light. I wasn't the girl with stars in her eyes, the one in the Beatles song that Saul had pinned on me—"LuLu in the sky." Instead, she was, and I loved her for that. Everything was scattered and out of sorts, but with Rainey, as long as she was with me, I felt sure.

The light pink sheet fell over the side of the bed. I grabbed a corner and pulled it over us. Slowly it filled with air and tented, and we were underneath. It was dark and not dark, the overhead light sifting through.

"Where did you and your daddy go today?" Rainey asked.

"Into town," I said. "We spent most of our time sitting in the car."

"Why?"

"It was raining."

"Really?"

"Rainey," I said, "it poured all afternoon."

"Oh," she said. "Right."

"Don't act dumb." I kicked at the sheet and it billowed for a few seconds. "You know you're not."

"What are you talking about?" she said. "I just forgot, that's all." She paused for a second. "It did rain, though, you're right. Saul wanted to go out walking in it. I said no, and he went off without me."

I felt her breath. She'd moved closer. I thought of Saul, soaking wet and alone, traipsing through mud. But his being alone and my being with Rainey didn't make me any happier.

"I stayed here," Rainey said. She smelled like lilacs, almost too sweet. "Remember those games we used to play with our Barbies?"

"What?" I said.

"I thought of them earlier today. When I was looking in the mirror at the earrings you gave me. Before you left." She grazed the side of my face with her fingertips. "Remember, though? How we used to pierce our Barbies' ears?"

"You remember the weirdest things." I blew at her, and she pushed her fingers against my mouth.

"We used to take your mama's straight pins, the ones with the colored ends. We'd take them right out of her sewing drawer and give Stacey and Skipper earrings to match their outfits. Sometimes the pins would stick through their scalps, and we'd have to move them around until they didn't show."

We were silent for a minute, and then I answered, "Yes, I remember."

And I did remember. Mostly the way the pins rusted inside their heads and how it looked as though they had some horrible blood disease because their ears and the sides of their necks would get all streaked with blue-green marks.

I studied the side of Rainey's head, where the sand dollar earring fell and caught in her hair, the muted colors of silver and blond mixing. Before I wrapped the earrings in shiny gift paper, I held them up to my ears in front of my mirror. But I didn't have pierced ears, so I put the earrings back into their little box and closed the lid. Now I imagined them staining Rainey's earlobes and the lines of her long neck with angry bruised colors, blue-violet and black.

Rainey touched my cheek, and I knew she could tell I was crying. She pulled me closer, and we lay there under the pale sheet until we fell asleep. I dreamed of another birthday. And in the dream we stood together and saw how the world wrapped us up, like birthday presents, slightly undone, the writing on the pink envelope smeared. And then we saw how the world held us on its sharpest edge, judged us by how carefully we took the corners, and then dropped us to see how we fell.

ROCK SALT AND RABBIT

AUGUST 1971

There it is again. The sound of the mortars, fired overhead, hitting the target, this time a nearby village, sending red earth, fire, and smoke into the air. We are too far away to hear the cries. VC meet there at night, though intel is not always exact on these things. Especially when most of our information comes from the children—surveillance in return for sweets. I wake to the sounds, small arms fire marking the silence between blasts. A tracer sighs and I breathe in red dust and I'm up and out of my bunk and through the door, and only then do I realize where I am. In the backyard of the Florida lake house that once belonged to my grandfather and now to me.

The air is not as heavy here. The scent is not thick with the nascent trace of powder that lies everywhere in 'Nam. And there are no cries, except my own. I wake myself now. There's no one else to wake me.

I stand in the dark and the lake water shines like black oil. There is reflection and no reflection. The moon is out, but its light is dull, meaningless. August has become a month lidded with clouds, as if the world were canopied by MEDCAP gauze, gray-white and used up.

Over at the edge of the yard, the rabbits scuff about inside their hutches, the ones LuLu helped build. There are three hutches and three kinds of rabbits. I watch them from a distance. The brown lop-ears lie like lumps, sleeping, while the dwarf rabbits are hunched together at a corner of their cage. The male Rex is mottled with dark spots but mostly white; his eyes burn an empty space into the darkness.

The rising moon seems to warm the still air. I take up a canoe paddle that rests against the corner of the screened porch. Between the paddle's handle and a length of support beam, a spider has sewn a long web, which falls like sticky thread to the ground. Beyond the porch, flat green grass leads out to the lake. The rabbits clatter about, their white-gray-brown movements doing nothing to disturb the night—at that moment, there is only the lake, like glass. I anticipate setting the aluminum canoe onto its surface and breaking its quiet.

Across the water, a figure stands under a bright dock light. Lillian Walbright. She wears her white bathing suit and swims nearly every night. I will pass her in the canoe, and she will ignore me, the one-armed man who marks his passage with wide, one-armed strokes.

The canoe is facedown on the sand beach; nearby, a rock for ballast. I lift the canoe by the center yoke. Its keel line meets the water, and I set the wooden paddle next to the bow seat and the rock in the forward-facing stern, step in with one foot, and push away from the shallows. I sit backward in the bow seat so that the boat works with me, not against me. There is a new definition of balance in paddling solo, left-armed, sweep stroke, J stroke. I appreciate the lack of wind and spare black skies and pass the cypresses that edge the shore.

At the center of the lake, Lillian is swimming. Breaststroke. Her white bathing cap shines, and she creates a line though the water. I lean into the paddle, concentrate on moving forward, and Lillian disappears, first her shoulders and then her head. Closer to me, she surfaces. The lake is wide enough, but she is a strong swimmer and I am making good progress.

"Royal," she says, not out of breath, not ignoring me.

"Lil," I say, holding up my paddle, letting the canoe glide and slow, while the druggist's wife reaches up and touches the gunwale.

Her fingernails are dark with polish, and her fingers are long, her hands large.

"It's late," she says, then lets go of the canoe and treads water.

"Yes, it is."

Lillian looks past the floating dock, where daytime swimmers rest and sun themselves, in the direction of my house, one of the only ones on that side of the lake. "Things we do in the dark." She laughs a quick, breathless laugh and then sighs. "You are something, though, I have to say. Cutting straight across the lake on your own."

"I could say the same about you."

"Well, I guess we have something in common." She leans onto her back and raises her arms, one after the other, in a beautiful backstroke.

I smile and remember what it felt like: the unparalleled backward sweep across the water while watching the sky.

Another thing that the doctors and therapists say I'll never do again. I hope to prove them wrong.

It's not every day your husband returns home with one arm less than he once had. Or is it, these days? We're all lacking something we once had. Arms, legs, egos, energy, will. Will. Sheer and impossible. Try to climb it. Like a plate glass window, straight up and slick. You can't climb it, but you can see yourself in it. Whatever's left. You can see that.

The month before I shipped out, September 1967, Minnie held me to a promise. We were alone, the kids spending the weekend with friends, and dusk hung on, the evening taking its time. From the stereo in the living room Percy Sledge belted a series of songs, and beyond the open sliding doors of our bedroom, the lemon and tangerine trees looked almost too green. Minnie breathed against me. "You have to come back," she kept saying. "You have to come back the same. Don't let anything over there change you." Her hair was in my eyes, and side one repeated.

Afterward, still naked, Minnie got out of bed and slipped through the open doors into the grove. She came back with an armful of tangerines and dropped them beside me. They fell into the folds of the sheets, between my legs, onto the floor. She sat, peeling one after another, eating sections, offering them, stems and skins falling on the floor. The bitter scent of citrus penetrated the air, and seeds littered the bed. And then Minnie leaned over me and made me promise again. I did, and down the hall the song ordered that I do her no wrong.

Minnie volunteered at the VA hospital and knew what might happen. Already, boys were coming back, riddled with anxiety, misunderstood. Some without faces, some without family. She made me promise because that's all she could do. She didn't depend on hope; hope was something different. She knew better than that. She grabbed on to what she could, and at that moment, she held on to me. Clothes draped over chairs and across the floor, doors open throughout the house, and empty bottles on the bedside table—wine and then whisky. And so the evening went forward into the night, into the next day. The weekend ended and the kids returned, and the next month came and I took up my duffel to leave.

Her last kiss was fierce. "Don't you forget," she said. Her eyes narrowed into shards of blue and she tried not to cry.

In the yard I sit and smoke and watch the moon sink. The canoe leans on its side against a paper birch. I'm alone, but not left alone. Minnie comes around when I'm not home and leaves baskets of clean laundry, bottles of wine hidden in the bottom. She takes up my worn clothes and the cycle keeps on. The scent of soap powder and perfume, the bottle of Barolo. How a woman can be so damned domestic and sexy, all at the same time, is nearly beyond me. But that's Minnie. Lingering in my world, while she's asked me to exit hers.

In a few hours the sun will come up, marking the beginning of a Thursday morning, and I'll finally sleep. The rabbits are still, until a sound by the house makes them jump. The screen door is opening. I can tell by the long sigh of the hinges, and over my shoulder I see someone go inside. I field-strip my cigarette and stand up slowly. Someone is on my porch, and none too shy, rattling something heavy onto the pine floor. I make my way from lawn chair to porch. A flashlight comes on and shines across me.

"Lord!" The light lowers, and I know my trespasser is a woman.

"Who's there?" There's a strange wet smell to this stranger. Algae, lake water.

"Royal?"

"Damn straight." I push open the door and step onto the smooth floorboards.

"I'm bringing things over. Damn it, you scared me."

I pull the cord that drops down from the ceiling, the porch light clicks on, and there she is. Lillian Walbright. Blue shorts, white blouse, loafers. Her hair is slicked back and at her feet is an ice cream bucket, the kind with a crank, the kind that asks for rock salt and physical labor.

"What the hell?"

"You're still having that picnic, aren't you?" Lillian's eyes are wide, rimmed with red, and she's taller than I remember.

"Not until the weekend." The lightweight door bumps behind me, and there we are, boxed in. I let the silence snake around us until it gets too strange. "You know how to use that?" I say.

"Of course I do. It could be fun. You'll have your kids here, right?"

"Sure." I think of LuLu and Saul and Rainey, all arms and legs and probably more in the mood for their own parties. Teenagers who moved on from ice cream and backyard picnics a long time ago.

"You like strawberry?" She nudges the bucket with the side of her shoe, not nearly the same woman who spoke to me earlier. Under the half-lit moon, out on the water, she seemed to belong to the night. Under the electric light, she disappears.

"LuLu's favorite. I like it fine."

"All right then." She moves to go, but I don't make room. I'm in the doorway and she's trying to leave.

"Breakfast?" I say. "May as well. You came all this way, lugging that thing."

Lillian looks as though she doesn't know which way is up or down. "I couldn't."

"Well, you could. I've got eggs, bacon. A new percolator."

I move away from the door, and she raises her face, looks straight at me. She brushes her damp hair back and finally says, "That sounds nice. Thanks, I'd like that."

We move inside and, while rashers of bacon heat up in the skillet, don't talk. I feel her eyes on me, taking in my work at the stove, one-sided, deliberate, less than new. In the corner behind a curtain is my unmade bed. In the center of the room are a sofa, stacks of books; on the only side table, a tall lamp and a level that shows the floor there is uneven. The room changes as the night becomes morning, crazy with birdcalls, and the coffee kicks up, bitter-smelling and brown. We eat our eggs and toast, and Lillian stares out the big windows that look over the lake, back to where her house and dock and long green lawn all lie. She stares and she breathes like she's underwater.

June 1969. Quảng Ngãi Province. Vĩnh An, a village at the mouth of Song Trà Bồng. The days were sweltering, leaning into each other like unbathed bodies. Sunk inside a bunker were sleeping pallets, men slung over them, those who had been on patrol during the night, and the heavy odors of breath and mildew. A radio droned. In July, astronauts would land on the moon. Every day men landed and walked the DMZ without the benefit of zero gravity.

USMC, Combined Action Patrol, I Corps, TAOR, Tango, Tiger Papa, one thousand klicks from home. Walt sat propped up and fingered his Guild, the wide strap across his right shoulder, the strings slightly rusted but still taut enough to play. His music, lean and raw like Hank Williams's "Your Cheatin' Heart" and "I'm So Lonesome I Could Cry," stretched into the wide unending afternoon.

PFC Titus Shields leaned over and pulled a dented can of beer from below his bunk. The gold sheen glinted between his enormous brown hands. He pulled the tab off and pointed it at Walt. "You have to play like that?"

"You don't like my playing, Tight-Ass?"

"Don't mind the music." Titus smiled and drank from the can. "Just mind the sound it makes."

"Throw me one of them." Walt nodded at the beer, and Titus threw the metal tab at him.

Maurice pulled his hands over his eyes and moaned. "Why don't you farm boys shut up? Trying to sleep in this mess is hard enough without all that noise."

Maurice was the only man in my squad from north of the Mason-Dixon. New York City. The rest of us came from small towns. Bogalusa, Eufaula, Dawson.

"I believe we've been insulted." Walt put the guitar down and threw his legs to one side of his cot. "Hand me one, Titus man."

"This here's the only one." He stretched and handed it to Walt.

I watched the men, dozing, drinking, from over the notepad propped on my knees. A letter I'd begun again and again but hadn't had a chance to end. Another letter to Minnie. I wrote about my squad, the hamlet children, the school we were building. I didn't write about the patrols, the coconut mine that took down Jimmy, changing our number from seven to six.

"Where'd you get this shit, man?" Walt wiped his mouth with the back of his hand and tipped the beer to pour it out.

"You crazy?" Titus grabbed the can. "Same time, same place, same shit. From that little girl and her brother. Where you been?"

"Mm-hmm," Maurice said. "You boys better watch out. The suds don't kill you, that girl's mother just might."

"Girl's okay," I said.

She was thirteen, granddaughter of the district chief. A little twist of a girl. Small, but long-limbed. Good at climbing trees. Not afraid of pushing her way into tunnels. She had short black hair, a pigeon-toed run, a laugh that rose in spirals.

"Her mother is the one sending the kids out with beer and cigarettes and anything else she can find. Your American dollars at work." I pulled my last cigarette from a crumpled pack and waved it in the air. The last time I'd asked her mother to keep her home, she'd yelled. Something about peace and quiet. Later, I'd understood the girl's name, An, meant peace.

"Maurice, you're on surveillance tonight. With Pete and McPhee."

Titus looked at me, smiling. "Then we're gonna need more beer, Sergeant."

A month later, once we'd landed on the moon, once Walt was gone, caught in a haze of crossfire under a tree covered in yellow flowers, Titus stopped drinking. Along with his M-16, he now carried a quiet kind of desperation. An's younger brother, Walt's go-to boy, now followed Titus, his hand held out, offering him tree frogs and crickets when cans of beer were turned down. "You take," Huy said. Titus always refused, until the boy brought him a small rabbit from one of his grandfather's hutches. Wide-eyed and dark brown, the rabbit disappeared inside Titus's large hands.

Years later, when the man on point doesn't go back to Dawson, Georgia, and ends up in the yard of my lake house, I hear him laughing. He stands before the open door of the rabbit hutch and takes out a dwarf rabbit the color of cocoa. He holds it high and then tips it into his top pocket.

LuLu questions me, like any teenage girl would. She sees past the old and the new—three years lost while I was in-country and then in rehab—and then kicks her way through the rest of it. The garbage she's read and heard about the war, the shift in her mother's skirt length from high to higher, the shit her brother gives her, the fact that I came back and then left again. She kicks past it all like she used to in her swim class, way back when she was a minnow. Graduated from dolphin to flying fish ages ago, her suit with the YMCA swim patches outgrown, she busts through the water like she can't go fast enough, and even then she hardly causes a wake. She glides through life the same way. My Lu-girl.

Arms folded across her chest, Lu didn't want to come with me in early April when I added the Rex and several lop-ears to the collection of dwarf rabbits.

"You still haven't told me why you keep rabbits," she'd said.

"To raise them," I told her.

"I think it's a dumb idea."

"Well, you're entitled to think what you want."

"Which means you're going to keep on doing it anyway. Stuff the hutches with cute little bunnies that will make more cute little bunnies. And then what?"

"I'll sell them."

"Well, it's still a dumb idea."

I haven't told Lu about the villagers in Vĩnh An and their mangy hares. Long, stringy animals with wild eyes. Not good eating, but we ate them out of courtesy, one less C-ration, one more hot meal.

"Why on my birthday, then?"

"Something to do besides cake and candles. Your mama takes care of those things."

Truth is, a hammer and a handful of nails, a cane pole and a tin of minnows are teaching her what she needs to know. Birthdays are just another day on the calendar. And I need help now and then. Last summer, she managed fine with the hutches, from holding boards while I tacked them together to angling their roofs at a pitch where the rabbits stay dry even when the wind drives the rain broadside.

This year, in late spring, after one of those rainstorms, Lance Corporal Titus Shields landed on my doorstep, Walt's guitar hanging from a strap across his shoulder. For days he slept on my couch, that dwarf rabbit nestled inside his hands. Lu seemed to find his endless sleep a great puzzle, and she whispered things over him, touching his face and the guitar frets, and then said loudly to me that he should wake up. And finally he did.

And then, under a ceiling of blue skies and lengthening days, as if to make sure that days were for waking and nights for sleeping, Lu, lugging a tool-belt like she knew how, announced the next project. Along with me and Titus, Saul, and one of the Callahan boys, she took on the porch, tearing down the old structure and then deciding on a red tin roof, the yellow pine flooring, the cypress beams for the new one. Titus stayed through the end of June and tried to teach her to play the Guild in the evenings, and she seemed to get the hang of it. "My dog has fleas," she'd say out loud, trying out the strings. And then at me, "Your bunnies are gonna have fleas, for sure."

"Not mine."

"Yes, yours."

And Titus, holding a sweating Coca-Cola, would say, "A lot of talk about nothing. Give me that guitar and y'all shut up and listen." He played songs by some new band that played up in Jacksonville, by way of Georgia—"Where I'm from." He'd smile and pull blues out of the box, the same one he'd complained on when Walt had played those long afternoons, below the South China Sea and above the backyards of the Binhs.

"How come you know the Allman Brothers?"

"How come you ask so many questions, girl?" Titus was still as sore as he'd been in Vĩnh An, but now he had something to curl his hands around, something that would mostly keep folks quiet and listening to him.

"You know Duane and Gregg Allman are from Daytona Beach, don't you?" Lu narrowed her eyes at Titus. "Not from Georgia."

Titus smiled. "Darlin', you know a lot more about those boys than you probably should. What's important is they're brothers, like I got brothers and you got one, too. Brothers staying together, keeping each other good. You know? Now settle down."

Titus's words were strung with something bitter, something steely. More than anger. Whatever ailed him was deep down, but pushing at the surface. He bent over the guitar and struck blues chords, forcing the conversation to a close. Lu eyed him and hushed, a frown across her face. Still, she folded her arms around her legs, rested her chin on her bent knees, and listened, eventually falling asleep on the sofa. Not long after, I sent Titus to bunk in my bed. In the kitchen I sat and smoked with the lights off, letting the dark sift around me, thinking of where I'd been and where I'd come back to.

With Lillian, I feel like a coin found on the tracks, flattened, but still of some value. She stands next to me and touches my arm. Her fingers press through my shirt and there's weight and warmth behind them. She slips out of her loafers, then moves across the room, pushes past the curtain, and lies down on my bed. Each loafer is lined up, the heels and toes a lighter color, worn from all the slipping on and off.

"You shouldn't smoke in bed, you know," she says. I hear her moving the glass ashtray, the sound of solid glass against the bedside table's surface. And then the click of my lighter, the odor of butane. "You could burn the place down." Her voice travels across the ceiling and back to me.

"I'll try to remember that."

I wonder what Titus would say to this woman in my bed. Titus, who comes and goes, who never stays around for too long. Then I know he wouldn't say much of anything. He'd just climb in next to her.

I leave the breakfast dishes on the table and go outside on the porch. The bin of feed is there, and I take up a large scoop and head outside. The sky is threaded with thin lines of white, no chance of rain. The grain falls into each bowl, and the rabbits gather, bumping heads. With the hose I replenish their water.

I turn around and Lillian's there.

"Need help?"

"Sure," I say. And then I see Saul sitting in a lawn chair, watching us.

"Morning," he says. He's wearing the cutoffs he always wears, and a T-shirt, faded brown, the words *TUMBLEWEED CONNECTION* across his chest.

"Hey there, Saul." Lillian approaches him and he smiles.

"What are you doing over here?" he says to her.

"Having breakfast."

"Awful early." He glances at me.

Next to the chair are a small pail and a cane pole, one of mine.

"What'd you catch?" I motion to the pail.

"Bluegill."

"You coming to the picnic?" Lillian touches his arm, and I realize this is just something she does, nothing special in the way her hand grazes and rests, then finds another place to fall. She holds on to the back of Saul's chair and leans down to examine the bluegill.

Saul stares at me like I am this morning's biggest problem. His hair has gotten longer, nearly to his shoulders. Lillian's question remains unanswered. Saul doesn't acknowledge her and instead points to the scoop in my hand.

"What's the point?" he says.

"The point?"

"All those rabbits. What's the point?"

"Does there have to be one?" He looks at me, his eyes lidded, that same blue as his mother's. "Yeah," he says. "There does."

"There isn't one. Just there to remind me." I thought of An and Huy, their rabbits. Titus's little brown one. "Here." I pitch the feeding scoop at him. "You're in charge now. Mornings, so I can sleep in."

He catches the scoop.

"All right," he says. He seems on the verge of telling me something else, something I have no idea about.

I know I won't be sleeping in. It's just a reason to keep an eye on him, and by the tone of his acceptance, I can tell he'll be doing the same. Keeping an eye on me.

Saturday afternoon is blazing, the air motionless, the sky stippled with clouds. I lie on my back in the lake, floating, balancing, trying not to tip to one side. The right side. No one is around. No one would want to see the scars, the man who moves through the water and the world at an angle different from the way he once did. The sky flips yaw-ways and I get a mouthful of water. The soft, green taste of algae brings me upright, treading water once again with my left arm, my legs. I breathe, lie back, straighten out. I frame the possibility of pulling backward, slowly, steadily, to the opposite shore, to Lillian, watching from her dock and waving me over. And then I raise my arm a few inches above the water, legs outstretched and ready, but I fall once more to the side.

"What the hell are you doing in there?" Titus stands on the narrow strip of sand that leads down to the lake. He shades his eyes but still squints. "Looks damn foolish."

I pull myself to shore, kicking until I find the soft sand bottom where I can stand and walk. Titus is grinning, the sole of his square-toed boot against the upturned canoe. He throws the towel I left there, and I catch it.

"Thanks." I run it over my hair and let it fall onto my right shoulder.

"Looking good for an old man."

Titus isn't looking too young himself, tired around the eyes. Those eyes that drilled through black nights and heavy white days. On point, or bringing up the rear.

We walk up the sloping lawn, the grass going bald in places, Florida soil too thin to keep it tamped down. By the hutches, LuLu is leaning in to check the Rex. His double coat, like velveteen, always tempts her.

"Rabbit girl!" Titus says. His call reaches up and over, the same way his singing does, teaching the day another tone.

LuLu bumps her head on the top of the little doorframe. "Titus—" She holds her head and looks annoyed. Then she smiles. "Hey, Daddy. Thought we'd surprise you." She shuts and latches the hutch door and walks over to us. She's seen me before without a shirt, but the marks are too definite for her not to stare.

"Well, I am surprised. Here to help?"

"'Course we are. Brought things from the store like you asked. Coca-Colas and ice. All the things you wanted." She points to the porch where grocery sacks, buckets of ice and bottled drinks, and a bag of charcoal are lined up.

Saul stands inside the screen door, and I realize they've all come together. Titus's truck is parked in the drive under the stand of pines. On the driver's door are the words *TROUBLE NO MORE*, painted in slanting black capitals.

"When did you get here?" I ask Titus.

"Last night. I went for a swim, met up with Saul. Stayed over at your house on the other side."

I think about the other side. How I want to swim halfway there, stand on the floating dock, and shout for another chance. Scream past the rooftops to the heavens for another chance.

I nod at Titus. "Minnie let them get in that truck with you?"

The screen door opens, and Saul stands at the threshold. "She doesn't care where we go. And she thinks Titus is just fine. Likes talking to him, feeding him pie, hearing about his family back in Dawson. About his brothers signing up and about going back himself to hunt down more VC."

"You are such a liar, Saul. Titus did not say that to Mama." Lu tugs on Titus's sleeve. "Did you?"

Saul stares at me, and I can tell he's not lying. He's pushing the truth as hard as he can. Only this truth belongs to Titus. Titus and Walt and Jimmy. Titus and his brothers. And Titus will spin the truth.

He puts his arm around Lu and shakes her a little. "Not going there. No, uh-unh."

"Come on," she says. "You promise?"

"Told you, girl." Titus squeezes Lu and she leans into him. "Not going there."

Titus is spending time with my family in my house on the other side of the lake. Saul recognizes this, too. I can't, though. The words across the truck's door would then be meaningless.

Soon Lillian will be here with strawberries and cream. The Callahans and Lingstrums will arrive with their large dishes of potato salad and their lawn chairs and wonder where the beer has been stowed. Vita Hull is certain to bring kielbasa and her small white poodle, red bows tied into his curls.

Inside, I dress, and shirt buttons slip between my fingers. Every extra moment I take for the simplest tasks is set in a heap of all the extra moments. I remember Minnie, her fingers unbuttoning, buttoning, following the edges of a shirt until it was undone, done. I think of how she reels me in and then pushes me away, and I pray she doesn't come.

Outside, I hear Titus pouring charcoal, Lu asking where the sparklers are. Titus tells her they are still in the truck and what's the hurry anyway. "For later, when it gets dark," she says. I hear a Frisbee hit the side of the house and Saul laughing.

The clock shows that it's nearly four. I look around and empty ashtrays, clear books off the floor, slide the kitchen chairs under the table.

Lillian pushes through the doorway, a large basket in one hand. The promised berries, the cream, eggs, sugar. She piles them onto the kitchen counter and waves me away.

"No," I say and touch her elbow. "Show me."

"All right then." She smiles and pushes my hair away from my forehead. I imagine she's done this with her son, not her husband. The gesture, and the recipe. "Watch first."

There is the process of making the custard: a saucepan, a wooden spoon, the stirring. Lu bumps her way into the kitchen, and I quickly take my hand away from Lil's back. But she's seen. Her scrutiny is wide and her eyes won't meet mine. She leans over to peer into the pan. Lillian hands her the spoon and Lu stirs, letting the custard burn just a little.

"I'm going back outside," she says to me. "I know how to do this already," she says to Lil.

"LuLu," I call to her. I wonder when she started lying. Her mother knows how to get around in the kitchen, but Lu is never there, except to tear open a cereal box, spoon her way to the sugared milk in the bottom, and then leave her bowl in the sink.

From the porch comes the clatter of the rock salt and the ice. I step out and LuLu is telling the Callahan boy to get out of the way, she can do it herself. Salt and melting ice cover the floor, and Todd Callahan stands there, holding a watermelon against his chest.

"Nice, LuLu," he says, sets the melon down, and backs out.

"That's enough." I try to take the bag of salt from Lu and she throws it down by my feet.

"That's enough yourself."

The screen door slams and she heads across the lawn.

Lillian takes a broom and I hold the dustpan, and together we clean up the mess, setting up the layers of ice and rock salt inside the ice cream bucket.

"She'll be fine," says Lillian. "We'll all be fine." Her gaze meets mine, and she shakes her head and smiles. "The custard needs to set a while. Go on and greet your guests."

The Lingstrums all stand in a semi-circle, and their youngest, a granddaughter, runs to LuLu. Lu scoops her up and shows her the rabbits. She unlatches a door and takes out the smallest dwarf, dark brown and all eyes. Its ears lie flat and it doesn't move.

"What's its name?" the little girl asks Lu.

"My father didn't name them."

And Titus is there, leaning over and stroking the rabbit's head, its back. "This one's Huy." He winks at the little girl and Lu frowns.

"Since when?" Lu says.

The rabbit stretches, sniffs, and hops. The little girl squeals and laughs. The afternoon is a bright, uncertain thing filled with those arriving, waving and calling. The heavy smell of charcoal caught in flame, a plane overhead, the sound of a Volkswagen. Someone hands me a beer, and I turn to see Minnie climbing down from the VW bus.

She is always beautiful. Beauty crossed with anger. She wears polka dots and stripes, her hair around her shoulders. And like Lillian, she carries a basket, but hers is filled with wine and shortbread cookies and a carton of Lucky Strikes that she will leave on my kitchen table. She nods to me, mouths my name, and walks into the house.

I follow, but stop shy of the doorway when I hear their first words—*hey* and *what are you making?* I picture Lillian looking up from the colander of rinsed strawberries and Minnie standing still, trying to decide on where to set her things. I should follow Minnie, but what would I say? That I'm trying to move on, that some days it's easy and others impossible?

The Lingstrum child is crying now and LuLu is kissing her finger. Titus holds the rabbit and it burrows against his chest. Across the yard, Saul sets the kielbasa on the grill, and the picnic table is crowded with dishes, and Vita Hull and Esther Wild are mixing drinks. Mrs. Laurent, our elderly neighbor who rarely leaves her home, sits in an aluminum chair and closes her eyes, then leans her head back, her face to the sky. No birds, only bare cloud lines and a swatch of blue. The lawn lies green and sparse under sandals and sneakers and bare feet, the lake is level behind the standing and sitting and roving guests, and the screen door yawns and slams.

Minnie is beside me. Lillian is crossing the lawn to join the ladies with their tall drinks.

"Hey, baby," I say.

"Hey, R3." She blinks and smiles.

Her perfume reminds me of our past, and I'm sad and filled with longing all at once.

"You invited everyone, didn't you?"

"I did. Didn't mean to, but it just happened. To be honest, the kids had more to do with it than me."

"I know they did. They even found your lance corporal and brought him." She points in Titus's direction. "I think Lu's kind of sweet on him. But she's way too young, and he's a good boy. Treats her like a little sister. Nothing going on, don't worry." Minnie reaches for the second button of my shirt, where I'd given up, and holds it between her fingers.

"I wasn't."

"No, you weren't." She lets go. Grins at me. "But you should. Especially if he keeps on hanging around." She brushes her fingers against my sleeve and moves toward our friends, our neighbors, stopping at Lillian's side to laugh and put her arm around her.

The evening closes in and the party's laughter opens out. Fireflies dart and spin in the dimming light. Cream custard and berries are working their way around the cold interior of the basin, which rests in the bucket of rock salt and ice. There is uncertainty in your mind, about what you have chosen from this life, and you try to move forward, past all the thinking and back into this yard full of friends enjoying themselves. But the uncertainty persists. Uncertainty combined with the acrid scent of mosquito repellent, the ladies downing their fourth and fifth drinks, Lu watching Titus as he plays the guitar, Saul sharing a moment with Minnie and Lil, the Lingstrum child running across the lawn to you and the ice cream bucket, begging for a chance to turn the crank.

◊ ◊ ◊

Things you cannot do with one arm: hug your daughter, drive a car, carry a load of firewood, row across the lake, turn the crank on an ice cream bucket, build a porch, shoot a rifle, make love, make amends. This is what people think. This is what people will tell you. You never argue. You never disagree and muddy their misconceptions. You let them have them. With ice and rock salt at your side, you invite them over one day. It is summer, and they are neighbors and old friends, and they comment on the rabbit hutches, how your stepson must have helped construct them. You nod, knowing that he did, for a day or two, then disappeared long enough that you tried to finish them on your own. And then your daughter showed up because she knew her brother had abandoned you. Even with a tool belt at your waist, there was still the need for another pair of hands.

On your porch, the floor still smelling of new pine, the screen door sighing but not yet creaking, you carry out the bowl of chilled cream custard, the sugar and strawberries. The metal basin is waiting inside the bucket of rock salt and ice, its sides glistening with condensation. The little Lingstrum girl looks up in expectation and you say, "It'll be a while yet." Still, she stands by the bucket while you pour the bowl's contents into the basin, add the dasher, and cover it tightly with the lid and hand crank. She reminds you of LuLu at age five, all wide eyes and curiosity. She touches your empty sleeve, and you smile. The crank goes around easily, your left hand on the handle, until you feel a little hand on top of yours. It is small and warm, with the barest weight, and you remember the weight of your rifle and the way there was never a breeze, the weight of your new wife in that first week after your wedding, the weight of your dreams that come every night.

You wish for better things. Friends that laugh without worrying how you will take their jokes. Lillian's smile when she looks up from her dock to see you out on the water, your single oar angling alongside the canoe, sending you across to the other side, your direction straight and steady. The moon crossed by cirrus clouds, rabbits resting in their hutches, the breath of night deep in your lungs.

The small hand is still over yours, helping you turn the crank, not taking anything from you and giving you nothing you'd asked for, but there, slight and new, returning again and again with each revolution, bringing you both closer to something sweet and unexpected on this still afternoon.

WAKING

JANUARY 1966

"Sleep, sleep, sleep," my mother says. But I cannot help thinking about waking the next morning. To the white-and-pink light, to the green-winged pigeon's murmuring, to the breathing of my brothers, to my uncle already speaking his mind to the pig. To rolling from my sleeping, my twisted covers, my corner mattress. To touching one toe to the floor, my own luck for the new year.

Tet is coming. Our village is scented with plum blossoms, sweet mandarins, the burnt-sugar aroma of lotus-seed candy, the thick pungent air of sticky rice and pork for the *banh chung* we will eat. The days are full of so much doing, getting ready, and the nights come too quickly.

Outside, in their hutches, the hares and rabbits bump their wooden bowls. I hear my grandfather telling them secrets, the sound of a latch opening and closing, his footsteps coming closer. "An," he says, calling to me, his face in the window above my bed. "This one is for you." He shows me a small brown rabbit, the size of a teacake, its ears short and straight, its nose moving and moving. I reach up to feel its whiskers and my mother stills my hands and my grandfather smiles and is gone. Only his soft voice separates the day from the night.

The moon rises, round, the color of an almond cookie. I think of taking it into my mouth, whole. Of chewing and chewing until the night is swallowed up in darkness and I am the only thing shining, my belly full of moonlight. I would open my mouth and laugh out loud. And then my brothers would know I'd eaten the moon by the way I glowed, my skin giving off pale yellow light.

"Sleep," my mother says. She strokes my back, the place between my shoulders, the place where I imagine wings will grow if I do things right. If I listen to her tell me about how to fold the banana leaves around the rice cake, how to tie them up with brown string. If I listen to grandfather leaning over the rabbit hutches, describing the difference between breeds, how lop ears and the thickest, darkest fur might explain the meaning of life. If I listen to uncle telling the pig about his first wife, how she was no good, but he loved her like his heart might burst. If I listen to my older brother's advice about riding a bicycle, and I teach my younger brother about the way the wheels turn once your feet press against the pedals, how the wind goes only as fast as the pedals turn and the wheels spin.

The moon is like an old woman, laughing, her mouth wide, her eyes closed. I reach from my covers into the cool January sky, and my fingertips graze her cheek. She opens her eyes and looks at me. "Tomorrow, to welcome Tet, the eldest boy must touch his feet to the floor first," she says. "Boys have the luck; girls must not be so bold." I take my hand back quickly and feel my mother's calm strokes across my neck, the back of my head.

In the morning I will touch the floor first, just a little, and then I will wait until my brothers stretch and set their square feet down. My own luck will mix with their luck, and the lunar year will begin with a new kind of brightness. The old woman moon will lay her face in the fields and close her eyes. No one will know.

SOMETHING FOR NOTHING

APRIL 1972

On the drawbridge that crosses the Halifax River, we have to wait for a shrimp boat to pass, its nets raised, its deck littered with lines and the gleam of the thundering rain. LuLu leans out the back window of the VW bus and yells at the tanned deckhands to hurry up. They call her "sweet baby thing" and blow kisses. A shade past fourteen, Lu is more like a flat-chested ten-year-old, small like our mama, tough like Royal. I tell her to put her head back in the window, the bridge is lowering.

"Shut up, Saul," she says, but she listens when Rainey echoes my words.

The waterway between the beach and New Smyrna's oyster bars and chicken-and-biscuit joints is busy with fishermen coming home, most of the boats small and singular, no more reason for the bridge to raise. LuLu stretches out on the bench seat behind Rainey and me, the soles of her feet up on the windows, her hands drawing imaginary pictures in the air. On the radio the Rolling Stones' intro to "You Can't Always Get What You Want" starts up, and when Lu chirps her high-pitched imitation of the choirboys' falsetto notes, Rainey turns around and tells her to please stop.

The evening sky closes in, the clouds an intense black smudge. We head out of New Smyrna, its main street crowded with bright umbrellas, parents in search of supper, a way out of the rain, their small kids pointing at shop windows crowded with beach floats and oversized balls. And crossing in front of us on skateboards, older kids in cutoffs with long, wet hair bleached from too many days in the sun. Kids like us.

I light a cigarette and exhale toward the ceiling. Rainey glares at me, waves the smoke away from the passenger side and back in my direction. She doesn't do anything that her mother does; smoking is one of those things. Lu, on the other hand, not wanting to be the baby, smokes like a chimney whenever she thinks no one is looking.

Soon, fields stretch out on either side of the road, and unlit billboards rise up, blank and massive, their messages unreadable through the downpour. The highway is dark and wet, and the night is heavy with the sound of rain, windshield wipers, and soaked asphalt under the tires. At the intersection where I have to head south, I take the curve too easily and the VW bus fishtails into the opposite lane. Rainey holds on to the dashboard handle—the "Jesus handle," Mama calls it—and stares straight ahead, through the windshield wipers flipping from side to side, her eyes on the path of the high beams.

"Slow down," she says. She leans back, raises her legs onto the seat, and wraps her arms around her knees. "It doesn't make any difference how late we are because we're already beyond late."

It was Mama who sent us to New Smyrna, to have a day of it, some fun. LuLu and Rainey and me. "Act like teenagers, why don't you? Quit moping around here." Her only rule: home by supper. And now it's well past supper.

Earlier in the day the beach was crowded, the ocean gray-green under thick white skies. The afternoon grazed over us in heavy breaths with wind and gathering clouds. When the rain finally came, it coursed down. Crazy walls of rain. We ran to the VW, but it was too late. Our legs and towels were plastered with sand, LuLu shivering, Rainey complaining that her thighs were sticking to the vinyl seat.

Now LuLu has settled behind us on the bench seat, finally quiet, asleep under a damp towel. I glance back at her and Rainey says to keep my eyes on the road. Sometimes my baby sister seems younger than fourteen, especially when she's curled up and dreaming, her fingers near her mouth. And Rainey, she seems older, more like sixteen than barely fifteen. She fidgets with her hair, braided and trailing over one shoulder, and then fools with the ties of her swimsuit top, the ones at the back of her neck. The ones I've fooled with too often. I glance at her and then back at the rain-drenched road.

Ahead are the signs for Lake Monroe and Lake Jesup and Lake Mary. I regret heading home, inland, to the part of Florida pocked with lakes and overgrown with orange groves. Across the sky is lightning, the horizontal kind that seems to strike sideways, reaching too far to find ground. The thunder is distant. Rainey counts to nine and then gives up. I think of lightning striking the beach, how a woman was killed at Cocoa last month, walking alone during a storm.

"What kind of idiot walks on the beach in a thunderstorm?" I say out loud without meaning to.

"My mother," Rainey answers. "That kind."

"Really?" I pass a pickup loaded with melons and going barely forty, the back end dented in at one side and the tailgate tied loose. In my mind, I see the rope coming undone and the melons rolling out onto the highway.

"Really," Rainey says.

Rainey has been living with us since she was ten, sharing LuLu's bedroom. My mama and Rainey's mother, Eva, have some sort of agreement. Nearly four years ago, just weeks after receiving official word that her Army husband had gone missing, Eva dropped off crates of books and china, waved to her daughter and then kept on going, like she was out searching for something and a kid might slow her down. Checks came in the mail, postmarked West Palm Beach, Coral Gables, and Islamorada. But Eva stopped coming by. Excuses like *better schools, friends your own age, that nice neighborhood* came inside envelopes addressed to Rainey, Eva's handwriting large and linear. Little packages came, too, with gifts inside. Rainey would open them and barely consider the contents—bracelets, earrings, tie-dyed dresses—and either give them away or put them back inside their boxes, a stash of secret things under her and LuLu's canopy bed. She kept only one thing—the thin gold chain with the ruby that traced her throat. "My birthstone," she told me, pushing my hands away when I tried to touch it.

Last summer when Rainey turned fourteen, her mother didn't even send a card. Rainey grabbed under the bed for the little boxes and filled the kitchen trash with all but one. The one Eva hadn't sent: made of cloth, light blue, hinged at one side. Inside, the MIA bracelet stamped with her father's name and rank and the date he'd gone missing. Like my father and my stepfather, he'd enlisted, but in the U.S. Army instead of the Marines. She told me how her father had sung to her, not in a wavering voice, but in one that burst open, loud and clear. She said he'd worn a buzz cut. All of our fathers had buzz cuts, but not all of them sang.

Rainey turns up the radio whenever Eric Clapton comes on. This time it's "Layla," and I wish she'd turn it back down. The way the guitar curves and Clapton's voice strains around the instruments—he just tries too hard. Girls love him for that.

Rainey thinks the music I listen to is too sentimental—"all that Bernie Taupin stuff," she once whispered, her face close to mine, her breath like licorice. She thinks I need to learn to like what she likes, what she is teaching LuLu to like. Music with an edge. What she means is music that's one step past the blues. But she doesn't understand that yet. What Eric Clapton did for Cream is fine, but I'm just not all that interested. Rainey seems to hear only the instruments, while I hear the words. Clapton's desperate chorus circles around again, and then finally the ending, instrumental, which sends Rainey somewhere else. Rainey knows I still feel bad, for wanting her, for her ignoring me, for the rift I've created by being that much older, seventeen, a year away from being drafted. I leave the lyrics to themselves, like they're lost chances—the begging and pleading and repeating better left to strangers on the radio.

By the time we head past Casselberry and Altamonte Springs down through Maitland, the rain has lightened, and I have to adjust the wipers, on again, off again, every few minutes. Mama would say I've taken the long way home, and she'd be right. I turn left onto Webster, a street which points back to the ocean, back where we've come from, and drive past the cemetery. Rainey stares out the window at the black streets. Not a light is on in the entire town. No streetlamps, no porch lights, only dark squares of house windows.

Mama is certain to be searching out kitchen matches and hurricane candles, cursing quietly with no one else to hear. That we're coming home late won't help. She'll most likely praise the Lord for gas stoves, then reheat supper and set out our plates, a tongue-lashing our only punishment. Since she pushed Royal out of the house, she's gone from disappearing into her bedroom for days at a time to leaving us on our own for entire weekends. She shops before she leaves—a warning sign—the cabinets stocked with cans of beans and soup, boxes of saltines, the fridge loaded with sliced cheese, half a baked ham, soft drinks. We don't ask where she goes, and we give her room when she returns. These days she sends us off, to the lake, to the beach— "anywhere there's swimming and sun," she says—like she needs to air the house of our all-day TV and laundry-covered floors.

LuLu stirs in the back seat and sits up just in time to see Mama standing in the driveway, all lit up from the headlights.

"She's probably got the leather belt out," Lu says, her voice soft, her tone mean. "Forty lashes for you, Rain-Rain. Fifty or more for Saul."

"Always exaggerating," Rainey says over her shoulder. "Like she's ever done that."

"Just not to *you*." LuLu leans forward and swipes at Rainey's unraveling braid and along her shoulders and arms.

"Quit it, crazy," Rainey says, and wards off Lu's half-assed swats.

I shut off the engine and then the headlights, and Mama disappears for a second, then reappears, a dark glimpse of herself, still standing there, waiting for us. Her arms at her sides, not crossed one on top of the other in her usual way, she now motions for us to come inside. "Supper" is the only thing she says. She moves into the house in front of us, the screen door bouncing.

Rainey says, "See?"

Lu only looks past Rainey, her eyes wide, her mouth a straight line, then drags her dirty beach towel out of the VW bus and along the wet drive.

We are all three still damp and caked with sand, which Mama won't know until the morning when she walks barefoot into the kitchen and feels the soft grit under her toes.

Later, after supper, Rainey leaves a bowl of strawberries by my bedroom door. It's nearly one in the morning, and I hear her set the bowl down and I know it's the same one as before. A shallow yellow bowl with handles, the one she took from the crate marked KITCHENWARE in our garage. The same crate her mother packed with teacups and tissue paper before finding a way to leave and not come back.

The berries are bright and small—like rubies, like Rainey's mouth. And when I take one and press it against my lips, I wish for her mouth more than the crush of fruit, the stain it will leave. Eventually, she will kiss me again. And eventually she will wander into the basement rec room of a boy named Timothy, just because his eyes are huge and she's curious about his silence and the size of his hands. Soon enough, I will lose her, to so many others, and she will come back, and I'll lose her again. But for this moment, I know none of this.

For now she is here, on the other side of the hall, whispering things to my sister. And for now I have this bowl of berries, one leaning against another and another, their scarlet syrup circling into the bottom of the bowl.

I can tell it's morning because they're yelling.

"Cut it out!" Rainey is shouting at LuLu, and Lu is silent.

Rainey rushes into the hallway between our rooms. My door is halfway open and from the edge of my bed I can see her. She's wearing a sundress, the straps falling off her shoulders. Thin straps, like the red twine around the package in the top of my closet. The small, square package, rescued nearly four years ago from a shelf in a military warehouse, with my father's personal effects inside.

Rainey stops and stands there in the new quiet, looking at something. She seems to follow the floorboards, the strips of light falling across them, to the empty yellow bowl next to my bed. And then she's in the doorway, pushing the door wider, looking straight at me. Her eyes are the strangest color, a pale blue-green that sometimes darkens.

My stereo is turned low, playing the song that always makes me think of her. From across the room she smiles like she knows I would meet her halfway. Wherever she wants. It's never for sure, though. I can never tell with her what is for sure. And then that's what makes me love her, makes me wish for another afternoon at the lake.

She sits down on my bed. The space between us is narrow and full of breath and rumpled sheets. She is wearing the MIA bracelet, the one that's stamped with her father's name and date of disappearance, and she traces her fingers back and forth over the engraved letters and numbers. I know there will be hell if Mama catches us. Screaming and hell. Me in shorts and no shirt, and Rainey with her dress straps falling down, both of us sitting on my bed.

"Why does LuLu always have to act so crazy?" she says.

"I don't know, Rain. She's just like that. Full volume, all up in your face."

She smiles. "She's not *just* like that." Her hand presses down on the mattress between us. "She's *just* LuLu."

"Sure," I say. I feel the space between us. Only inches. The space between me and Lu feels immense, even though we're related. Different fathers, same mother.

"You always listen to this album," Rainey says. "Over and over and over." Her fingers lay flat against the sheets. No rings. Not like other girls. Bare fingers. Bare feet. Bare ankles. She laughs.

Around her throat, a sliver of gold, a teardrop ruby in the hollow. The necklace from her mother.

"Saul," she says.

My name in her mouth.

And then a door slamming open. LuLu. She is just like a rabbit the way she jumps around.

"Hey!" she cries. She's high. "What are you two doing in here?" Joyride high.

Rainey stays on the bed, trying not to blink and gathering fistfuls of sheets. LuLu pounces onto the bed, pushing between us, her hands slapping at my chest.

"You," she says to me, leaning closer, breathing in my face. "You, Saul, are practically naked!"

"You wish," Rainey says.

"I do," she says back. " I do!" She laughs and nearly falls on the floor. "And I know you do, Rainey. Don't you?"

"Right," Rainey says.

The flat sound of her voice hits me hard. I don't know if it's for LuLu, this act. They each have an act. I know Lu's already. How she's mad at everyone and wants to make us all disappear, and each tiny pill she swallows is supposed to do the trick. Lu's act is loud and clear. But Rainey's isn't.

Lu turns up the volume on the stereo. There is a slow moment of the needle against the vinyl, scratching at the space between songs. And then, too loudly, the lone piano and the voice. Rainey glances from me to the turntable and walks away, and LuLu is still jumping up and down on my bed.

"LuLu and Saul!" Mama is in the hallway. "I will not have all this racket in my house. Do you understand me?"

LuLu sinks onto the bed, knees first.

"Yes, Mama," she says.

I can tell she's trying not to laugh. Her mouth meets my shoulder, and I can feel her starting up. She stops herself by falling over and smashing her face into my pillow. I lean over her to turn the stereo down.

"LuLu."

"Yes, Mama?" she says, her voice muffled.

"You and Rainey clean up that room of yours today. *Before* you go anywhere, young lady."

I turn to face Mama, but she's already gone. Her bedroom door shuts with a click. This morning Mama makes herself scarce, only showing up to put out our small fires.

LuLu still has her head against the pillow, her legs tucked underneath her. Across the room on my dresser are open rolls of Life Savers—peppermint, the kind Lu likes to nab. Blue marbles, some pennies, a black comb. Mama's words echo in my head—*clean up that room*. These days, she rarely comes into mine, so I guess she doesn't care about the clothes lying on the floor, or whether the dresser drawers are closed like she wants them, or how many towels are thrown over the foot of my bed.

I want Royal to come back and take charge of Mama and Lu and the meds he left behind. It's been almost two years since Mama asked him to leave, the door yawning wide, the vials of painkillers buried in a bedroom drawer. I want him to take Lu to his lake house where they can work on carpentry projects with tools and two-by-fours, where they can fish with cane poles, where he can keep her out of trouble.

I nudge Lu and she groans.

"Stop," she says.

"Get off my bed." I push her this time.

She lifts her head off the pillow and stares at me. "Make me."

I grab her by the wrist and pull.

"All right, all right. I give up." She jumps off the bed and smiles. "Asshole," she says from the doorway and then runs down the hall.

When I was ten years old, I wasn't very tall and my father—the full six feet, five inches of him—towered over everyone. Isaac Finch Edwards. Mama called him handsome. Tall, dark, and handsome. All Mama's friends did, too. "So handsome, that Isaac Edwards," they said. In their church pews, down grocery aisles, at the lake. Back then Mama still acted like she owned him. Even though they'd been divorced a long while. Even though she'd been married to another man for seven years. Even though she had another child to worry about.

He came over that night like he was timing it. Like he knew just when Royal and LuLu had stepped out the door to get a quart of vanilla ice cream. Mama had made a peach pie, which sat cooling on the kitchen counter, the top crust latticed and golden. When my father came in through the kitchen door, I guess Mama thought it was Royal and Lu. I heard my father's voice, a drawer open, the sound of a plate being scraped. And then I heard my father calling me again and again.

"Goddammit, son," he called. "Get out here now."

It wasn't the first time I hid from him. I was under the bed and breathing dust.

"Isaac," Mama said. "Leave him be."

"Get out of my face, woman," he shouted. "Don't tell me what to do."

"Isaac." And then the slap. And then the bare silence and the crying. Always the crying.

He reached under the bed and pulled me out. Later, between his tours in Vietnam when he knew Royal was still overseas, he'd come by the house and pull cans of Schlitz, one after the other, out of the fridge, the silver ring tops left on the kitchen counter. His hand cradled and then crushed each can into a flat disk. His hand could have circled my forearm at least twice.

He didn't have any words for me. Words were not his thing.

The belt burned when it first landed. My shirt ripped, and I leaned over and gave him my back. It wasn't the first time he'd found me.

"You come when I call you," he said.

He turned the belt around and used the metal end.

"You hear me?" he yelled.

The buckle bit into my side. I knew from all the other times there was nothing I could do, and so I did nothing but take it, while Mama lay on the floor and cried.

Afterward, when Royal and Lu came back, the kitchen was empty, the pie on the counter, the latticing broken and one piece missing. Mama had locked the bathroom door, and she bathed me. I pretended not to wince, and Mama promised things she shouldn't, like we'd leave and she'd never let him hurt me again. But even then I knew if she'd really meant it, we would already be gone. Driving away in the middle of the night, the headlights showing us the dark, long road. And Royal swore that we didn't have to go anywhere, that he'd kill Isaac if he ever showed his face again. I blinked against the sound of his voice. Unlike my mother's, bruised and hollow, his was edged with certainty.

Lu is outside in the orange grove, sitting up in a tree and smoking the cigarettes she steals from the 7-Eleven. She has a little black duck call in her other hand, and between drags she presses it to her lips. It no longer makes a sound, and I know it's stolen, too.

I've even caught her taking things from our mama's dresser drawers, including the pills Royal left behind.

"Don't you think Royal needs those?" I asked her back in December, when school was out and she was beyond bored.

She was lying sprawled across the shag carpet in her room, the Stones turned up loud, shaking the plastic bottle to the beat of "Gimme Shelter."

She eyed me and said, "My daddy would've taken them if he needed them. He's not dumb. Not like your questions."

"Maybe we should take them to him, instead of you taking them yourself." I tried to twist the little brown bottle from her fist, but she only held on tighter and laughed.

I thought about telling Mama, but knew that soon enough the pills would run out. Besides, I almost liked Lu high. Too bad she kept on with all that little sister crap.

Rainey was careful and avoided Lu when she was messed up. The pills would appear and Rainey would disappear. Not that she thought she was too pure. She just said she didn't want to join in. She didn't need anything to quiet or rouse her. She was like that already, the way she listened. Lu should've taken lessons.

Through the blinds I watch my half sister smoking in the orange tree and feel the day press down. Everything is heavier now—my thoughts, the weight of my sheets at night, the spring heat, the yellow bowl in my hand, the strawberries against my tongue, the endless body counts, the box tied with thin red twine sitting on the shelf in my closet.

I think of the twine and the straps of Rainey's sundress, and I remember the time Rainey went out in the canoe with me. We paddled for a while, and then drifted. I pulled her into the curve of the canoe, and she lay next to me, quiet, her eyes closed. We said nothing: there were only the sounds of lake water lapping against the sides of the canoe, of our breathing. Skin, warmth, and then a sad exhalation. The smell of metal was all around us—metal and mildew. And I remember her hair brushing my face and the taste of her tears.

I close the blinds and leave my room. The morning has disappeared into one of those nothing afternoons. A long Sunday afternoon meant for wasting. The sky has a blue-white wash to it, and the air is warm. I walk down to the lake and lie on the dock. I smoke and look out at the cypresses, the boathouses, the blank sky repeating on the lake's surface.

There isn't a single canoe out there. I think about flipping over the old aluminum one that rests on the lawn. I know it will smell of damp green things, and the oars will have to be taken down from the shed. But the day is calm, and I don't want to ruin it.

A few nights ago, I went out alone. I listened for voices moving over the lake from the shore, and I rested the oars whenever a conversation drifted out to me. The Lingstrums' laughter. Lillian and Jack Walbright's voices, low and serious, until Lillian shouted and Jack slapped her. Their dog, Lyman, barking once. A wash of silence, and then a night heron's calls. The darkness settled, and an uneven sky dipped down. I raised the oar. Long strokes. And then just the sound of the water. Nothing else.

Later, as I paddled toward the dock, I saw Rainey and LuLu, swimming, diving, holding their breath, linking arms and floating together in the moonlight.

Once, we knew nothing about the world, only the lake, and Alan Walbright was still alive. That was another time all together. In less than a year, I could be called up and shipped out to that world where bombs fell, where children burned alive, where villages disappeared overnight. But here, two girls swam together, and there were only distant sounds—an outboard motor, Lyman's barking, and here—right here—two girls treading water.

Now, the lake is still. The smoke from my cigarette rises, the whiteness nearly matching the sky. A large white bird takes off, and a stand of brown cattails shifts. A bare foot nudges me.

Rainey stands there. Her long beach-brown calves stretch up, and I follow them to the hem of her dress and farther. Underneath, the pink bikini underwear she wears. I reach up and touch the inside of her thigh.

She stands there, looking out at the lake. Barely breathing.

"LuLu went in your room this afternoon," she says.

I let my hand fall down to her ankle.

"Lu doesn't go in my room when I'm not around."

"Sure she does." She looks down at me. "She goes in there all the time."

"Well, she never messes with anything." And then I remember the peppermint Life Savers.

"Today she was searching for something. And she seemed bent on finding whatever it was."

I imagine my sister, her short blond hair flying, searching drawers, pushing marbles and pennies onto the floor. But I can't imagine what she might search for.

Rainey kneels next to me and traces my forearm with one finger.

In the closet are my father's dress blues, the white cap on the shelf above. After he died, the Marine Corps didn't know where to send his belongings, but finally found the one address that made sense. Mama probably thought she'd thrown away every last thing. I found the box, though, and saved it. The pack with all of his personal effects: whatever he hadn't been wearing that day, including photos—of Mama, and another of a girl, someone from over there. Nothing much saved from nothing much of a man.

Rainey takes my hand inside of hers. "What was she looking for, Saul?"

On the closet shelf with the cap are his belt, shoes and all. And the pistol. Not my father's, my stepfather's. A Browning semi-automatic Royal gave Mama when he shipped out for Vietnam. Insurance against Isaac, in case he came back when Royal wasn't around. Black and heavy, far too large for Mama's hands. She never touched it, afraid to. Had me empty the chamber into the kitchen trash, each bullet thudding against orange rinds and coffee grounds, and asked me to put the gun away. And so I did. In the farthest, highest corner of my closet, up high, out of sight. And it was still sitting up there, inside the box with my father's things.

Rainey winds her fingers through mine and holds our hands to her mouth. "Hmmm?" she asks. I feel the vibration of her question and the warmth of her breath.

Even if Lu kept on looking, she wouldn't find the rounds. Why the hell had we kept this pistol anyway? Royal should've taken it back. He never should've given it to Mama in the first place. We didn't need it.

I don't want to think about Lu going through my things, through my father's things. I let go of Rainey's hand, and she stays next to me; she stays there and just lets me be.

There was the time when I thought about the gun. I was thirteen and trying to make sense of things. Like the box secured with red twine, the pistol inside, the absence of rounds. October 1968—the one-year marker of Royal's departure, the one-month marker of my father's death. November came, and then December. The months when no one seemed to give a shit and the nightly news told us as much. Hueys evacuating the dead and wounded; Walter Cronkite announcing serious setbacks for the U.S. due to losses in Khe Sanh; old Vietnamese women as small as children leaning over and praying; children running and screaming along dirt roads; villages set on fire, the smoke like a thousand blackbirds beating their wings against the glass of the TV.

All winter I slept with the Browning under my pillow and dreamed of bullets. Bullets, a beach, lines of men. I walked LuLu and Rainey to their grade school, and then I walked on to the junior high. A boy from my class sold me the bullets from his father's gun. And an extra box, just because. Same sidearm, standard issue. I paid a month's allowance, then considered the real cost and buried the rounds in the orange grove.

At night I'd take the empty pistol out and hold it against my right temple. To see what it felt like. I'd imagine the crimped safety lever unlocked, the trigger pulled and then released. My bedroom door, closed and locked. LuLu and Rainey running down the hall, shouting and laughing. And the click.

My father almost made it through his second tour in Vietnam. Grenade, rocket fire, mortar power—whatever killed him killed him. We weren't told the details. Gunnery Sergeant Edwards died for his country. That's all they said.

When Rainey and I get home, we find Lu standing in front of the full-length mirror in her room, wearing nothing but my father's white dress cap and a pair of Royal's uniform socks, waving the Browning around like it's the latest boy in town. Lu is fucking looped.

"Jesus, Lu," I say. "Give me that." I look away, embarrassed to see her naked.

Rainey stands back in the hallway outside the bedroom, looking over my shoulder.

"Make me." Lu is tiny and bare and points the gun at my chest.

"Give it to me," I say. I force myself to look at her, make my gaze steady.

She traces the barrel between her small breasts. I watch her and realize how gone she is. Mama is missing and I wish for once she weren't. And then I remember the bullets. I turn down the hall past Rainey and slam the back door open. At the edge of the backyard where the grove begins, where I buried them, there's a mass of dirt and a hole. Lu must have watched me bury them from her bedroom window. I should have known. She is always watching.

"LuLu!" I scream, running, skidding down the hall. Rainey's sitting on the floor now, and I slide against the wall to get around her to the bedroom door and Lu.

She's sitting on her bed, lifting dark pennies and dirty bullets and letting them rain down like beads onto her quilt.

"Lulu, please?" I can't breathe.

She holds the pistol out to me, like it's a gift. And I take it like it's just that, like it's the best thing she's ever given me.

"Saul," she says. My little naked, blond-headed baby sister. She lifts her arms over her head and releases a rush of pennies and ammo into the air. And it all comes flying down, landing everywhere, bouncing against the bed, our feet, the floor.

"Lu," I say. "What the fuck?"

"You shouldn't hide things."

"You shouldn't take things."

She picks up a handful of .45s like she's going to throw them, casting her arm backward. "You shouldn't either," she says, looking straight into the hall at Rainey. "You know, just a little something for nothing. Right, Rainey?"

"Please give me those." I hold my hands out.

"No," Lu says. "I get to keep these." She lets them fall again, and they clatter together with a hard metal sound that scares me.

"They're not yours."

"No, they're not." She winces. "But I'm still keeping them."

"What else did you take?"

"You are such an asshole, Saul." She sits up on her knees, and the bullets roll around them. "Don't act like you care."

"Where's Mama?"

"Off somewhere."

"Looking for you most likely."

"Maybe."

The back door slams.

"Oh," says LuLu. "Better go see what's wrong with Rainey. You don't want her to be upset. That'll ruin things for you."

"What the hell is your problem?"

"You are! You fucking are!" And she cries then. She curls into a little knot and cries.

I cover her up with a blanket and wait. I sit on the edge of the bed and check to make sure the Browning isn't loaded. And then, when she finally calms down, I reach around her legs and scoop up the bullets. She is still so small.

There is no going back to my room, blinds closed. To a bowl of strawberries left by the door. And I don't want to be in charge of what's left at the end of a day that started out with yelling and is now mute. I feel the load of the bullets in my pocket and try to understand what my father knew in the last moments of his last day. Was the sun shining down, reflecting off the waves of the South China Sea? Did the stripes across his sleeve feel like accountability, like the weight of someone else's life? Did he see me in the slant of light, the glimmer of the raised rifle, across the beach that day in Qui Nhơn?

Outside, I try to find Rainey. The backyard is empty, and the sun is starting to fall below the lowest trees. Soon it will be dark. Soon it will be pitch black, with stars that go on and on—endless, hopeless little stars. I remember how yesterday the sky was covered in clouds, the road wet and black and drenched with rain, and how we took the long way home, driving west, then south, circling back east in the direction of the beach, like we were starting all over again.

Rainey will come back, long before summer flocks of blackbirds weigh down the orange trees and before the boy named Timothy smiles from across a crowded classroom. And so will Mama and Royal, and maybe even Eva. One at a time. For now though, it's too hard to think, to know that I can't leave. That I have to stay here for Lu. At least until she wakes up. Until I've sunk every last pill and bullet in the depths of the lake. Until I can get through another nothing-for-nothing Sunday. Until all the nothings finally become something.

LA LA MEANS A THOUSAND DIFFERENT THINGS

SEPTEMBER 1973

The bright yellow telephone in my living room has an even brighter ring. In the early evening a call will mean one thing—a gentleman caller. So when the fellow from *Look* phones to ask for an interview, I pause a slight moment, listen to the silence between us, wait for his breathing, patient and faint, and then I say yes. He's heard about my shows at the Poinciana Club in the Royal Palms Hotel. Classy song-and-dance acts, performed mostly for men in uniform and the company they keep—their lovely brides, of course, and then those local girls, regulars, bejeweled and made-up like *Vogue* models. Why, my audiences are stacked with celebrities, though the days of JFK and Jackie are long over. I've become a bit of a celebrity myself, my voice said to be as sultry as Dusty Springfield's. Mr. *Look* tells me this will be his big break, a solo assignment, and seems intent on writing a feature article, something to the effect of "Eva Ives McPherson, the officer's wife who has taken fate into her own hands." The cover has even been promised, in color, along with a large sum of money for showing off my legs.

The sliding doors that lead to my terrace are open and a breeze travels through my rooms. I walk to the doors to close them, but stand there instead, staring out. Before me, the West Palm Beach clouds laze and skid across a sky that stretches on and on. The world over, the heavens must seem the same. The same strain of blue, the same tapestry of gray. Whether here or there. Whether today or tomorrow or twelve years ago.

These days I linger in the past far too often and have to force myself to remember that life doesn't lie there. That Will left for Vietnam in the fall of 1966—before our tenth anniversary— and went missing soon after, that Rainey is out of sight but never out of mind, that I am on my own—this is where life lies. Concentrating on the here and now, the moment at hand, the rum and lime with a perfect little orange umbrella—that's how I bring myself back. Attention helps. Of course it does. Dancing with my hand against a broad back, sequins, songs, pretty things. They help, too.

The days flip forward, and I wait on my veranda for the *Look* reporter and wonder what questions he might ask, what stories I will tell. The motel where I live faces the beach. I rent by the month, so it's really more like an apartment. Families come for the week, couples for the weekend. Twelve bungalows in all, the Seaglade Motel is a tiny affair but likes to think of itself as a resort. Palm trees, a curved pool, and shell-colored stucco cottages with terracotta-tiled roofs and terraces all around, facing the lawns and the pool and the ocean. I walk out of my front door and over the wind-blown dunes, and there is the Atlantic, sweeping on into forever. I met Will on this very beach. It's strange that I came back here; lots of things are strange, though. I work at a hotel and live in a motel—isn't that strange enough?

The writer from *Look* arrives right on time, all clockwork in schedule and appearance. He's attractive in his dark blue suit, buttoned up like a proper wind-up toy. Tall and tense, ready to go. I study him briefly, then I invite him in.

"Take a look around," I say. "I'll get us some drinks and we'll sit by the pool."

"Oh, nothing for me, thank you." He holds a pad and pen at his side, and a camera hangs at his hip from a thin shoulder strap. "I don't drink this early in the day."

"It's just iced tea. My goodness."

He may be zipped up a little too tightly, this Mr. *Look*.

"It's like summer outside," I say. "Plenty of ice, a little lemon. Do you good." I glance at him peering around the living room.

My cottage is small, but certainly the Seaglade's most elegant, furnished by admiring naval commanders. Most of the rentals are simple, meant for vacationers who don't expect more. But mine is elaborate, revealing the generosity of those who love me. The chaise with the silk throw from Bangkok over one arm, the Murano chandelier above, the champagne chilling in the fridge. There are only three rooms, the walls lined with art and low-banked bookcases, the bedroom partitioned by a curtain of bamboo beads. Above my bed is a photo by another photographer, taken on the beach years ago for *Harper's Bazaar*. A photo that made the magazine's August 1967 cover, a scant year since Will had gone missing, and a session that broke any promises of propriety I'd ever made him. I sit on my knees, facing sideways, wearing a strapless swimsuit and a *non*, a bamboo farmer's hat from Vietnam. In the corner above my profile and the conical hat are the handwritten words, *In Vietnamese, La La means a thousand different things.*

Nearly everything I own has been a gift. My clothes, my jewelry, the record albums I endlessly play. It's all part of the package. The colonel who loves my eyes but never touches me, the ensign who adorns me with jade necklaces he can't afford, the supplies officer who makes paella after making love. The thrills and throes of war—martini glasses, first editions of Hemingway, brandy bottled in commemoration of V-J Day, even things that I refuse that stay in my dresser drawers until I can give them back. Sometimes the men don't return and I don't have the heart to take their gifts to the trash, but eventually I do.

Men love me. They compare me to Dunaway, even Bardot. And I love my things. They are as refined as they are outrageous and excessive. To be sure, I pause at times, fingering the gold bracelet before handing it back. And inside all the excess is a vast emptiness.

"Let's sit outside," I say to the man from *Look*.

He remembers his manners and holds the door open, allowing me to lead the way and choose a shaded table. Tall glasses of tea at our places, I settle into a lounge chair and face him and the sun. It is ten in the morning and a warm autumn breeze slips over the dunes. I understand the dress I'm wearing is fine for now, but he'd like to get some photographs on the beach and at the club. I'll be changing several times. The revealing red swimsuit will surprise him, I'm sure.

"Right then." He clears his throat. "Some warm-up questions to start?" He opens his pad and grasps a sleek black pen. "How long have you lived here?"

"It's been six years now," I say. And then, "Oh, no. I'm wrong. It's been nearly seven. Rainey, my daughter, just turned sixteen. I still gauge time through her birthdays, rather than my own. Safer, don't you think?"

He laughs, then looks out at the ocean and back to me. "Where is Rainey? In school?"

The warm-up questions veer away from what I'd expect. Still, I invited them and so I answer. "Well, yes, she's certainly in school. She doesn't live here."

"Oh?"

"She lives with friends of mine in Anna Clara. It's a sweet little town, surrounded by lakes and citrus groves. It's easier, you know. I'm working at the Poinciana. So I do count on my friends."

"Rumor has it you count on those who come to your shows as well."

I know what he is implying and don't shy away. "Rumor is such a bad source, don't you think? Besides, why complicate things, it's the simple truth. Heavens, I can't even remember them all. They just swarm in, and then of course they ship out. Vietnam—the other woman—she's still out there."

"So you like to shock people?"

I lower my sunglasses. "What do you think?"

"I think you like attention."

"Well, that's why you're here, isn't it?"

I raise my glass to him.

Mr. *Look* smiles. I admire his straight teeth and then his silence.

"You want me to be honest?" I ask.

He nods.

"I may sing with the likes of Dean Martin, Sam Butera, even Louis Prima. On stage, of course. But really, in truth, I'm on my own. My husband is missing in action, my parents are gone, and I've a child to support. There you have the facts. So here's the real question: would I be working if I still had a husband to support me? No matter what anyone says, we are simply left alone. Military benefits? What are those? I may not be a war widow and my husband may still be out there somewhere, but it's been over seven years."

I think of patriotism, of the morale-boosting moments I've given to the boys, the soldiers, who have no idea what they've gotten into. I think of guilt—a mother's, a daughter's, a wife's. I have plenty. Sure, I dance and sing at a nightclub. A secretarial job won't pay for the life I want, and I'm fine with playing West Palm Eva against Hanoi Hannah any day.

When Mr. *Look* asks if he can quote me, I smile, thinking of the story he said he came for and the one he will get. And then I tell him, "Of course, but maybe we should start at the beginning." And then I tell him what he really wants to know. I tell him about the man I married.

I was twenty-two and working nine to five as a secretary for an insurance firm, which catered to some of West Palm's wealthiest. Seriously. From the Kennedys on down. In on the most confidential of meetings, I sometimes received invitations for drinks and dancing, for a modeling job on the side that promised extra cash. Who could refuse? The touch of a hand on my waist— at the office, on the dance floor.

Weekends, though, were reserved for time alone, for things I liked to do, with mornings in the art museum and afternoons on the beach. Long, cool museum corridors led to rooms of radiant, light-filled paintings. The beach was lit in the same way, with springtime skies so brilliant and unbelievable and blue that I could barely breathe. May was immeasurable and at that point I thought the same of my life. The sun, the sand, the sound of the waves.

One memorable afternoon I fell asleep, lying on my stomach, and when I woke, I knew that someone—a man— was standing over me. I reached out and touched the sand near his toes, then sat back on my towel, my arms wrapped around my legs. My white bathing suit was new, and I'd bought it thinking of Marilyn Monroe, wishing to impress someone, perhaps a client, and now felt less than daring.

"You are the most beautiful girl on the beach," he said and sat down right next to me. His brown hair was incredibly short, and his gray-blue eyes startled me, their glimpse more than inquiring. "I'm Will. First Lieutenant William McPherson. And you are?"

"Excuse me?"

His legs were long and muscular and very close to mine.

"Invite me to dinner," he said. His words were clipped yet elegant, the intonations spelling out possibility.

"I don't know you."

All around us were people reading, their sunglasses in place, their children building sandcastles. Only the gulls faced into the wind. No one looked in our direction.

"Seriously," he said, "you are stunning. Look at those legs. They go on and on."

"Don't be ridiculous." I waved him away, but he didn't quit.

"I'd guess you're a remarkable dancer. Though everyone would cut in and I'd never have a chance. Why don't we give Ta-boó a try? I'll pick you up at eight. What do you say?" He held out his hand, as if inviting me to dance right then and there.

I knew how to play this. I kept my eyes on the horizon and tracked a lone surfer, who rode a wave nearly to shore. The first lieutenant seemed to follow my lead then, slowing down and leaning into the laze of the afternoon. He surveyed me, his right hand still extended, palm up, the lifeline deep and truncated.

Again I said, "I don't know you," and noticed the delicate laugh lines around his eyes, how they remained whether or not he smiled.

When I still didn't take his hand, he said, "Invite me to dinner. Then you will know me."

Afterwards, I thought he'd been incredibly forward, and later I realized he'd meant to be. The summer was just beginning, but Will had only weekends free. He'd finished officer training and was working his way up, for the time being at Pinecastle Air Command in Orlando. Perhaps he wasn't a true catch, but as I said, weekends were reserved for things I liked.

At dinner he gazed in my direction and said it had been a long time since he'd met a girl who knew so much. About Palm Beach personalities and art and which wine to order. He didn't know what I'd committed to memory—conversations overheard about the beach villa crowd, bits and pieces on contemporary art from museum brochures, orders from permanently reserved tables at the best restaurants in town. His hands rested in his lap and then moved to the table, as if he were slowly trying to determine our distance, one gesture at a time.

We shared a platter of shrimp and crabs, the delicate pink and bright orange shells slowly mounding to one side, and one bottle of wine led to another. Ta-boó was the most popular scene in West Palm, and I wondered how he'd managed a last-minute reservation. Will was impressed that the waiters knew me and that several parties waved while passing by to their usual tables.

"Well, looks like you should have made this reservation."

"You did just fine on your own," I said and touched the crisp cotton of his sleeve. I had to admit, he knew how to dress, when to smile, what to order.

Our table faced the dance floor, the retractable roof open, the first stars coming out. A few couples were already dancing, but most guests were chasing their prime rib with drinks, loud talk and laughter rising from their tables.

"You're not really just twenty-two?" he asked.

"I'm really fifty-five, but look good for my age."

I didn't know how to wink or even joke very well. Still, he laughed, his arms against the table, which rocked in his direction and then tipped toward me. Of course, it all happened in slow motion—the wine glass slipping to one side and the empty shells cascading to the floor. The waiter didn't even blink. A new wine glass appeared, and before my glass was even refilled Will was on his feet, leading me to the dance floor.

The music was lively, a sort of big band sound, and we fell quickly into step and swept around the room. We came close together, tight as a top, then away, spinning out and back in again, only our faces in focus, the world flying around us. Cha-Cha, Swing, the Bop.

"I was right," Will said. "You are the best dancer in the room, and maybe even in this town."

"And you're a regular Fred Astaire."

I grinned, maybe a little too much, as he twirled me around. People had begun to step aside and watch us, tapping their feet in time, clapping their hands. And soon enough the spirited, quickstep tunes ended, and the crowd melted back to their seats or together, murmuring. The band began to play a song from *Guys and Dolls*, the one Sinatra sings, the one about love. Will knew the words.

"No singing," I said.

"Why not?"

"Too soon for things like that."

"Never too soon."

He pulled me closer, and I gave in a little, resting my head on his shoulder. I hadn't planned for this; I had other things in mind, things like jewelry, fine clothes, a large beachside house complete with staff. For now, though, this was nice. More than nice, this was something I could get used to. Will kept surprising me throughout the evening, then throughout the weekend, and a series of weekends began. He said again and again, "Life is too short, so why waste it?" And we'd be off, swimming in the ocean at sunrise after staying awake all night, then dancing on the beach in soaking-wet swimsuits.

One afternoon at the museum of art, he pointed out a painting by Edward Hopper. "More like where I come from." He hummed a tune that matched the canvas, dark and brooding, an absurdly sad song. A New York boy, he couldn't help himself. He loved Rodgers and Hammerstein and knew songs from nearly every musical I'd ever heard of.

Summer turned to autumn, and Will received transfer orders that would take him clear across the country to Fort Lewis. I couldn't believe he was leaving and I was staying. He surprised me with another long evening at Ta-boó, and inside the embrace of a dance-floor song, slow and sultry, something Lena Horne might sing, he asked me to marry him. I didn't respond at first, my head on his shoulder, thinking how his whispered question completely swept away the best-laid plans for landing a millionaire. I had no idea how far away Tacoma was. Once we were there, it felt as foreign as the moon. Beautiful, but so different. The air felt thinner, more crystalline. And soon enough I was pregnant, and when Rainey arrived the years spread out before us, measured by her first steps, first words, first impressions, in a world as new to me as it was to her.

By half past eleven I am posing on the beach for Mr. *Look*. His camera is built like him, slim and angular with a wide lens. He promises results as he aims and clicks, aims and clicks, my red bikini in the center of his viewfinder. He is still wearing his light wool suit.

"Are you afraid of the sun?" I ask him.

He asks me to smile more dramatically. I find myself laughing and looking at the line of pelicans flying overhead. Pointing at each one, I count twelve. Rainey loved watching them, when she was nine and we first lived here, after Will had left for Vietnam. I shake my head when Mr. *Look* asks me to tell him what I'm thinking.

"No," I say. "How about I tell you something else, something you'd never know otherwise?" I sit on the sand and motion for Mr. *Look* to sit next to me. He not only sits down in that dark blue suit, but he crosses his legs like a child. Those long, ridiculous legs crossed and his attention all mine.

"There is an afternoon I remember when I was ten or so and my father took me out fishing. He had hopes of catching sea trout and mangrove snapper, and I was sent along to keep him company. My mother reminded me to breathe in the sea air, as this prompted good health, though she never went on these trips herself."

"So you grew up in the area?" Mr. *Look* is squinting and truly curious.

"Of course I did." I smile. "Florida girl. Born and bred. Listen and I'll tell you."

I describe how I held on to the sides of the boat as we skirted the inland marshes, and each time I turned my head, my chin touched the padded collar of my life vest. The wind reached around us and my hair flew every which way, but I felt safe inside the quilted vest. Our aluminum boat drew a clean line through the water, its outboard motor, an old Johnson Sea-Horse that my father put to its limit, raising the boat's bow and bringing salt spray up along the sides. Little islands lined our route, and further in, we slowed and the rushes and sedges loomed up, green and alive. A heron fished in the distance and seagulls looked like Vs against the bright sky.

Mr. *Look*'s notepad lies in his lap. "Sounds beautiful," he says.

"It was beautiful," I say. "I know we fished, but I don't remember catching anything. My father reeled in his line regularly and I stared over the side at large minnows and fiddler crabs."

Mr. *Look*'s pad falls onto the sand as he raises his camera and starts taking one photo after another of me. I point straight up at the noon sun and explain how that day the sun crept through the water like a spotlight, at times fading, the shallows darkening as clouds passed over.

"Something caught my attention," I tell him. "Something that floated but was partly beached. Brushing against the marsh grass in an indented part of the shoreline was a section of driftwood. I thought it was driftwood at first, but it was limp and lifeless and immediately made me sad. Unbearably sad. The pelican's long bill was open, the eyes like glass, without anything more to behold. And there I was, just an unremarkable little girl, staring over the edge of a tin-colored boat."

Still, the camera continues. A forward spin of film, sure to reach its end.

"It's strange how death affects us, isn't it?" I say. "At one moment twelve pelicans draw a line across the sky, and then there's the memory of a blackened version lying forsaken in an eddy, as if it had never been alive at all. So strange."

Mr. *Look* holds his camera, turning the lens, opening and closing the aperture. Perhaps only the smallest thread of light will make it into his mind, onto his typewritten pages, and out to the newsstands. A flicker of who I really am, the Army wife gone astray, the mother without a child, the woman who entertains crowds and pleases men, even this one, for a price.

"I don't even remember the rest of that day," I go on. "I don't remember seeing my father clean the fish once we'd reached the landing and were back on shore. I'm sure other fishermen were there as well, calling to each other, talking about their catches. I don't remember much of my childhood, though, especially after that. I'm sure it was mundane, a dreary thing. I only hope Rainey's having a better time of it. I wonder what she remembers about her father and her first day in school and the mountain we could see from our windows, the one that gave me her name. But I haven't really told you about that, have I?"

In Washington State the air was cool and the mountains rose up into the clouds. You could look out past the sheer blue, and the sierra seemed to reach on endlessly. Mount Rainier was out there, wide and lilac and ghostlike. After all my years in flat, sea-scrubbed Florida, I'd never seen anything like that. Will and I settled down, and I grew accustomed to the whispery light of Tacoma.

In the summer of 1957, Rainey was born—Adelaide after my mother and Rainier for that mysterious summit. She was a beautiful baby and grew into a pretty little girl. Her first years flew by, and the minute she was able to climb into our laps, she took over with her hold-me-daddy moments. Will was completely taken with her. He'd swing her up into his arms, mesmerized. I'd hold her and feel beguiled, then look away, past the brilliant blue sky awash with clouds, beyond my daughter's blond head. There were no sensations, no impressions of emotion, not even anger. Instead, I felt deprived and numb and a touch reckless.

Here I was, halfway across the universe, well beyond the world I'd once desired for myself. Evelyn Bridget Ives had disappeared, replaced by Mrs. William Sean McPherson. An officer's wife, complete with child and military housing, I'd had another life in mind, one more refined, filled with sophisticated people and their parties, with travel to beautiful places. I ransacked my mind for where that had gone.

The war came along for those of us at Fort Lewis, and by 1966 we knew the weeks were numbered. Will's orders to ship out had arrived. Rainey was nine, and her playfulness distracted her father. She twirled in her pleated skirt and tiptoed around, catching his eye when I needed him the most. He was leaving soon, and so I arranged for our things to be sent back home to Florida, where we'd live with my mother until Will's return. And then, thinking in straight lines, I made plans to send Rainey on ahead. She cried and carried on about going. I gave her a charm bracelet and told her to count the charms, one for each time she missed me.

"But I'll miss Daddy, too," she said.

"So will I, baby," I said. "So will I." I held her wrists, their fragile bones, the gold flowers and seashells of her bracelet softly tinkling. She wouldn't look me in the face. "Don't fret. I'll be there soon. Just as quick as you can wink. And your grandmother is so happy she'll have you all on your own. She hasn't seen you in such a long time."

"I want to stay here with you and Daddy." Rainey crossed her arms, but not in the tight and insistent way I'd expected. Her attention seemed far off, and her dress folded around her. There was a loose delicacy about her, which infuriated me. "I don't want to go." She looked up at me, unblinking.

"Come on now, Rainey." I reached out to hug her and instead traced the line of her cheeks to her chin and kissed her forehead. "Chin up, my pretty girl."

Mr. *Look* holds a new glass of iced tea, and we move to my terrace out of the noonday sun.

"Would you like a sandwich?" I ask, setting a tray of deviled eggs, Spanish olives, and sandwich makings on the table.

"You are accommodating, aren't you?"

I laugh. "I'm fixing one for myself. Would you care for one?"

"Is Rainey as beautiful as you?"

"You don't know how to say yes, do you?" I arrange four slices of bread on two plates. "Rainey is lovely. Same eyes, same long legs. Yes, she looks like me. Lucky girl. I'm sure, when the time comes, some young man will be smitten. Just as Will was with me."

"So life is all about appearance, beauty, not at all catch-as-catch-can?" His eyes follow the length of my outstretched arm and stop at my throat, my closed mouth.

"Here." I hand him a plate. "Chicken salad on wheat. Lettuce leaves, a little curried mayonnaise. Rainey's favorite, last I heard from her."

"Last you heard?"

"It's been a while. She's busy with school, and I'm busy at the club. It's fine," I say, knowing full well it's not fine at all.

Rainey did get on the Pan American flight, her little hand held by a stewardess who promised to look after her. Her dress was a pale blue, a breathless color, and her hair fell onto the collar so that I wished we'd spent more time tying it back. She barely glanced at me as she climbed the last steps into the cabin. I held my hand up to wave, but she was already gone. I visualized how she would peer out the window as the plane crossed over the Rockies, how she'd not be able to understand such height, how she'd close her eyes and lean against the cool window, her raggedy toy rabbit tucked under her chin. How she'd fall asleep and not wake up until the captain announced their slow descent over southern Georgia, how those on the left side of the plane could glimpse their first view of the Atlantic. Whitecaps, little fishing boats, a school of dolphins—too far away to see.

I pretended not to worry about Rainey and went on with my days, preparing myself for another sort of good-bye. I hadn't ever thought of Will leaving me. It hadn't occurred to me that I was married to a career officer who might be called up in the event of war. And I didn't try to understand the goings-on in a country so far beyond my own experience and a world away. Vietnam. I'd never heard of it until the evening news began to cover events—South, North, Ho Chi Minh and his strange ideas, the lovely French and how they had failed, the saffron-robed monks, the Catholic priests, the peasants in their rice paddies.

Will became reticent. We ate our meals, took walks together, moved through the days and nights in a semi-hushed state. It seemed that if I breathed too deeply, if I sighed, I would take up too much air, and there was so little air left between us. I began to think that he resented me. He kept to his side of the bed, and he ate less, spoke less, wanted less.

"Are you all right?" I asked him.

We stood outside the little house, surrounded by other small, unadorned officers' houses. The dinner out we'd just had seemed to have happened on an entirely different night, sometime in the past, in another life. Before us, the street curved, and the mountains seemed too bright against the autumn sky, whitewashed and distant.

"What?" he answered and gave me a sharp, haphazard look.

"Where are you these days?"

"Thinking about things."

I pulled at his arm, and he struggled with the effort of not wanting to be touched.

"Thinking about things?"

"I'm sorry," he said. "I know I'm not entirely focused on you. I've made you the center of our world. But the world now involves sweeps and air strikes, not just martinis and supper." He opened the front door to a house that would be ours only a few days more. "I'm leaving soon enough, and then you will, too. Let's make the best of it." His expression was drawn, his tone forgiving and tired.

I kept talking about everything and nothing, about how I'd worry, how I couldn't accept what was happening.

Will shook his head and went inside the house. The door was wide, and I could see him stop beside a chair and take his jacket off. He stood there, holding the dun-colored coat. I wondered at his stance, at our military-issue life. I wanted to ravage the regulations and keep my husband all to myself. How unpatriotic, how ridiculous and unseemly that would be. I wanted Vietnam to disappear. But I couldn't send the war off to Florida to stay with my mother.

Feeling hurt and slightly unhinged at Will's distress, I went straight to the bedroom. And just as I knew he would, Will followed me in. I sat on the bed with my blouse unbuttoned and my stockings and high heels on the floor. He stood behind me, slid the blouse off my shoulders and kissed the very top of my back. And then his hands rushed over me.

Three days later Will boarded a transport plane that headed over the Pacific, opposite the direction the Pan American had taken Rainey. But before he left, for those three days—endless, tangled days of wishes granted, pausing only for scrambled eggs straight out of the pan, for another bottle of Chablis—he'd been entirely mine.

It's late in the day, nearly dusk, and I begin to acknowledge what is private, what was given to me without expectations. "I do miss Will." I say this before I can stop myself, and the words are muted and seem to spin into the air.

Mr. *Look* ignores my confession and asks me to dress in something black and elegant. Rhinestones edge the thin straps of my heels and long earrings fall nearly to my shoulders. He's asked for a plunging neckline but to keep my neck bare. The sun is dropping, the days shorter now, and pink light pours across the pale tiled floors. I suggest we do this at the nightclub, where the curtains are gold and the stage offers better light. But Mr. *Look* has other ideas. To stay here, uninterrupted, to reach further into the personal story, rather than the glitter and personality he thought he'd come for.

I distract him with Sinatra on the hi-fi, and the lyrics glide into the room, suggesting mistakes made, then laughed over. Frank is singing with his daughter, something I could never do. The lamplight is at its lowest setting, and so are my words.

"You know, I try to do the right thing for Rainey. I send her money every month—for school, for dresses, that sort of thing. And there's the money I've put away for her—for college. There's a nice liberal arts college in Anna Clara, and she's smart enough. Sometimes, I wonder if she misses me. She's always been a thoughtful girl. Occasionally, she seems down and out, but for the most part she's—well, as I said earlier, she's lovely. Once, I knew everything about her. The way she'd twist her hair around one finger, how she'd lean backwards to scratch behind one knee, and the tunes she'd hum so you could barely hear them, so you didn't really know if she was singing or humming or if you were simply losing your mind. I wonder if she still does that. That breathless singing. Really, though, she won't answer my phone calls, and I rarely make it over to Anna Clara. I suppose I know practically nothing about who she's becoming."

"Do you miss her?" Mr. *Look* asks.

His face is hidden by the camera, which strobes and flashes. I look away.

"Of course I do. What an absurd question. But I can't have her here, especially now that she's a teenager. That would be pure trouble. I've promised to visit her when I can."

I cross through the beaded curtain to my bedroom, motioning to Mr. *Look* to follow. He hesitates, his hand against the curtain to quiet its clattering, then peers through. I reach for a framed photograph of Rainey, a recent one I didn't take. I'm not at ease behind a camera, only in front of one. The thought of prisms, light, shutters, and speed presses in on me. I position the photo next to my cheek and smile.

"Promises," echoes Mr. *Look* as he approaches to catch a close-up. "Aren't they meant to be broken?"

"What is it about men?" I say. "Why aren't they good with promises? They never hold up their end of the bargain, while women are simply swept up and practically become the bargain itself."

Mr. *Look* places his camera on my dresser and sighs.

"You don't know what I'm talking about? Well, that just proves my point. You're a man, after all."

"I'm amazed at how much Rainey looks like you." He takes her picture from me to examine it.

"She does, doesn't she? But she still counts on men too much. Still waiting for her father to come home. Though there isn't really a home to return to. She'll figure it out eventually."

I sit on the edge of my bed and take off the heels. The satin covers are pulled back, and Mr. *Look* sits beside me. There's a lamp nearby, but I don't turn it on.

"I don't know if you heard me earlier." I can barely see his face in the dimming light. "I do miss Will. This beach, the men, the nightclub—all pure distraction. If I start believing Will is in limbo in some godforsaken jungle, then I can't do what I need to. Rainey's young and naïve. Why shouldn't she believe that her father might return?"

"Do you think he's coming back?"

"It's been seven years. What do you think I think?" I wait for his response, knowing there won't be one. "No," I say, "he's not coming back. And that's off the record. Rainey will learn far more than she needs to, if she reads your piece. And that's fine. Maybe I'll be less mysterious, less of an enigma."

Sinatra sings the last song on the album. Waving away love, fortunes, the sway of it all. His voice sweeps over us, the past recalled, the future clear.

I consider how less would be a wonderful thing. I could take my chances with less.

The bed shifts as Mr. *Look* stands.

"Eva Ives McPherson, West Palm's most beautiful entertainer, how does her story end?" That's all he says. No mention of more questions, another day, the promised cover shot.

He leans down and touches my cheek, and I see that he's smiling. He crosses the floor, his camera in hand, and the door closes behind him. Through the window he becomes smaller, and the night pushes in, its skies starred and strained against a backdrop of diminished and darkened blue. The only light is the one glowing at the bottom of the pool. No one is swimming, and the water is still and luminous. The turntable's arm lingers for a moment, its needle coasting the grooves beyond the final song, then swings back into its resting place, and my rooms are filled with breath and waiting and unyielding silence.

TWO GIRLS LAUGHING

DECEMBER 1973

I heard them laughing.

I was standing in the garden, holding a long-handled spade, staring without looking and trying not to think. Lately, thinking made me speak aloud without knowing it, until I did know it, always horrified at whatever I was saying. This sort of thing was happening more and more, and I preferred to move through the moments of confusion with a task, like trimming back the overgrown ginger lily or taking in newly fallen grapefruit, the ones that crashed down from the highest branches, those I couldn't reach.

The Sybelia grove separated my backyard from the Blackwoods'—one of the many families in the neighborhood whose men were called away to war. I could tell the girls were under the twisted limbs of the orange and tangerine trees. Their voices at first sounded soft, like murmurs, and then loud and lilting, the way one laughs when terribly amused. I caught myself trying to hear what they were saying, and then

I let myself walk closer, into that part of the yard where the camellias grew, so that I could find a better place to listen. I propped the spade against the fence and leaned on its handle.

The camellias were still closed—small, imperfect, creamy buds. There was a slight breeze, and the buds nodded against the dark green leaves. By their size they would open before Christmas, a little early. I touched one, a soft feathery burden, and it fell from the bush and landed beside the low fence.

"Typical," I said, trying not to speak too loudly. The tortoiseshell cat, the one that lived in the space between yards, leaned against my calves, and I swatted it away.

For a few moments, it was utterly quiet in the grove. Perfect stillness. And then the rushing sound of someone moving through the low-growing palmettos. Rainey pushed her way through the weave of trees, only yards from me. She stared straight at me, unmoving. She smiled with her eyes—bright, extraordinary eyes—and mouthed my name, "Hélène." I heard myself saying the words "bright, extraordinary."

And then I heard them running. Through the trees I could barely see them, their long, teenaged limbs, all angles and grace. Sneakers and breath and long hair caught in thin branches and LuLu whispering. And Rainey slowing, releasing her hair from where it had tangled, and then running, but not really.

I had to admit that I watched them. I listened to them. And I remembered being that age, the days measured like sugar. Long, luxurious trails of it. Swept into my tea, stirred, savored. So long ago.

Indochine, 1921. Compared to our life in France, the days in An Lộc were slower, more drawn out, less expectant. If one of the cooks made a brioche, we felt lucky for days. We grew used to tea, mangoes, fish steamed with tamarind, lime, and chilis. In the south, fish and royalty had too much in common—they were both loved and celebrated. Carp filled the rivers, and processions of the royal family with silk parasols, outspread fans, and bejeweled elephants made their way around the grounds of the Imperial Palace. The Nguyen Dynasty still resembled a government, pretty but powerless; but it was the Vietnamese Restoration League the colonialists worried about, my father among them. The nationalist movement was led by men like Phan Boi Chau—educated, passionate, imprisoned.

Later came the Viet Minh. What came after that—well, perhaps it was what the Americans didn't know that helped the revolution. Ho Chi Minh was already old by the time they arrived. He could only have smiled at their view of the world, of his world. Two thousand years of dominance, of others laying claim to a land so unlike their own, of peasants living under change that had little to do with the seasons. Two thousand years of preparing for independence. Of course, the Vietnamese were patient.

My cousin, Simone, came for the summer. As children we had been inseparable, our mothers sisters, and we eventually like sisters ourselves. Sharing dolls and sweet cocoa, then necklaces and secrets. My father arranged her visit, and I recalled the last time we'd been together, how she'd already turned to boys, always looking for the ones with lovely hands and insolent faces. Nearly seventeen, she wore dresses and cloche hats; barely sixteen, I pulled on trousers and left my hair in braids.

Years before, we had moved from France to Cochinchina, near An Lộc, a village in Bình Long, a province in the south, so that my father could run his family's plantations, and in the beginning it was a paradise for us all. But then the seasons and the humidity and the strange looks from the workers became tiring to my mother. She complained of the sun and then of the rain, the lack of good butter or decent wine, until my father finally gave in and sent us back home to France. I went often to see my father, to the big house surrounded by verandas, and Simone came for holidays and even grew to love the sweet stink of rubber that mingled with the scents of tea and mango from our kitchen.

Simone had always been fascinated with the unending rows of the rubber trees—how the trees were spaced so evenly, one from the other; how the bark was carefully scarred with incisions that spiraled around the trunks; how the milky sap followed the grooves to collect in ceramic bowls tied at the base of each tree. But that summer, she wandered past the paths where tree roots trellised under the soft dirt and toward the buildings where the sap was processed into lengths of rubber. Her pale eyes and her light, bobbed hair made the workers stop and stare and sometimes laugh behind their hands. And there was one who continued to stare even when she looked away. I didn't think anything of it, until later, when I would wake, the shutters slightly open, her nightgown lying near the foot of her bed, and the hanger where her dress had hung bare. She'd go out into the dark of early morning, the time when things looked blue and insubstantial, and I always woke to see her and the boy who trailed her, two figures amongst the trees, with only their secretive laughter to give them away. Moths flew up and past my window into the silver darkness, heavy-winged, without direction, no candle to catch and burn them. I thought about following Simone and the boy, but I never did. I didn't want to find them, her long back pressed against a tree, his hands at her waist, his delicate mouth against her throat. Things I wanted for myself, things I was afraid to have.

The eldest cook, Lam, saw Simone return every morning.

"She walks through the kitchen," Lam told me, handing me a cup of jasmine tea. "She sings, your little cousin-girl, and she has dirty feet." Lam's eyes, the color of yellow quartz, flashed when she spoke, and her face was all wrinkles. From too much smiling, my father said. "And she takes fruit and eats it walking through the house. I tell her, stay, eat here. But she always goes, always with a persimmon. Who eats a persimmon walking and singing? She's crazy, your cousin-girl."

The tea was bitter, and I drank it slowly. Lam leaned over her board of mint, onions, limes, a knife angled in her hand and her smile running through the day, through all the days of her long life. Later there would be *pho*, with noodles and broth, beef and chilis, but now there was a slice of baguette with the marmalade Simone had brought and that Lam said was an insult in her kitchen.

Upstairs, Simone slept, her face against the pillow. But she would wake in time for the *pho*, its scent circling through the rooms past the bedroom shutters. And when she came to the table, Lam would offer her a bowl, smile and say, "No singing."

The summer would go on that way, the days scorching and the monsoon rains heavier and Simone's walks out into the dark more frequent. No one ever questioned the outings, though everyone seemed to know. My father, who knew she'd be returning to France soon enough. Lam, who began to slice the persimmons and leave them on a dish where they would bleed, sticky and sweet, more golden than red.

"Where do you go?" I asked.

Simone brushed her hair and ignored me.

"You must go somewhere." I was furious, impatient. Everything seemed unfair. Simone's visit was nearly over and she'd spent it wandering around in the dark, in the rain, and then sleeping away the days.

She laid down the brush and pointed at me with her hand mirror. "You should know. I've seen you watching us."

"I only see you leaving, you and that boy." I thought of the first day Simone saw him, his bare chest, smooth and brown, and the white trousers that were rolled above his knees.

"Lam knows who he is. She doesn't seem to mind. Why should you?"

"I don't mind. I don't mind at all." But I did mind.

Simone walked through our summer, with her love and her persimmons, as if she didn't care. She took what she wanted, not once considering me. And then she left. The cousin-girl with her hand mirror and empty marmalade pot and stories to tell.

She left behind unread novels and a cotton nightgown and a pretty pair of shoes, cream-colored *peau de soie*. The ones she had given up to walk barefoot with the boy. She left me behind as well, the one who truly loved her, more than the boy with the white trousers and the delicate mouth ever could. And then the nights grew longer, the air thinner, and the boy below my windows never glanced up. He never noticed that I was still there, that I had always been there. His chest no longer bare, his long sleeves dragged over his wrists, he never knew what he had stolen.

More and more I called up memories of my mother, strolling our parterre garden in France, so exact, so different from the gardens in Vietnam. She pointed out the bright roses, the boxwood hedges, the mounds of lavender, all in need of tending and trimming, and the gardeners nodding in agreement, then whispering to each other. She'd become more demanding, more repetitive. My American doctors laughed when I told them this. They promised that it was only natural to become forgetful at seventy. "Not uncommon for someone your age, Mrs. Laurent. You may want to find a companion, someone to check in on you now and then." Perhaps they were right, but I wasn't fond of company and spent a lot of time inside so that no one would catch me wandering or mumbling or looking for something I hadn't even lost.

And then one afternoon, Rainey stood at my backdoor. Tall, bashful, far too quiet, like a shadow against the threshold. I had no idea she was there. I'd expected to meet her eventually, but not standing on my porch, not in a way so startling. She'd cut her hand and held it out to show me, her long fingers curled slightly around the wound. The blood came easily and pooled, her curved palm like a saucer.

"What did you do?" I said.

She only looked at me, her expression pale and withdrawn.

"Come here," I said and led her to the kitchen.

At the white stone sink, she flinched as I held her hand under the tap, the cool water washing away the blood and revealing the depth of the cut. I pressed a tea towel against it, and there we were, face-to-face, never having met and now meeting. I remembered Simone in the way this girl held her head, glancing at me and then away.

"I knew a girl once," I started and then stopped.

"I'm sorry," she said. "I'm sorry to bother you."

"You're not bothering me." I smiled. "Not at all."

"I didn't know where else to go."

How odd, I thought. "And you live over there?" I motioned with my eyes, out the window toward the clutter of dark-leaved trees, the rooftop beyond. "I've seen you and the Blackwood girl together. And I've heard you calling each other. Her name is LuLu, and yours is Rainey, yes?"

I tried to understand why she had come to me, the old woman on the opposite side of the grove. She pressed her lips together; I had no idea of her pain, if she felt any.

"No one was home. I thought you could help me."

"That's fine," I said and tried to smile and realized I was. "You're a smart girl. You know what to do when you have to. Don't you? And you even know my name."

"Yes," she said.

I thought she might cry. This tall child with a long, curved back, long legs. Not a child at all. A girl like I'd been, like Simone had been.

"Sometimes LuLu and I look through your mail," she said, a little too sweetly. She told me they'd wished for a name as lovely and uncomplicated as mine, that they'd practiced pronouncing the syllables, in the soft way they were meant to be spoken. And then she commented on the shape of my eyes, my small nose, and how my smile changed them, making them no less pretty but different.

Her shyness edged forward into careful amazement, five-pointed, a stellar thing. I released her hand for a second. The cut was clean and thin and followed the lines of her palm, replicating their angles in a more dramatic way, a dividing line. Again, the blood rose inside the seam and I replaced the towel with another.

"Hold this tight," I told her. When she did, I noticed the thin gold bracelet around her wrist, laden with little charms. Flowers, stars, the smallest of shells.

My kitchen wasn't bright, but this child cast something into it that reminded me of candles and the way they pushed away darkness. She reminded me too much of many things. Including Simone.

She stared at the towel. I wondered if she ever smiled, though I'd heard her laughing many times.

She explained that a globe had fallen from the ceiling. When she bent to retrieve the biggest shard, she realized it was already done. She stood up and knew the piece was buried in her hand and, frightened, quickly pulled it out. A mistake.

"The other pieces are still all over the floor."

I listened and nodded, aware that she lived with a family that wasn't her own, that her own mother, a bright silhouette, came and went.

"You may need stitches," I said. "But that's not for me to decide." And then I thought to ask, "Where is your pretty mother?"

"Away" was all she said.

Her face dimmed, and I thought of other questions.

"How do you and LuLu get along?"

She responded in a vague, dreamy way, telling me that in the grove there were birds that shouldn't have been there. Starlings and terns. That once LuLu, out of anger or mistrust or perhaps just out of meanness, had thrown a collection of scallop shells, pink and orange and cream-colored—the ones Rainey's mother had brought long ago—into the tangerine trees, and how now and then they surfaced, always among the tree roots. That LuLu's brother, Saul, had discovered a cluster of white spider lilies growing in the crook of a dead oak at the far end of the grove, where the orange trees were older and larger and where tree frogs gathered during rain storms. That sometimes she saw me standing by the camellias, watching.

After that, we heard a screen door slam and LuLu calling.

"Too bad," I said. "I was going to offer tea. I have some nice jasmine."

Rainey handed me the towel, a checked piece of linen, now splotched with dark stains. I made her keep it, and at the door, she promised to come back.

It was the winter of 1922 when Lieutenant Laurent first came to the house to visit my father. I was seventeen and I quickly learned that he was twenty-two, young for a naval officer. His uniform white and his face tanned, perhaps from so much time on deck. He didn't notice me at first.

I was reading on the sofa that faced the windows. From there, the distant rubber trees looked gray, their branches lacing upward, the air around them tinged with smoke. The familiar smell of rubber clung to everything.

The volume of *Night and Day* that Simone had brought on her last visit—a book my father disapproved of, and then ignored when he found it lying open on a chair—felt awkward and heavy in my hands. I tried to focus on the pages before me, but soon became disengaged. The lieutenant's voice carried from the next room, and I repositioned myself to better see him. Though a stranger, he spoke clearly, as if he knew my father well and was simply adding to a conversation they had already had. Something about the number of hectares, about allegiance and engagement. I could see his back, a glimpse of the epaulette at his left shoulder, the way he reached to shake my father's hand. I thought the visit was to be brief, that he would then leave, but my father ushered him toward the veranda, to see the view no doubt.

Father had his back to me, but the lieutenant could have glanced in my direction. Instead, he stepped past the wide threshold and stood before the wooden balustrade. Everything he regarded I'd seen over the top of my book for hours, I'd known for most of my life. And now I saw only the white back, the stiff collar, the broad shoulders, the cap he held in one hand. My father was rarely silent, but now he didn't speak. There was something between the two men that felt decided, a rope of understanding that coiled around their collective thoughts. The afternoon folded in on itself, the unsure and the sure moments meeting and then disappearing, undefined and small. I didn't know what was about to change, but I was sure that something would.

The sun tried to push against the clouds, but the day remained white and drawn. My father pointed to the buildings where the long swathes of rubber hung from the rafters. Lieutenant Laurent nodded. Though he'd not once taken notice of me, I knew he was appraising my presence against the surrounding silence.

The lieutenant came again and again to our bungalow, but not to see my father. His voice resonant, carrying through the long days of 1922—while Ho Chi Minh remained in France, months away from Moscow and Lenin's ideas of worldwide revolution—the lieutenant made it clear that he would court me. I allowed him the privilege, finding his manner more French than military, one that spoke a relaxed sort of elegance against the crisp, uniformed angles. Gradually, in the tropical heat, his voice, and even the shape of his uniform, would soften, never relaying details of duty, but those of heritage and legacy, his hopes for the future. I thought of how, if given the chance, I would dash these hopes, my legacy limited, only my mother knowing the truth of my unproductive ovaries, how I'd never have children.

I learned that he came from an old French family, one in which the men devoted their lives to the Marine Royale, and that he was named for his mother's father, Frederi Michel Bertrand, an admiral who knew the pitch of the sea better than his own daughter's laugh. "I would never do that," he said, taking hold of my hand. "I would cherish a daughter, not leave her to chance." I smiled but said nothing. The young Frederi assumed things I could never promise.

We took long walks, mostly in the afternoon, the balmy winter air warming to a tropical spring. In the meadow, past the workhouses and the lines of rubber trees, he taught me to shoot. "You have to know these things," he said. "How to aim and never to fear what you're aiming at."

The Ruby pistol, cold and strange in my thin hands, had a rose patina and was, as Frederi promised, easy to manage. "An intuitive mind like yours is suited to this sort of sidearm." He held my wrist firmly, showing me how to sight the target, angling it just above the red and blue glass bottles that I'd eventually shatter. While the recoil was slight, I still startled at the enormous, singing explosion that I created by pulling the trigger.

Frederi was patient with me, reminding me that he'd spoken to my father about our situation, the nationalists surrounding us, the men and women who collected the ceramic bowls of rubber sap under the pretense of allegiance to the French flag. It wouldn't be easy to tell where loyalties lay.

I held the rose-colored handgun and imagined aiming it at Simone's lover. And then at Simone. I didn't know which of them I'd shoot first.

Rainey and I sat on my porch. Several days had passed, and she still wore a bandage around her hand. Underneath, seven neat stitches ran across her palm. Steam curled from our cups of jasmine tea, and Rainey stared into the backyard. The thin china felt too delicate in my hands, which had begun to tremble in the cooler weather. I chose to blame the season, the weather, the charmless Christmas wreaths on neighbors' doors, rather than my own deterioration.

"Do you know Saul?" Rainey asked.

"Who?" I said, a little too loudly. I had wanted her to come and now I felt irritated with her voice, my hands, the day.

"Saul. LuLu's brother."

"Oh, the Blackwood boy." Of course I know him, I thought. I'd seen him at night, in the grove, running, secretive, burying things. "He's older than you girls, isn't he?"

Impatient with the conversation, I spilled the tea on my trousers, trying to place the cup into its saucer. "Oh, what a mess."

"Here," Rainey said, handing me the linen napkin I'd given her.

"Thank you." I did feel grateful, between the tremors and the strands of annoyance, moving slowly, like snails under my skin.

"Saul is a little older, but not much." She played with the bits of her bracelet, its silvery song inching along my spine. "He's always liked me."

"Sounds complicated," I said, not smiling. I thought of Frederi and his wishes, how I could never grant them.

"It is." She sipped her tea. "I think I've always liked him, too."

"And what about LuLu?"

"What do you mean? LuLu loves to pretend she hates Saul."

"What about you and LuLu, then?"

I thought of sisters who weren't sisters, husbands who wished for daughters, daughters who disappointed fathers. How Simone had smiled when it hurt the most. How I hadn't been the one she loved, though I'd loved her. How I'd married the man who'd taught me to shoot, my father standing alone on his veranda on our wedding day. How Frederi had inherited the large house outside Paris with flower gardens and fruit trees and airy rooms, the perfect house for children, a lively pair of daughters, perhaps a son, knowing in time that we would have none.

"LuLu," Rainey said. "LuLu will hate me now."

"I suppose he's already kissed you."

Rainey hid her face in her tilted cup, then put the cup down, smiling, trying not to smile. "Yes. Out in the grove. A secret place."

"I'm sure it is." I thought of the veranda at An Lộc and the first time Frederi kissed me, of watching Simone and the boy disappear into the mist, of hearts and tremors and love in the shadows of the trees. I knew then that I would go there, I would find the spot where the shells were scattered, where tree frogs gathered in the rain, where kisses were given for free.

The afternoon turned quickly into evening, the night sifting in, hours passing since Rainey had gone home. Something she'd said had opened a long, winding corridor of memory. There was the dream, the moment of sitting up in bed, recalling the boy in his white trousers rolled to the knee. And then no recollection of climbing from my bed, opening the back door, and following the sandy path into the grove. I stood outside in my nightgown. In the darkness I found the oak tree and knelt down where Rainey's seashells lay like litter against sandy soil and tree roots. The ground was soft and the roots had surfaced, thin and sprawling. I didn't know how I'd get back up. It wasn't so easy anymore. The tortoiseshell cat lay lengthwise across the slim branch of a nearby tree, her eyes glinting like citrine.

The air felt heavy, the sky a peculiar, thin stretch of violet. Nearby, buried at the base of a gnarled orange tree, were the brass-and-copper bullets. Years ago, I'd seen Saul in the thickest jungle of citrus trees, digging with a shovel and then with his hands, desperate. He deposited a handful of bullets in a shallow trench, and once he'd left, I uncovered a few, noted their shine, their weight, and placed them back beneath the sand, tamping it down a little better than Saul had. I wondered what had happened to the gun that once held them. Something black and heavy, no doubt. Surely military issue, given the uniformed men coming and going from the Blackwood house.

As if to give a purpose to sitting in the grove in the middle of the night, I knew I had to find that gun, those bullets. I found a low-hanging branch and pulled. The branch swung and I ended up on the ground barely any distance from where I'd started. I sat there, thinking loud thoughts, muttering *mon dieu* and *merde*, until I found my knees. The cat jumped from her perch and clambered in my direction, and as I pushed myself to standing, she circled my legs and then followed me back to my yard. The long-handled spade leaned against the fence, exactly where I'd left it just days before. I picked it up, and the cat raced back into the grove.

It was then I heard laughter. High and sudden. Then nothing.

"Lam?" The distinct smell of *pho* mingled with that of ripening and rotting oranges.

I followed the cat back through the labyrinth of low branches and walked past thick-limbed grapefruit trees. The rows of rubber trees and the nights I'd refused to follow Simone and the boy came back to me. How they'd laughed, how they'd disappeared. I imagined Simone sitting in an orange tree, swinging her legs. But she was dead. She'd died alone.

There was a slight breeze and it was cool. December. The end of yet another year.

"Eventually you will die alone, too." I was talking out loud again. No one else was outside in the middle of the night. The laughter I'd heard had surely been my own.

Haphazardly, I dug holes around the maze of tree roots and palmettos. I didn't find the bullets, or the gun, which would have been ruined from the wet, sandy soil. Still, I would have known how to clean the magazine, the internal striker, the barrel. Frederi had taught me.

Frederi and I married in August, nearly a year after Simone left. 1922, the year a rare orchid had been found in the forest near our plantation. Frederi said I should wear one in my hair for our wedding, but Lam brought me persimmon blossoms. At first I laughed, but my mother, returned to An Lộc for the celebration, found the gesture meaningful and arranged a few of the coral flowers around my veil. I thought about the stains Simone had left on her sheets after crawling into bed with her dish of persimmons and was relieved she hadn't come. She was in Paris, studying literature at the Sorbonne, spending time with American expatriates. Writers, of course.

"You know you're returning to France?" my mother said. Her wedding ring had caught in my veil and she was trying not to unravel the lacework.

"Not until after the honeymoon," I answered, blinking.

My mother's hands flew around my face and her breath smelled of lavender pastilles. Whenever I remembered my wedding, I saw her delicate hands and recalled the scent of lavender. And in the distance my father's silhouette. Everything else was forgotten.

Frederi wasn't the love of my life. But he never knew.

For our twenty-fifth anniversary we took a trip to Cuba and then to Florida. We fell in love with the tropics all over again. I didn't mind leaving France. After yet another war, she seemed ravaged. The bright sun of Florida and the surrounding islands brought me to my senses, a glorious slap in the face. Her pink and coral houses lined the streets like confetti, and my mind widened at the possibility of a life with larger skies, with trees that would bloom year-round.

Frederi taught me how to head in new directions in the same way he'd shown me how to aim the Ruby pistol: without fear, with precision and a little ill will, even malice, at the intended. We walked along the streets of Key West and stood a long while at the southernmost point, looking back in the direction of Havana. Frederi noted the sunlight on the water, how the reflection changed with the current, ocean and gulf meeting, deciding. All the way up the coast, under the sparse shade of coconut palms, we drank daiquiris, sharp with lime and white rum. Frederi seemed happy, a calmer, less determined version of himself, and I thought perhaps this was fine, this holiday. Deep-sea fishing one day, bare feet in the sand another. I bought a new pair of sunglasses in Miami, and from the beach in Jupiter we watched an enormous pod of dolphin swimming along in the dark blue waters of the Atlantic. Across the same ocean was France, a home I didn't miss.

We drove north to the lakes and stopped in Anna Clara, where white stucco houses with red-tiled roofs were surrounded by enormous oaks and Spanish moss. Something told us to stay and we did. Frederi chose a one-story cottage with screened-in porches facing out onto a large garden and an orange grove, not too far from Lake Sybelia. He planted fruit trees, including the persimmon that never took. When it began to droop and lose all its leaves, he looked so disappointed, unlike the man I first married. The man who had expected children and gardens burdened with flowers and fruit, who I'd thought found success in the expectations, if not in the outcome.

"It must be the soil." I patted him on the shoulder and tried to be matter-of-fact, though I was glad to see the thing wither, the memory of the sticky blood-orange fruit, its bitter musk, from Simone's final summer in An Lộc.

"Perhaps," he said.

He asked neighbors what they thought. They only shook their heads. Then he asked the neighbors' gardeners, but they only paused from their pruning and raking to answer openmouthed, "Persimmon?"

I wondered if Florida had been such a good decision after all. Only ten years later, Frederi died of a heart attack while standing in the garden, looking up into the blank, blue sky. From where I stood on the porch, his officer's back never curved. He fell in a perfectly straight line as if he were measuring the length of our lot, or perhaps the depth of his own soul.

At the gravesite, I listened to the priest reciting prayers and thought of my dead husband lying in his casket the same way he'd lain in those final moments on the ground, clover and roots and thin, yellow grass around his unmoving body, his ending exhalation like a sigh. I tried to remember the last time we'd made love and couldn't. A week later I had the dead persimmon tree removed and planted my camellias, layered and complicated, unlike the frilly, lacy persimmon flowers that Lam and Simone and my mother loved so. Frederi thought I'd loved them, too. I'd never told him differently.

The camellias budded early, only months after their planting, thick knobs of dark and then lighter green, eventually unfurling into alabaster and cream. Just as I'd expected, their blooms turned out to be resplendent. Even in their immature days, they improved the view.

I walked back to my house, stumbling, stopping by the camellias. Even in the darkness, pitched now with a black serious ceiling, they were visible. The outermost buds had opened into wide spirals and pulsated with blanched light. They trembled in the rising wind. I thought of the ocean Frederi had given up for marriage, for me. Of his French navy, of trim white uniforms and sails, of his cutlass and compass. Of how he lay beneath a swell of earth, a gravestone to mark his direction. I considered the possibility of bullets still under the citrus trees, somewhere in the soft sand. It would be so easy. To lie down one last time.

Rainey hadn't broken her promise. She'd come again to visit me, for the shared pot of straw-colored tea. Then she returned nearly every night, always late, but not to see me. She and Saul, together on my porch on the rattan settee, talking in close whispers, and not talking. And tonight they were there, leaning into each other, the outline of their bodies like one. I eased the door open, trying to slip through, the memory of the small rose-gold gun in my closed palm.

Like my father's veranda, the porch was long and narrow, with a sofa and chairs on one side and the entryway on the other. A few nights before, I'd first seen the young couple there from the French doors that led from my living room. I'd watched them, remembering the long divan at the house in Cochinchina, the way Frederi once held me. We were almost as young.

Now I entered from the yard and stood across the porch, no dividing doors, no barriers between us. I walked across and stood next to them. Their eyes closed, they pressed against each other and the darkness, and I remembered candlelight and the sound of moths caught in flame, the dust from their wings torched, the palest ones turning immediately to embers, the darkest ones reeling back into the night.

They returned and returned. They were so young, and finally I recognized them. The boy and Simone. The shirtless boy with his gleaming white trousers, his sweet mouth, who had chosen my cousin, the girl who was mine to love, not his. And Simone, who had forsaken me, who desired the boy instead. There they were, her light hair trailing, his dark hair and bare back. In my dream, I had raised the Ruby pistol and aimed it at the base of his neck. And before I could put pressure there, before I could release the trigger and watch him fall to one side, the boy turned and clasped my wrist, and I awakened, so very sorry I hadn't completed the task.

And here I stood, about to touch his long, dark hair. And here, as in the dream, the boy turned and held me by the wrist, but just as quickly let go. I fell, the porch's stone floor hard and cold, and when I looked up, the boy was Saul. He rose to help me, upset, asking if I was all right. I shushed him and waved away his helpfulness. Rainey stood over me, too, her eyes enormous and sad.

"You aren't Simone," I said. "She was never sad."

Saul insisted that I stand and checked to see that I could.

"You startled us," he said.

"I did?" I looked up at him, then at Rainey. "I don't remember."

I remembered Lam, the cat, a scattering of shells. In Cochinchina I wore a robe over my nightgown. I watched from the upstairs windows. Below, Simone and the boy walked out into the dark night. I held on to the sash that fastened the robe in place and tested its tightness. I climbed back into bed and the sheets swallowed me like flower petals, sweet, cloying, suffocating. There were things I had always wanted, things that were forbidden, and they appeared as two girls laughing, as at last I fell asleep.

ROADSIDE FLOWERS

FEBRUARY 1972

Hoa leaned down and snatched another stem. Her fistful of flowers was leggy, tattered, but brilliant. Gold, orange, red. Just seven years old, she stood in the center of the path, her toes sunk into the fine pale dirt. She waved the flowers at me.

"Jaymes-man," she called. "You take picture?"

Earlier in the week, I'd let her wear the lightweight camera around her neck, its leather strap shortened, and take pictures of her father and mother, her aunts and uncles, the cooking fires, the rice fields, earthenware bowls of *pho*, even me. I'd developed the film and made enough prints to share. From each, faces peered, looking down, laughing, pointing. In one, Hoa's grandmother offered a bowl of steaming noodle soup, fogging the lens and catching the moment before everyone squatted to eat. In another, a baby brother was hidden under his mother's blouse, the blur of his small kicking feet a contrast to his mother's still gaze. And one without faces, only cumulus clouds, sunlight, a sweep of green grass and purple cattails.

Assigned to my battalion as a photographer, in the field I carried the Kodak I brought from home, a dozen film canisters, an M-16, ammunition, and a pair of canteens. I'd signed on as an infantryman, but my CO caught wind of the camera, decided I was better suited to capturing images than VC, and put me in charge of changing the mood. "I'm talking morale, Williams. Get these men's fucking bravery and honor covered; you'll do better there than covering their asses." *Stars and Stripes* published nearly everything I gave them, only a tenth of the photos I took. The other percentage was out of focus, or out-of-bounds, the negatives sealed in envelopes and filed in heat-resistant boxes.

It was the Year of the Rat, and we all became water rats, sinking in rivers and rice paddies, my camera and film bag held above my shoulders along with my rifle. We had wit and curiosity, and we were nervous and aggressive. Tagging along behind the point man, itching for a fight, smoking in order to stay quiet. Waiting, listening. I measured my steps, I refocused, I balanced my load, so much lighter than some. The light meter gave me a reading; I adjusted the viewfinder; I pressed the shutter release, advanced the film, and just as quickly discovered the next image, a fraction of the field before me, the picture as contained as the war was wide.

Sometimes you have to go away to come back.

My orders were to honor men and make them noble by documenting their actions. "Now let's get this straight,

Williams! We are not talking about combat. We are not talking about the goddamned beauty of the battlefield. We are talking about survival and making sense out of this mess." My orders were to look through a lens into men's souls. "These are not your friends, goddammit! These are heroes. Make it so." My orders were to hump into the hills with my own platoon, with my own rifle, with my own canteens and 35 mm camera, but not with the lump in my throat that came from seeing and hearing and disbelieving.

I tried my best, and still the CO kept on yelling.

"He just loves you, Williams, bro," Shields promised. "He just wants to get all up inside of that sweet, shiny lens himself."

"Why don't you get some pictures of the girls for us, Jamesy-boy?" McPhee licked his fingers and squeezed one eye closed, as if he were aiming a camera instead of an M-60. "Slide up under some *ao dai* and see what they have to offer."

I did take pictures of women, in silhouette, from afar. Women in yellow, red, white *ao dai*, like flowers, their long black hair swept under their conical hats, shadows over their faces. They walked through the markets and called out to the merchants, laughing, taking green papayas into their arms, silver fish into their baskets. Sometimes they looked at me—me trying to frame their eyes, their burdens—but mostly they looked away.

I was the grunt, the new boy, the one chosen to shoot pictures, rather than people.

The children in the villes found me curious and stared and followed me when their elders let them. Children standing at the front gate of a school, waving and calling out until their teacher called them back inside. Children in flooded rice fields, their trousers pulled waist-high, catching crabs and small fish. Later, these same fields were flooded with light, that of the moon and artillery fire, the petals of water lilies scattered with the scales of dead fish, the carcass of a buffalo calf, and men's bodies hidden beneath the tall, silent grasses.

I'd heard about the bamboo jungles, tigers that appeared shining like bright butter in the forest when all was quiet. I'd heard of the meadows of poppies, opium available in rooms above the bars in Saigon, a long arm's length away from Long Bình Jail. And I learned there were tunnels that reached under the earth for miles and miles, and pits covered in thatched grass to hide the punji stakes. Firsthand, these became my education, better than that of a classroom, and I memorized each breath of each day, laden with salt from the salt tabs in our packs, laying low under sniper fire, old-timers telling me to stay down if I wanted to see the sun set.

"Williams Jaymes-man," Hoa said. "You come home soon?"

I had been in-country for barely a month and had almost the full tour still in front of me.

I knew how to fish in Florida mangrove swamps. Hunting for Charlie was something entirely different. The underwater roots of the Vietnamese mangroves hid leeches, not bonefish. Straight from the bottle I had my first taste of backwash whiskey, on the banks of that brown-water stretch of river, in a downpour that outclassed any thunderstorm in the Keys. No matter the tropical heat, I shivered under the standard-issue rain poncho, in a daze of fever and confusion, not sure whether to hold my rifle or the camera.

"You got to take your Monday pills, baby boy," Shields said.

Monday pills. CPs. Chloroquine-Primaquine. Anti-malaria pills. Another standard-issue item that hadn't gotten lost in the mail between boot camp and the boonies. I had been given the dosage, same as everyone else.

I shook harder, and Shields raked me with his stare.

"You think you're going somewhere, Williams? You ain't going nowhere, man. You are staying right here in this shithole, just like the rest of us."

McPhee was bad enough; Shields was worse. Shields was bad news, trippin, kick-em-til-they-die crazy, one re-up too many. Sly slept with one eye open, Torchdog with the other eye shut—partners in crime. Tibbs wrote in a notebook that he rolled up inside his sleeve after each entry. Baker hummed under his breath and hid a harmonica in his pack. Mankiewitz kept quiet and then kept us all guessing.

Mankiewitz, who in the middle of one already miserable sodden night, sent incoming our way by yelling, "Come over here and light up my landing zone, little Miss Saigon!"

The same night Shields broke down and kissed the ground one final time. The same night marionettes danced in the jungle and not just in my mind. The same night the rain spiraled down in strands, like those beaded curtains in that one-time bar. The same night poppies grew from my chest and bloomed bright and vermillion right there in the mud. The same night the dust-off flew out one KIA and one WIA.

"Jaymes! You go away long, long time?" Hoa stood on the road and waved her flowers. I held up my camera, but didn't wave back.

ST. LUCIE

DECEMBER 1973

Outside, pine tops, longleaf and loblolly, cut across the thin blue horizon, and flat yellow fields fell away from the edges of the road. A Texaco gas station, a fruit stand selling grapefruit the size of babies' heads, a woman standing beside her open mailbox. I pictured how she'd stand there in the cloud of dust we left behind, then snap the metal door shut and lift the red flag to alert the postal truck of outgoing letters. The air inside the bus wavered over each passenger, the sliding windows cracked open here and there. The weather was too warm for the holly and tinsel decorating the street lamps of Christmas, Florida, and I wondered if the town looked that way all year round or just the month of December.

This whole trip was Rainey's idea and she was sleeping through it. By the time the lakes and streets of Anna Clara had slipped away behind us, she'd closed her eyes and pulled her long legs onto the seat and fallen into that other world, the one that left me more tired than rested. Sleep, for me, was a fitful place where I didn't want to spend much time. For Rainey, though, sleep seemed to untie all the knots in her mind, her expression calm and light, even when the world tipped against her. Her fingers splayed against her thighs, and her hair fanned in long, pale strands against one cheek and down onto her shoulder. I knew Saul was infatuated with Rainey, taking his chances as her on-again, off-again boyfriend. Still, I doubted he would miss her.

I'd paid for the bus tickets—one-way to West Palm Beach, a place neither of us had ever been, with transfers in Melbourne and St. Lucie. Unaccompanied teenaged girls, we'd surely be in trouble from both ends, my parents on one and Rainey's mama, Eva, on the other. I pictured how Eva's face would open, puzzled, and how then she'd toss her head and laugh, mystified by the sight of her daughter. And then later, after our visit, she'd wave and throw kisses from outside the bus that would take us back home, my mama would throw a fit once we'd returned, and my daddy would stay out of the fray but wonder why we'd taken off without telling anyone. Saul would lie and say he hadn't even noticed we'd left. But right at that moment we were in the middle, between two places, without anyone to tell us what to do, surrounded by vacant morning light and the dull vibration of the engine.

I nudged Rainey slightly, and she leaned into me. She knew the route to Melbourne; maybe that's why she slept so easily. Even as we swung onto Highway 1, past Cape Canaveral and Cocoa Beach, she coiled herself tighter, separating herself from the blur of travel, of whatever the end of the ride might give or take away.

Rainey had a history with buses. Barely ten, she'd arrived with her single mother in Anna Clara, the bus station her first impression of our town. Several months later, after Eva left for the Atlantic coast where nightclubs were hiring, Rainey wandered from our house on Sybelia Drive all those blocks back to the station and slept on one of the benches until a ticket agent found her. When she was eleven, she followed a family onto a Trailways bound for Miami, blending in with the children and then finding a seat by herself in the back row. No one noticed her until the Melbourne stop, and then it was my mama the bus authorities called, not Rainey's. Eva never seemed worried about Rainey's disappearances or embarrassed by her own absence, and Mama never spoke of it. Instead, she included Rainey as if she were her own daughter, more her daughter than me. Birthdays, picnics, Sunday mornings at church—Mama laid claim to Rainey and there was never any talk otherwise. She was one of us, one of her own. On loan perhaps, but that was understood and left unsaid.

It had been more than a year since Rainey had heard from Eva, and only weeks since the December 1973 issue of *Look* had landed in our mailbox. The article wasn't long, but the photo spread went on for pages. Mama read aloud, stopping to laugh, and said, "Why, this writer must be head-over-heels. Just look at his praises!" *Eva Ives McPherson takes on West Palm Beach!* The enduring spirit of the military wife; the long years of not knowing the whereabouts of her brave husband, the Army captain, who'd been missing in action since 1967; the sophisticated, even patriotic stance she'd given the nightclub revues. There were lists of popular songs she'd performed, accompanied by famous singers, all men. There were angled shots of Eva saluting the camera or performing for enlisted men, and posed ones: Eva waving from an open convertible, Eva walking on the beach, Eva in the company of Navy officers, their white uniforms as brilliant as her smile. But among all the captions and quotes, no mention of Rainey. No one would even know she had a daughter.

Rainey had flipped through the pages with me gazing over her shoulder, and then left the magazine on the couch where my daddy found it later. "Well, look who's in *Look*" was all he said, other than whistling a few times. I glanced across his shoulder, too, still amazed at the resemblance of Eva to Faye Dunaway, from her slim hourglass shape to her angled gaze, but more so the striking way in which Rainey looked like her mother. The bright face that could suddenly turn ashen, the eyes that widened in contemplation or creased with laughter, the pained appeal for more quiet when hours of silence were forced open by the simplest sound—a door opening and strains of Saul's stereo edging into the hall, the TV turned on to the lowest setting, the kitchen faucet turned on quickly to wash out a juice glass.

Rainey was our precious girl, the girl whom we pulled into our lives without her having any say. The girl who settled on whatever she could find, from the reflection of our faces in the lake to a boy's kiss to a handful of seashells, sent parcel post from the beach outside her mama's apartment. She was the girl who found solace on buses, in the thrum of moving along a road, always looking for a way home.

Ahead, a few rows up, a small girl with wide brown eyes and tiny black braids popped up and down in her seat. Her round face appeared and then disappeared and her laughter flew up the aisle. After a few minutes, her mother told her to sit back down and stay down. "Stop all that fussing." The girl seemed no older than four and stayed still for a little while, and then her hands reached up to the light switch. Just as her fingers brushed the ceiling, her mother slapped her. "I told you!"

The old man across the aisle looked over at them with a slow, sad stare. He coughed without seeming to need to, the wool above his eyes furrowing. He mumbled something I couldn't hear, but which the girl's mother did.

"Some people need to mind their own affairs," she said to the seat back in front of her. "Some people have no idea."

The old man coughed again and turned toward the window.

The bus slowed for our first stop—Melbourne. I wondered if Rainey would remember where the restrooms were.

We wandered through the station, and a transistor radio's tinny sounds pushed around the thin crowds, lyrics straining to be heard. I caught a thread of them and thought it was strange that, of all bands, Cream should follow us. At home Rainey listened to Jack, Ginger, and Eric all the time. How she could swoon over Ginger Baker was beyond me, but he had that emaciated, I've-already-lived-an-entire-life look she loved. Why she didn't go for Jack, with his wide eyes, or Eric, whose voice could wrap around a room, I had no idea. Maybe it was just the name, Ginger—sweet and subterranean.

Rainey pulled me through the dingy terminal, which had a stale smell that reminded me of boredom. Paper cups and cigarette stubs littered the floor. People with vague expressions waited in red and orange seats, the molded kind that you slipped into. There were glass-windowed ticket counters like at the movies, without the lines, and a wall mural made of colored tiles, something that was supposed to make us think of traveling across the country: sunrises, fields, farms, beaches, happy families waving hello and goodbye. The vaulted ceiling made everything echo, from high heels crossing the hard floor to announcements for buses arriving and departing.

My satchel was heavy with extra clothes and that Eva issue of *Look*, and it kept slamming into my side. The little vial of pills surfaced, an expired prescription of Nembutal I'd taken from my mama's bedside table. I thought of how Mama had given me one of her edgeways hugs that morning, the way she could kiss without ever laying her lips on my cheek, the way she'd full-out kiss Saul on his forehead or Rainey just at the corner of her mouth, and I pushed the pills underneath a rolled-up pair of jeans.

"Come on, LuLu," Rainey said. "I thought you had to go."

We turned a corner into a dim hallway that led to the public bathrooms. A silhouette of a lady in an A-line dress on one door and one of a man in square, high-water trousers on another. Toilets flushing, mirrors that didn't reflect, the mother and her little girl washing their hands together at a sink. The mother lathered her daughter's small brown hands with her own large ones. The movement seemed brusque and hurried, and I tried not to stare. The mother glanced up at me and then back to the running water. By the time I came out of the stall, they were gone.

Rainey was leaning toward the stained mirrors trying to put on lip gloss. I felt wound up, the way I did when I'd sneak into Mama's room and steal her sleeping pills, the excitement of taking things that weren't mine and then swallowing them. Rainey and I'd find a place to go, whether the lake or a party or the end of our driveway, and the night would rise up like a dare— unfurling, unspeaking, and dark—and the everyday would become something much more. And then what happened depended on the pills. Either the world spun faster, the water's-edge willows and birches taking on new roots, the stars expanding, or the dark grew and billowed inside our heads, laughter turned loud and heavy, and we'd find a corner to hide in. Afterwards, always, we'd be so tired, the next day drenched in exhaustion and bad moods.

I didn't know if it was such a good idea—our standing there in the public bathroom, twisting off the cap and taking one Nembutal each, looking at each other in the discolored mirror, and still heading out to find Eva. But we boarded the next bus, the one that would take us to St. Lucie. Rainey hesitated for a moment on the bus steps, and I stared at the flowered patches on the back pockets of her jeans. At the top of the steps, I saw the holdup. Ahead, the little girl stood in the aisle. She had dropped her doll, and her mother was pulling her into the seat.

"Sit down now. And hold on to that baby doll."

The little girl sat still and patted her pale doll so that its eyes clicked shut. I tried to smile at her, but she looked away. Her mother rustled through sandwiches wrapped in wax paper. Rainey had chosen our seats, so I followed her. Across the aisle a soldier, dressed in drab-colored fatigues, unloaded his duffel bag and edged past. On the side of the olive green canvas were three stamped lines: JAMES A WILLIAMS, USMC, and a set of numbers. He looked over at us and then turned to watch something out the window. Moments later, the bus pulled out, the thick smell of exhaust welling up around us. And there was Cream again, their restless song moving around in my mind, making me look for an exit when there wasn't one.

"How did we end up on the local buses?" Rainey sighed and pulled her legs beneath her. She was in the window seat, and I had to look out into the noon glare to face her.

"I had just enough for these tickets, Rain," I said. "Babysitting money doesn't buy express."

"Oh," she answered, her response quiet, more an idea than something spoken.

"Well, I guess you're welcome," I said.

Sometimes she infuriated me. Her breathless act of unknowing, as though she had no idea of anything. The way she lingered on a thought and the way she moved with her slow, careful stride, always trailing behind.

Rainey was sixteen, almost a year older than me, but every year between my birthday in April and hers in July we'd share the same age, and then when the summer days grew longer and hotter, she'd move ahead again. This past summer I'd finally caught up with her in size, and having been the shortest, smallest kid out of all of our friends for the longest time, I was still getting used to it. Mama had groaned over my need for all new clothes, three sizes up. I ended up borrowing Rainey's gauzy things so I didn't have to face the shopping mall. I considered what I'd borrowed, what she'd borrowed. Later we'd probably get hungry and then the three remaining dollars would be gone, too.

"Rain, you know that money was nearly all I had."

"I know, LuLu." She exhaled, and her words rushed forward. "God, you don't have to keep reminding me. As if I don't already owe you for everything." She looked past me at the sticky gray floor and over at the soldier, who was turning a slip of paper over and over in his hands.

A glimpse of the ocean skimmed the window, and I pointed. Palm trees, tall and spindly, crowded the edges of the highway. Green signs read DIXIE HIGHWAY: EXITS SOUTH TO MALABAR, ROSELAND, AND OSLO. I turned these towns around in my mind and then tasted them—the rich, sunny, bitter taste of these towns. I'd never been anywhere, other than New Smyrna Beach, which lay north on this same road, and I remembered the briny smell of the fish stands that surrounded the pier. It had been a while since Saul, Rainey, and I had spent a Saturday watching the surfers and lying too long in the sun.

"Do you think Saul misses us yet?"

Rainey rolled her eyes. "Why would he?"

Rainey'd had Saul on her mind for nearly ever, but she'd begun to notice other boys looking at her. Like Timothy. The one with eyes the color of lake water. She mentioned him more than once. That he'd never spoken to her but was always around. I saw him, too—at parties, at the 7-Eleven where we got Cokes after school, on the walk home. He gave me the creeps because he was too closemouthed. And Saul had begun to edge around Rainey. He'd brush past her, singing that Moody Blues song about another Timothy, just outside and peering in. And that gave me the creeps even more and I ended up watching the windows, expecting Timothy with his liquid eyes, staring through the blinds.

The bus pushed past low, flat-roofed buildings and ugly signs. Rainey turned her head to look, too, and I realized Malabar was not the pretty place it should have been. The streets scudded by with rust-colored cars parked alongside and the sky took on a wan, lusterless tone. I leaned on Rainey's shoulder and she took my hand in hers and hummed a little tune that reminded me of sun and dolls and things once treasured and now lost.

Right around the end of November, Rainey had started listening to albums by Cream and Blind Faith, even Traffic, anything that let her lay around in bed half the day. With a strand of hair twined around one finger and her legs stretched up the wall, she sang along with Steve Winwood. To me, it always sounded as though he was calling from the bottom of a well.

As we crossed the bridge leading into Roseland, she murmured words that reminded me of wide bell-bottoms, the lilac pillowcase doused with her *Charlie* perfume, and staying up too late—"Up, down, and around. The lights don't make a sound." That she'd listened to the album endlessly and still didn't remember all the words was just so Rainey.

Below us, the bridge stretched over the bay, and the road surface hummed. The water had a bruised, swollen look, and I could tell the wind was picking up from the pitch of whitecaps. Farther up, the little girl slept with her head on the armrest, her mother now across the aisle. The old man with the woolen brows wasn't on this bus. I wondered if he was home, settling into an easy chair and watching the weather change through a picture window.

"Better get up off the ground, or else you're gonna make me frown." Rainey didn't sing; she pretended to sing. And I joined in, "Or else you're gonna make me frown, ooh, ooh." The little girl's mother turned around. She wore reading glasses and peered over them at me. "Ooh, ooh," I sang again, this time more quietly. I thought she'd tell me to hush up, but she simply turned back to her book.

"I don't even like that song, even with the words all lopsided and wrong," I said to Rainey.

"How can you not like "Badge"? George Harrison, your hero, wrote it with Clapton."

"And Clapton is your hero?"

"He could be." Rainey smiled and pushed against me with her long fingers. She still bit her nails, something she'd done since I could remember, and the edges were jagged. She traced the outside of my face with a middle finger and said in a fake sad voice, "Sing me something you like, then."

We were sliding into that happy, unhurried place, the pills doing their tricks.

I sang the beginning of "Two of Us," the Beatles always foremost in my mind, the idea of never arriving brightly colored and bittersweet.

Rainey laughed and tried to remember the rest, and I noticed then how she looked past me at the soldier. He turned to listen, to watch us, even through the silly whistling part, though neither of us could even whistle. He half smiled, more at Rainey than me, and I realized how young he was. Though the duffel marked with his name looked worn, JAMES A WILLIAMS was barely older than we were. The moment should have been slick with uncaring, weightless joy, where nothing else mattered, but something else was happening. A pale, shallow color had come into the day. The soldier blinked, and Rainey laughed louder than before.

I remembered the afternoon a week before when the latest Lingstrum grandbaby had taken her first steps. Her hands let go of mine, and she padded across the floor to Rainey. Her head so round and soft in the late angled light, and her steps so small. I realized then how everything seemed to go away from me and toward Rainey. It didn't make any difference. Not that I'd be grounded for at least a month and lose my babysitting job and any chance of earning back the money I'd used on our fare. Not in the composition of our friendship, the balance constantly shifting so that I felt like I was always falling, with every successive nod or turn or gesture, farther and farther away. Not even the idea of what might happen to Rainey once her mother opened her West Palm Beach apartment door. I imagined Eva stepping back and leaving us in the unsettled light of sundown, so that all she'd see were our silhouettes, diminished but together.

The war in Vietnam was still happening, even without my daddy there anymore, even with Rainey's father missing, even with the boy across the aisle on furlough. For Rainey and me, there were parties every weekend. All we had to do was walk out into the neighborhood to find one. And there was music. We heard it between the television broadcasts of the fighting, in the margins of multiple-choice tests, at our desks marked with Peter Max drawings, before midnight swims in the lake, after drinking too much and collapsing at the edge of the Callahans' lawn. Music wrung words into meanings that real life didn't seem to offer. And the paper cup was handed over, along with a palm of pills—bright little heroes. Blue, red, and yellow. Especially yellow.

Rainey didn't know much about heroes. The disappeared and returned fathers. The secrets we stashed. The boys we ignored. The MIA bracelet she'd hidden in a jewelry box years ago now clasped her wrist and left marks on the inside of her arm. Her biggest hero was somewhere out there, the evidence imprinted on the silver band. The new boys fawned over her, and the ones on album covers sang in questions, their endnotes rising up and sailing off.

Still, I loved Rainey, and what I loved about her were the same things I hated. The way she moved, so lithe and quiet. The way she stretched her long legs, the way she touched me around my face with the pads of her fingers, the way she let words fall from her mouth. Once, I wanted to own her, just crawl inside her skin and make her move exactly the direction I had in mind. That was so long ago. Fourth grade, fifth grade. The sound of pencils being sharpened. Announcements echoing down the long school halls. "Rainey McPherson, come to the office." But now I wanted her to float whichever way she wanted, so I could just watch in amazement. Only Rainey didn't float easily, like the autumn drifts of fallen cypress dust on Lake Sybelia, those feathery bits that glided down and rested for a while, that we plucked from the water before they sank. Instead, she liked to be rescued, and sometimes she was the one who rescued me.

The bus shuddered against the wind. Leathery magnolia leaves and torn newspaper pages blew past the windows. The first sign for St. Lucie was ahead, the sky behind it dark and mineral.

"Look," Rainey said. "You're a saint. St. Lu."

"Sure," I answered. I felt snug and complete, the shiny sun-colored capsule sliding into all the right corners.

Rainey folded the long, feathery tails of her blouse. "Remind me of your full name," she said. "Your real name."

"LuLu," I said, not playing, measuring her lack of insistence.

"Come on. I'll go first." She closed her eyes and then cast her name out into the air. "Adelaide Rainier McPherson."

"Whoa," I said. "I forgot about Adelaide. Jeez, Rainey."

"Quit." She smiled. "Now you."

"Oh, all right." I said the names slowly. "Lucille Flowers Blackwood."

The mother from several rows up revolved in her seat and nodded at me. She reminded me of women in church, not the ones who were friendly with my mother, but the ones who watched us with their eyes as if they expected us to suddenly explode.

"That's right," Rainey practically sang. "I remember now. Lucille Flowers Blackwood. Your name is so sweet."

"Shut up, Adelaide."

Outside, St. Lucie was sad and pretty. The mother woke her little girl, and I guessed this was their stop. Maybe even their town. The soldier pocketed his slip of paper, too small for a letter, probably a picture. The street signs were tipping and careening outside.

Was the bus slowing? The gears seemed to grind down. We swerved and I grabbed Rainey's arm, failing to remember the words to "Two of Us." Wearing rain hats in the rain? No, that wasn't it. I saw George and Eric on the side of the road, and Ginger Baker under an umbrella in the middle of the white dividing lines. The bus was listing, and Rainey's feet were flat against the seat in front of her. She was slipping away. We were no longer singing or laughing or quiet, and I didn't have her anymore. I only had the words. *Ooh, ooh, me-me mine. Inside, outside, and getting nowhere. Someday driving, never-ever arriving. Timothy's on the ground and making me frown.*

I opened my eyes. The little girl stood beside me, looking puzzled. Her mother gently shook me and asked me over and over if I was all right. But I wanted her to leave me alone. I wanted her to let me hear the music. Rainey leaned over me, too.

"It's our stop, Lu," she said. "You were sleeping. And singing. In your sleep."

Rainey looked like she was sleeping. Her fingers were so pretty, half hidden in her long hair. But she was crumpled. One arm thrown back over her head. A swimming stroke, I thought. Backstroke. And it was raining outside and inside, coming in through the bus windows. Why hadn't they been closed? Why was it raining at all?

"Rainey?" I looked up at her now.

"LuLu, come on. We have to get off the bus. It's St. Lucie."

The water was like needles coming in over us. Somehow, the windows were on the ceiling, and they were open and the rain was falling in.

"Rainey," I said, "you'll get wet. It's pouring, Adelaide." I started laughing then. "Seriously, don't get drenched."

There was a hand on my shoulder. It was warm and definite and wanted me in another place. The soldier tried to pull me up, and his hands were gentle and not very big. I remembered his name, stenciled in capitals—JAMES A WILLIAMS—and tried to whisper it aloud. The little girl's mother looked at me, and her eyes were enormous.

"Is she all right?" she asked Rainey.

Rainey looked like she might cry.

"Come on, honey," the mother said.

Rainey stayed next to me, her hands heavy with our things.

"Lucille Flowers Blackwood," the mother said to me. "It's time to go now. This is the last stop for this bus."

I decided I should listen and got up. James was there, letting me lean into his shoulder. He was tall, and my head rested on his chest. Rainey had my satchel, which I'd never buckled, and I wondered if everything was still inside—the magazine, the little bottle. We moved down the aisle, the mother and her little girl right behind us. Beyond the doorway, men in raincoats and women with umbrellas moved through the rain. They should have been blue and yellow raincoats and red umbrellas, but instead they were brown and gray and disappeared in the downpour. We climbed, one by one, down the stairs, out of the slanted bus and into the blackening day.

Inside the station, overhead lights buzzed and we moved to a row of benches in the waiting area. Against one wall were telephones, each with its own kiosk, each asking for one dime per call. I invented my mama's voice on the other end. "LuLu!" I could hear her yelling, and then my daddy taking the receiver because I could hear him saying not to worry.

"What did she get into?" James asked.

Rainey didn't answer, but I could see she was thinking about it, better than me at holding things together.

"Ooh, ooh," I said.

The mother held her daughter's hand and walked toward the terminal entrance. The little girl clutched her doll. Its hair wasn't even hair; it was painted on, a thin swirl of yellow to go with the blinking blue eyes. And then they were gone. At the door the mother quickly turned to look back at us, then pulled the little girl past the double doors and into a waiting car. The windshield wipers moved in time with the song in my head, and the car idled a few more minutes before pulling out into the dull, patterned day.

"Are you transferring here?" James asked us.

"What?" Rainey said.

"Are you getting on another bus, or are you getting picked up?" he said.

Rainey looked at him, and I didn't answer. I decided not to sing anymore. Instead, I decided to be mad. Things weren't going the way I'd imagined, and then I couldn't even remember what I'd imagined in the first place.

"Well, I'm going on from here." He shook his head then. "You all are something. You really shouldn't get strung out if you don't even know where you're going."

"We know where we're going, James," I said.

He didn't even blink when I said his name. "Well, that's good, Lucille. Where?"

"None of your business." I smiled without smiling, my eyes narrowed.

"Right. Well, have a nice trip."

He started to lift his duffel, but Rainey touched his arm lightly.

"Wait," she said. "We're going to West Palm Beach. Where are you—" She stopped.

"It's all right," he said. "Going home. Got lucky since it's nearly Christmas. My family's pretty happy about that." He searched the line of waiting buses. "We're probably on the same bus since we're all heading south."

"That's good—I mean, it's good you're going home," said Rainey. "Maybe you won't have to go back. Over there." She pulled at the ends of her hair.

"Doubtful." He looked from Rainey to me, then smiled. "'Maybe' is certainly an idea, though." He sat down next to me. "What *did* you get into? You look completely dazed."

"And confused," I said.

"A little." He pointed to the soft drink dispenser against the opposite wall. "Want something?"

I closed my eyes, but nodded. He came back with three paper cups filled with Coca-Cola and crushed ice.

"Funny," he said. "I haven't seen one of those drink machines since I was a kid."

"You're still a kid," I said, taking one of the cups. "A big kid."

"Nope." He shook his head. "Not anymore."

"I'm not a kid anymore either," I said. "And I'm LuLu, not Lucille."

"I know," he said. He held the cup to his mouth and drank nearly half of it at once. "Everyone on that bus knew. Both your names."

"Oh, yeah?" I noticed his eyes, dark and thick with lashes, and how when he spoke, he never looked away. His gaze felt level, but I didn't want to trust him.

"And you know my name, and where I've been, so we're even." He shook the ice in his cup and downed the rest of the drink.

Rainey seemed bewildered, so I pointed to his duffel, the USMC insignia much bolder than his name.

"My daddy's a Marine," I said without meaning to.

"In 'Nam?"

"Yeah. He's back now." I didn't want to tell anything else, especially not how he'd lost an arm, and how my mama had divorced him and then taken him back.

Rainey set her nearly empty cup on the floor by James's bag, and traced the block letters of his name, stopping at the middle initial. "What's the A for?"

"Alan. Not as nice as Rainier, I'm afraid."

"Oh," Rainey whispered. "We had a friend named Alan. He was killed in Vietnam."

"I'm sorry," James said.

"Seems like so long ago, but it wasn't really. Just three years. Alan was in the Army, though. Like my daddy," Rainey said. "Only, I guess my daddy still is." She'd returned to her breathless way of speaking, the way she spoke when doubtful or spaced out or when she met new boys.

James glanced at her bracelet, at the embossed letters and numbers, the name "McPherson" standing out.

"So, who's waiting for you all in West Palm?"

"My mama." Rainey seemed to consider the strap of her purse, tracing the worn leather. Everything she did was lovely, and James noticed.

I curled my fingers around my drink. The paper cup felt cold and strange, and I realized I was spilling the contents. The day was letting me down all at once, and I had landed in an indistinct and angry place. I thought of Alan, the lake, wet towels around our waists, his laugh. The way he understood me and my anger, the way he watched me slide the little duck call off his bureau and into my fist, that night so long ago. The Nembutal slammed itself into corners, dark and angular and dizzying.

"Well, it'll be a surprise and all," Rainey went on, her words like bits of confetti sprinkled into the air. "My mama doesn't really know we're coming. She might even be more mad than surprised when we show up."

James stared at Rainey, resting his hands on either side of his seat, the one beside me, right next to my leg. Through my jeans, I felt how warm it was. Rainey didn't seem to notice and kept on talking, but I didn't listen anymore. I closed my eyes and wished I could disappear, then reappear in another form, something prettier, something boys would love.

"LuLu." Rainey stood over me.

"Where'd James go?" I said, not sure how long I'd closed my eyes. His duffel leaned against the bench. And then I saw him crossing the tile floor. A tall, long-legged boy, a boy any girl could bring home to meet her parents.

"I swear, LuLu," Rainey said. "They're calling all the passengers for our bus. We're not going to get a seat together."

I thought about how she'd probably rather sit with James anyway. I was tired of buses and roads and the idea of Eva's expression at the end of the day. We ended up in the back of the bus, where the seats were higher and stretched all the way across, above the engine and the back tires. I threw myself into a corner and glared through the window.

"Happy?" I said to Rainey, as James pitched his bag on the opposite side and sat next to her.

"You're obviously not," she answered.

James ignored us, reaching into his pocket, checking for the little photograph.

I decided to be mean, because being mean was easy, and because my mood needed a place to swing. I thought of the girl who was probably waiting for him, who had no idea that he was so friendly with other girls when she wasn't around. "Who's the picture of?" I said.

"A kid," he said. "Just a kid."

"Who?" I stretched across Rainey and tried to take the photo from him.

"You want to see?" He looked at me, half amused and perhaps suspicious of why he even liked me. I knew he did.

"Here." He handed me the snapshot, the frayed edges bending in his fingers.

Inside the white border was a Vietnamese girl with short dark hair standing on a dirt road and waving to the camera. Trees like the familiar spindly palms of Florida were on either side. It could have been a road in Anna Clara, spread with soft, shell-colored sand and laced with tree roots. The girl was small, maybe seven, and wore a flowered dress but no shoes. The biggest thing about her was her smile.

"Her name is Hoa," he said, stretching the single consonant so that it was clear. Hwa. "Since you like names."

"Why do you have her picture?"

"Because she and her family were my friends. They took care of me, and I took care of them."

"Were?" Rainey said.

"Yes." James's steady, unwavering expression was kind. Not sad, not angry, not even perplexed. I knew nothing about him, but I could tell there was no way he would show us how he really felt. He was like my father and Saul and even Rainey, who'd grown quieter and quieter over the years.

"What was she like?" I asked.

"She was funny, like you. She was sweet and angry and confused and, more than anything, curious. And she always seemed pleased with herself." He took the photo from me. "I don't know if I'll be sent back to her village, but I'll always be looking for her."

The bus started up, and the engine vibrated beneath us, muffling our words. Rainey and James kept talking, but I didn't strain to hear them. Outside the windows, St. Lucie slipped by in a haze of heavy rain, and somewhere ahead West Palm Beach promised to rise up like glitter, with its hotels and bars and Ocean Boulevard estates. I wondered if we'd ever get there and then if we'd ever get back home again.

Rainey's mother lived in a bungalow at the Seaglade Motel, too far to walk from the bus station. I'd spent nearly all my money on the bus tickets, so James agreed to come with us and pay the cab fare. He'd attached himself to us, maybe slowing the arrival at his own door. The rain kept on, slanting down, the view outside the taxi stormy and vague.

We pulled onto the street that led to the motel, and empty white beach and gray ocean stretched before us.

The driver stopped, and James leaned forward to hand him the money. Rainey opened her door and hesitated, rain flying into the back of the cab. I sat in the middle of the cracked vinyl seat between Rainey and James, and I pushed Rainey to move before we got any wetter.

"C'mon, Rainey," I said. "Get out."

She stepped out and ran for the covered passageway, and then stopped and stared. James and I caught up to her. Behind us, the sound of the taxi pulling away, its tires on the wet road, and in front of us, a lawn with palms and poinsettias, a pool surrounded by chairs and tables and closed umbrellas, and two rows of individual bungalows. And beyond, the Atlantic, unsettled and endless.

The twelve bungalows were identical, with red-tiled roofs and stucco exteriors, painted in alternating colors of cream, shell pink, pale peach.

"Don't you know which one?" I said.

James moved past me and took Rainey's hand in his own. "You okay?" he asked her.

Rainey left us in the shelter of the archway and approached the cottage at the very end, the one closest to the beach. She waited a moment, then knocked, her blond hair darkening in the rain. The door finally opened, and Eva in a pretty green sweater and slacks appeared. Though she was tall enough to meet her mother's gaze, Rainey stared down at her feet and backed away. Without hesitation, Eva pulled Rainey inside and hugged her. Half a second later, Eva leaned out and waved us inside.

"Come in!" she called. "Come in out of this awful weather!"

I felt uncertain, but James ahead of me obviously didn't. So I followed.

Inside, the television was on, a movie with Jimmy Stewart climbing an endless staircase, the blue light filtering through the dim room where we all stood. Eva switched on a few lamps and turned off the TV. I leaned my satchel against the wall by the front door. Rainey held her purse next to her chest and glanced at us and the floor and my bag and then her mother.

"What in the world, Rainey?" Eva said. "You came all this way without a word of notice. And you're soaked through. Let me get some towels." She disappeared through a beaded curtain, which made a soft clattering sound as it parted, and then was back with thick multicolored beach towels. "Dry off and sit down. Shall I make some tea? Oh, goodness. Of course I should. Oh, Rainey, I'm just so surprised to see you. And LuLu! And—oh, honey, what was your name?"

"James, Mama," Rainey said, her voice flat and unfriendly. "His name is James."

"Why, well then, James. I'm Eva, Rainey's mama. Sit, sit down please." Eva waved to the sofa and walked over to the little kitchenette tucked on one side of the living room.

A small table and pair of chairs were off to the side, and a slim modern chandelier overhead. I conjured up who might sit in the second chair. Somebody to take Rainey's father's place, somebody to take Rainey's place.

"You all have caught me on a rare evening off," Eva said. "How lucky! We can even have supper together. How's that sound?" She filled a kettle, opened a red tin of loose tea, spooned it into a tall gold-and-white striped teapot, and kept on talking without letting us respond.

Rainey pushed past the beaded curtain, where I guessed the bedroom and bath were, and James kept his eyes on the swaying strands as they slowed. He had his own family waiting on him, and yet he was still here with us. Avoiding one reunion and landing in the middle of another, a stranger's really.

Eva set a tray of cups and the teapot on the coffee table just as Rainey reappeared wearing another pair of jeans, her own, and a blouse, bright blue with polka dots the size of spotlights. Definitely Eva's. Eva didn't say a word about it, just kept on with her nonstop nothing talk, including highlights about the tea, which was jasmine, brought all the way from the Vietnamese highlands. James glanced up, but didn't speak.

"They say jasmine flowers are night-blooming, and so the tea is scented in special rooms with the harvested flowers at night." Eva poured the tea, pale and golden, into each cup and looked up at us. "Isn't that fascinating?"

"Mama, since when do you drink tea?" Rainey said. She had combed her hair and braided it across one shoulder. She held her cup, her fingers laced around it and through the handle.

"Oh, Rainey," Eva started and then stopped.

I took a sip of the tea and was surprised at the soft fragrance, the bright but bitter taste.

Suddenly everything was silence, and steam from our cups curled into the overly quiet room. The rain let up for a moment, and the quiet was too quiet. We had barely tasted our tea when Rainey held her cup high and then simply let go, the tea splashing against the table, the bright rug below, her jeans, and the china breaking apart into three neat pieces. It was like that—this trip, this attempt, this calm, this mess—all flying apart, pained and perfect at the same time.

Eva ignored the broken cup, though she did say "Oh, Rainey" several times. The day shifted then into something brittle and slanted, daylight long since gone and night edging in.

Insisting we all must be hungry, Eva took us to a place down the beach with bright red lanterns and drinks with little paper umbrellas, where we ordered egg drop soup and moo shu pork. Both Eva and James knew how to handle chopsticks, and Eva finally noticed James was in uniform. She chimed in with embarrassing bits of conversation—"things we do for our country, things we do to pay the rent, things we do"—and James smiled politely. Rainey twisted her napkin, and eventually tore apart her paper umbrella.

"Things you do, Mama. Not the same as things that James has done. Or that Daddy's done."

James balanced his chopsticks on his plate and set his hands on either side of his placemat, the paper edged with thin red lines and Chinese characters. His expression was too calm, and he wouldn't look in Rainey's direction. Rainey swung her feet under the table as if she might kick someone.

"Ma'am," he said to Eva, "we're all trying to do our best. Really, though, I'm just glad to be back."

"Well, of course you are," Eva said. "This damned war is endless, and your family must be thrilled to have you home again."

"Yes, they will be."

"You mean you haven't been home yet?"

"No, ma'am." He glanced down at his last few bites. "I'm on my way still. Just wanted to make sure Rainey and LuLu landed in the right spot. Pompano Beach isn't much farther though. I'll catch the local and be there in no time."

"Why, that's just down the road." Eva touched her napkin to the corner of her mouth. "We could drive you, once all this rain lets up."

"Seriously, Mama. James doesn't need you to take him home." Rainey glared at Eva and pushed her seat out from the table. A thin scraping sound flew across the emptying dining room.

"I don't want to make trouble," James said. "And the buses run fairly often."

He was so reasonable and unassuming and began to remind me of Alan Walbright. Tall, steady, interested in the world around him. I sighed out loud.

"Are you bored?" James said.

"Nope," I answered. "What did you do over there anyway?" I wondered if he'd ever come close to dying, if he'd been afraid.

"LuLu." Rainey pushed against me with the sole of her sneaker. "James doesn't want to talk about that. Nobody does."

"I did what I was ordered to do." James smoothed out a wrinkled corner of his placemat. "And I took pictures, of course."

"That's right," Rainey said.

"What in the world did you take pictures of?" Eva leaned in. "I'd love to see them."

I imagined our table covered in small, square photos, trimmed with thin white edges. Kodacolor images of tangled jungles, fields of grass bowing to the wind, a sky crowded with helicopters and herons. And then black-and-white prints of faces—soldiers in full battle gear, women in black pajamas, children alone on a road—like the one of the girl James had shown Rainey and me on the bus. Except for the last, I knew all of these from the news, from stories my daddy had long since stopped telling, from my own mind.

James tried to respond, "I could show you—"

But Rainey interrupted. "Maybe James will show you someday." Her voice didn't waiver. She had no room for Eva. None at all.

The waitress came with a teapot and realized none of us were drinking tea. Eva asked for the check, and the waitress nodded. Her black hair was twisted tightly at the back of her head, and we all watched her walk away.

Later, I knew the trip had been a mistake. That Rainey was moving on, into a place that was crowded with anger. She'd been crushed and was finally done with all that. The future was spinning out before us, faster than I could understand, and the day had darkened, misunderstandings and lies and wrecked promises like flotsam. Eva would always be Eva, on the lookout for that wealthy husband, trips around the world, beautiful things. That she was looking in the wrong place seemed clear, but she did love a man in dress whites, the Army having forsaken her, the Navy picking up in its stead.

The convertible Eva drove was one of the many gifts she'd received from suitors, and tonight we sat inside with the top up, the rain drumming down on the cover overhead. Dusty Springfield sang on the radio: "I Don't Want to Hear It Anymore." Dusty and Dionne and Diana—the singers our mamas listened to. And our mamas, losing and leaving and looking for, pushing us out of the way while they did. I sat in the backseat with James, and Rainey up front with Eva. No one talking, just the song and the rain.

It was dark and everything glistened. We'd come this far and it didn't really matter. Hours ago, the bus had pulled away from St. Lucie, and the little town had lingered in my mind, even when the lights of West Palm Beach stretched before us, kaleidoscopic and distant. Now, we were surrounded by those same lights, which seemed there only to block out the night and the real reason we'd come.

The day had had too much motion, rushing, spinning, going away from instead of toward the very thing meant to be reached. The back of Eva's head, the curled, teased, fussed-with hair hitting her shoulders, the oncoming headlights shining through the loose strands, and Rainey's profile as she stared out the window—the strength and sadness, the way they kept withdrawing from each other. I realized then that retracing the way here was pointless.

We pulled into the motel parking area, and there was my family's Volkswagen bus, large and red, at the breezeway leading to the bungalows. The flame from a lighter lit up a figure in one of the back windows for a second—my daddy. Saul in the driver's seat, and Mama on the passenger side, sitting too straight and fooling with the radio dials.

"I'm leaving with LuLu," Rainey said.

Eva parked her car under a communal carport meant for residents. She turned off the engine and held the small set of keys in her hand. "Baby, you just got here."

"And I'm just leaving." Rainey opened her door and Eva reached over to stop her, to touch her cheek.

"Please wait." Eva stroked Rainey's long braid. "Stay the weekend. You came all this way."

James had his hands on the seat, on either side of his legs, his eyes down. We couldn't get out of the two-door car until Eva and Rainey did. Behind us, voices. And through the rain-smeared back window, umbrellas, and then Mama and Daddy peering in.

"What are you all doing just sitting in there?" Mama called.

Eva sighed and then waved. "We're talking, Minnie."

"Well, come on out." Mama had looks and determination and no patience at all.

I heard Daddy say, "Let 'em be a minute." He and Mama hadn't let on that they'd shared anything in several years, and yet they'd openly shared the same ride over here. I didn't blame Saul for staying in the VW bus, away from what was surely coming.

Eva smiled at Rainey, then opened her door and stepped out. Rainey stayed where she was, so once James had unfolded himself from the backseat, I had to climb out on his side. I barely had both feet on the pavement, and Mama grabbed me by the arm and said, "What are you thinking, taking off and not telling us where and why and what in the world for? You know how I hate all that leaving nonsense. Who gave you your marching orders anyway? Praise be to G, LuLu, you will wear me out."

Daddy didn't stop her from scolding like he usually did. He stood holding on to his black umbrella, waiting, like Mama, for my answer. But I didn't have an answer, so Mama zeroed in on James, who was trying to circle around us.

"Why is there always a uniform in the equation? Why, oh why?" Mama said. "What's your excuse, young man?"

"No excuses, ma'am," James said. He involuntarily came to attention, facing forward, much taller than Mama, who obviously didn't like looking up just then.

"What are we all doing standing out here in the rain and in the dark?" Eva said. "Let's go inside. Come on, Minnie. Give me a hug. You can yell at LuLu later on. Royal, look at you two together again. I love it."

"We are not necessarily together," Mama said. "We are just standing in line with switches for bad children. Lord have mercy, Eva!"

"Well, you always were the couple everyone adored. So in love, so gorgeous." Eva walked ahead with Mama, and Daddy stood back.

I pulled James over to him. "Daddy, this is James. He's come home, just like you did."

James saluted, and Daddy nodded, not one to salute anymore. We walked together, me and James and Rainey, Daddy a little behind us, bringing up the rear, keeping us safe. The front window of the Volkswagen rolled down, and Saul smiled at me.

"Seriously, Lu? You always find someone to share your adventures, don't you?" Laughing, he threw a glance in the direction of Rainey and James.

That this was Rainey's adventure didn't make any difference. Since I'd spied Rainey across the schoolyard years before, since I'd paid the bus fare this morning, since we'd left St. Lucie, it had been mine, too.

Saul closed the window again and climbed down from the VW and punched my shoulder gently, while Rainey and James moved past us into the breezeway. The wind had died down and the rain started to let up, and the surf grew louder. Our parents went into Eva's apartment, the lights sudden and bright through the windows, and their conversation punctuated by ice falling into glasses.

Outside, the four of us stood under the palms, their long trunks leading up to tattered crowns, and the sky opened wide with starlight and cloud trails and layers of unending darkness. Saul, Rainey, and I knew each other too well, Blind Faith and Beatles tunes falling from our mouths at the same time, and even James, whom we'd known only hours, fell into place, one of us. And still, at that very moment we hardly knew each other at all, that moment when Rainey laughed, the sound startling and sweet, promising nearly nothing and almost everything, lingering and fading into the night.

BUTTERCUPS, BEACH DAISIES, AND GOLD STARS

OCTOBER 1977

In our house on Lake Sybelia, the walls are covered with James's photographs. Not the ones that have won awards, but the ones we love—a white sky filtered through the branches of a lemon tree, the tortoiseshell cat sleeping across the long faded blue of James's threadbare jeans, my mother's lowered head in silhouette, cypresses that appear to grow from their own lake reflection, LuLu laughing in close-up with newly cropped hair. We have our favorites, of course. James's is the one of me lying in a field of buttercups, nearly asleep. And mine is still the one of Hoa standing on that dirt road, so far away.

Our house, a cottage really, is a gift from Mama. She's finally rich and famous, just like she always wanted. Of course, she still has admirers and suitors, but she doesn't need them anymore. That article in *Look* gave her so much attention that she's started touring, Las Vegas even. And I've thrown resentment to the side. James is the reason. "You carry this ridiculous load, Rain. Why don't you just let it go?" It took years, but he brought us back together. Mama was already trying, but I did need to see her from another angle before I could try. I suppose James's photographs allowed me to see another side of her. One where she wasn't posing and putting on a show; one I'd actually never known before.

In late August, after the SOLD sign was pulled up, the three of us sat on the porch with salted peanuts and beer, hoping for a breeze off the lake. Mama laughed and said how she never thought she would, but she loved a can of beer on a hot day. A transistor radio sat on the same table as the bowl of peanuts, "Don't Be Cruel" playing for the hundredth time since Elvis's death. I turned the dial, found news and baseball, and then switched it off.

"That man." Mama shook her head and drank from her beer again.

"Yeah, we know you loved him." I laughed and rolled my eyes. Mama had never liked Elvis. Sinatra was more her style.

"Show me your hand again, Rainey."

Mama reached for my left hand and sighed. She'd already said she thought the little ring odd. A glint of yellow sapphire, like the buttercups I'd laid down in.

"So pretty, so unique," she said. "Like you." Then she touched the small ruby at my throat, the birthstone necklace she'd given me for my thirteenth birthday. "And you still have this. You know how to hold on to things, don't you?"

"I hated you then," I said.

"I know you did, baby." She held her beer in the air, as if she might pour out the rest, dousing the porch floor. "I think we're making up for all that now, aren't we?"

I'd held on to bitterness for years, and it felt unbelievable to have cast it aside. It was true. I knew how to hold on to treasures and ire, like they were shaped in the same way, carefully, perfectly.

"Yes, we're making our way past all that," James said, scooping up peanuts and tossing a few my way.

He winked at me, surely noting the way I didn't answer. And I smiled, tucking my feet up, leaving the scattered nuts alone.

Lulu is coming home. For a visit, anyway. She's been in Venice, California. Wanted to see what "the other coast" was all about. Of course we had to make the trip worth her while. I suppose a wedding is close enough.

The Orlando Airport is crowded with coming and going, with families that have flown in from far-off places for a weekend at Disney World. I watch for LuLu. She would die laughing at these little assemblies, looking wilted in the autumn heat, standing beside mounds of luggage. A father checking his tags, a mother lighting a cigarette, a little girl holding the hem of her mother's floral dress and crying. And with the whirl of activity—people calling to each other, taxis pulling up, suitcases being loaded into trunks—I'm startled when LuLu runs through the automatic doors at arrivals and slams her palms up against the front passenger door, her hair still boy-short, close to her head, her gold-brown eyes bright. She's still punching her way through life.

She practically climbs through the window, shouting, "You have a station wagon? Seriously? You must already be married!"

I open the driver's door and run around the front of the car to where she's standing. "Give me a hug, crazy," I say. "And don't give me grief. The car's a hand-me-down from James's family."

"Lucky you, Rain-Rain." She tosses her blue suitcase into the backseat. "Let's go fill up the back of this monster with groceries. Let's fill it up with surfboards and booze and a giant wedding cake!"

"You really are crazy." I laugh and open the door for her.

"Let me drive this thing," she says. Her eyes crinkle up, and she has that look on her face like she's going to light something on fire.

"No way." I push her gently onto the bench seat. "You'd speed or sideswipe some poor old lady, and James would kill us both."

She smiles at me. "James? He wouldn't do that. He'd just shake his head, ask us what we'd gotten into, make us empty our pockets. He's going to make a good daddy." She laughs with her head thrown back, delighted with herself.

I circle around to the driver's side and head out into traffic, all of us funneled toward I-4, the more direct route dotted with stop lights and strip malls. The old Florida, Mama says, is disappearing, but she and Minnie still visit the bakeries and dress shops that cluster together in these centers. "You know how I love finding new adventures." That's Mama, of course. "Little hole-in-the-wall restaurants like Sing's—the best dumplings! Tailors who know how to take in a waist and shorten a sleeve in the thinnest silk chemise." And then Minnie has to chime in. "And for you, Rainey, cake shops with windows full of three-tiered beauties." They have their hands deep into the wedding plans, the way they once had flour up to their elbows in piecrusts and filling. Back when

LuLu and I were little and I didn't know what to make of Mama's long absences. But that was years ago. They've given up baking and rarely turn up the heat in the kitchen. These days they like to be served.

LuLu, I learn, is serving. She's been tending bar in some ritzy place in Santa Monica, awake all night and sleeping through the days.

"How can you stand that? Don't you miss the sun?"

"The sun is overrated." She pulls lightly on my hair, still straight and still long. "I had practically nineteen years of Florida sun. The sun is bright and hot and exhausting. Sunrise is fine. Sunset, too. But all that stuff in between, you can have it."

"You did used to hide inside a lot. Anywhere that was cool and cave-like. No wonder you like working in a bar. I'll bet it's modern, maybe even lit up in dim coppery hues?"

"Wrong," LuLu says. "And then again, right. Not modern, but dim. Like a speakeasy, all forbidden and shit. The crowd bores me. Lawyers and their clientele. I'm looking for another job. Anna Clara have any coppery, modern set-ups?"

I changed lanes and passed a VW convertible full of girls in sunglasses and short-sleeves.

"There we go." LuLu waves to the girls and blows them kisses. Then as we overtake the VW, she shoots them the bird. "And here we are instead." She motions to the saddle-colored interior around us, wood paneling inside and out, the biggest Estate wagon ever made. At least that's what James's father said when he handed over the keys. "Seriously, Rain, I have to drive this big baby before I leave."

"Don't talk about leaving." I pouted. "You just got here."

Our exit was coming up, and I thought about people coming and going. I always hated the going.

◊ ◊ ◊

LuLu stands in our living room and nods her head at the picture of me lying down in the buttercups. "Reminds me of when you first lived with us. The time you were sleeping and I chopped your hair off. All that long yellow hair swirling around your head, finally free." She grinned and then didn't. "You weren't even mad. You just couldn't believe I'd really gotten the scissors out of the kitchen drawer and made use of them."

LuLu reaches out toward my hair, her fingers like scissors, dramatically pretend-cutting great swathes. She stops at my ears and stares at my earrings, the same little silver dollars she gave me on my thirteenth birthday. Like the necklace from my mama from that very same birthday, I still wear them.

"I didn't know how to be mad at you," I say. "I was too scared and in awe of your daring. Sneaking around the neighborhood, stealing other people's things. It was like you didn't think before you acted, but then I knew you did. You admitted to me that you thought a lot about it, knowing on what night you'd steal from which neighbor, planning the theft inside your mind, then making it happen."

LuLu becomes hushed and turns back to the photos. She follows the edge of the delicate gold frame that surrounds the photo of the field of flowers. Certainly, she is thinking of taking it right off the wall and stowing it in her suitcase. James would notice the bare spot on the wall, the lack of bright color, and very quietly tell LuLu to give it back. She'd resist and then unzip her bag and, without a single iota of embarrassment, a laugh hidden beneath her smile, she'd hand it over.

"You must have thought we were all crazy," she says, her voice layered with something like memory. "But then, I suppose we were."

It wasn't so long ago. Did I think the Blackwoods were crazy? I tripped over their craziness until I learned how to sidestep or run or hide from it. And eventually I leaned into and loved it—the unpredictable sway of our days and months and years together. LuLu's rush into circumstance became mine, too. A tag-along, a shadow compared to her, I still followed, waiting to see what she'd do next. Sometimes it was completely normal, like going for an afternoon swim, and other times, traipsing into the dark, opening neighbors' unlocked doors, LuLu silently rifling through their possessions and pocketing the ones that appealed, no matter their worth.

"Do you still take things?" I think of the bits and pieces that crowded the corner of her sock drawer in our childhood bedroom. The glass bird, the seed packets, a gold pencil, marbles, pennies, amber-colored pill bottles, that pair of men's military-issue socks. And of course, the duck call from Alan's room. "What would you take now?"

James arrives from the kitchen with a tray. It holds glasses loaded with ice, vodka, grapefruit juice, and rimmed with salt. LuLu's favorite, the taste of citrus groves and the ocean all at once.

"I would take this," LuLu says, a glass in hand. "And I would take that." She points to a small photo in a black frame, a study in composition, a new one James added to the collection only days ago.

A couple sits side-by-side in lawn chairs, their backs to the camera. The woman is smoking, her elbow resting on the metal arm of the chair, her arm extended, wrist angled, her fingers long, the cigarette balanced between them. Her hair is pinned up, and long tendrils of it trail her neck. Very close beside her, the man is in profile, perhaps smiling, and he appears to be staring at her feet, or the grass around them. And then I look closer and see what he's really looking at, something I hadn't noticed until now—a small brown rabbit, asleep against the woman's left foot.

James hands me the tray, our two drinks steady, and removes the picture from its nail.

"It's yours," he says to LuLu.

And there she is, the girl I met all those years ago, lake swims and school days, drugs and hurricanes marking our years together. LuLu, all smiles. Sipping her drink and admiring the framed shot of her parents.

Hurricane Dolly blew through Florida in August 1968. Her rain drenched our yards and streets, and her winds rushed through Anna Clara, tearing away entire palm fans, shredding banana leaves, and littering the grove with green, unripe tangerines and oranges. I remember the sounds. The wailing, the unceasing drumming on the rooftop, the sudden crash of another gate flying open or another limb coming down.

Dolly was not the biggest hurricane ever, but she is the first one I remember.

Mama dropped me off at the Blackwoods, the family who for the time being, like ours, was fatherless. The war in Vietnam always the reason for everything: for how we waited for our daddies to come home; for how our mothers lingered over their drinks, laughing and laughing, and then sometimes crying; for how we spent too long indoors in front of the television, watching shows like *Lost in Space* and

Laugh-In; for how we felt lost or abandoned, though we'd gained each other. I'd gained LuLu and Saul and Minnie, and I was wary of them all, especially Minnie, who wanted me to call her by her first name. Back then, while I always did what she encouraged me to—keep quiet in the house, help her in the yard, answer sweetly when called—I thought of her as Mrs. B, that capital B creating distance where I needed it.

The Ford Fairlane, the only thing Mama'd kept of the small inheritance after my grandmother died, idled by the curb for a few minutes, just enough for me to slide off the bench seat and step onto the Blackwoods' front lawn. Mama had no time to stay and visit, since the weather was bound to turn bad. Mrs. B never questioned my mama's decisions, even heading into gale-force winds. And on this particular evening, she took my overnight bag, shut the passenger door, and waved to my mama, who blew us kisses and pulled out, her taillights gleaming in the wet evening light. Then, her hand on my shoulder guiding me forward, Mrs. B brought me inside for cold fried chicken and her lucky coleslaw, the kind she made when she wished for luck to change. I felt comforted and loved by this woman who'd become my mother's best friend, the way she'd include me like a member of her family, no judgment and no questions asked, though at times she frightened me with her anger. The way she'd yell down the hall, or raise her arm and point to our bedrooms, all of us punished at once just because she was in a mood. Like the storm outside, Mrs. B moved from calm into fury all too easily.

Strangely enough, Dolly and my mama were both moving toward West Palm Beach. In great sweeps of daydreams, I painted them hurling themselves at the coastline, pushing tidal waters inland, flooding the area. All for attention, their reckless bearings broadcast over every station, Mama coming from one side, Dolly from the other. And I came to associate this particular storm and all those that followed with cold chicken and my mother's absence. They settled on me, salty and undecided, and made me lean east, listening for my mama's singing inside the screaming wind.

LuLu sat at the kitchen table, elbows splayed, a chicken leg in her grasp. She took mincing little bites and chewed with her mouth open until her mama said, "Cut that out, Miss Lu." Everything on the table was cold, just out of the refrigerator. "If the electricity goes out, we'll be one step ahead," Mrs. B had said, piling plates of leftovers onto the counter. Biscuits, the chicken and slaw, sliced tomatoes and bread-and-butter pickles, pepper jelly and a pitcher of sweet tea. I loved Mrs. B's kitchen. Unlike my mama's, it was full of home-cooked food, always enough for a crowd.

"We get Dreamsicles afterwards?" Lu said.

"If you sit up straight and stop your foolishness," Mrs. B answered.

"All right." LuLu sighed through her words and sat up, elbows at her sides.

Outside, the wind began to pick up, blowing in fits and starts, sideswiping the wine bottles Mrs. B had hung from the oak tree in the front yard. Through the three floor-to-ceiling kitchen windows, I could see shapes of colored glass, swaying and swinging. At first, they called out with chimes and clangs, and eventually, they slammed back and forth, a few shattering. Mrs. B looked toward the windows, then lit a cigarette, waving the match well after it went out.

"You take care of those, Saul B?" she said, as usual emphasizing the family initial like it was an act of ownership.

"If I have to." He hunched over his plate, his mouth moving around a biscuit.

"Well, we're not going to listen to that racket all night." Mrs. B gestured with her lit cigarette toward the oak. "Just run out and untie them, and then you can come back in for a Dreamsicle with the girls."

"I don't need a damned Dreamsicle."

"Watch your tone, mister. Go ahead on and pull them down."

Saul left the table by sliding his chair back and nearly knocking it over. Even after almost a year of spending week-ends and sometimes weeks with this family, Saul still seemed mysterious and unfamiliar to me. He clipped LuLu on the back of the neck as he walked past, and she yipped.

"Quit, Saul!" LuLu acted utterly wounded.

"I swear," he said under his breath.

"Oh no you don't," his mama said back. "Not in this house. Be careful. I'll have you tape up all the windows if this storm gets any worse."

Taping Xs across windows was a precaution I'd seen in other houses. Even when her heart grew weak, the heart that soon gave up and stopped, my grandmother had been one to tape windows when a hurricane was coming. Mrs. B, I'd learn, didn't always pay heed to hurricanes and precautions. She'd fling her arms around, as if to remind us of the locations of all the windows in the house: the narrow floor-to-ceiling ones; the small, levered panes that cranked open; the sliding glass walls that flew apart, allowing entrance into the yards; the three diamonds cut into the front door.

Minnie inhaled and pointed her cigarette in LuLu's direction. "Your daddy had light and nature in mind when he built this house." She exhaled her smoke toward the ceiling. "Maybe he should have thought of the weather as well."

Coming back in, Saul slammed the front door, and Mrs. B called, "Shoes on the mat!" We heard them drop, one, then the other.

"You're welcome," he said, just loud enough for us to hear.

"That's right, sweet boy," Mrs. B said. "I am." And she stood up, opened the freezer, and pulled out two Dreamsicles. And then a third for herself.

The taste of cold orange-and-cream, the texture of the wooden stick underneath—these still remind me of the days of Hurricane Dolly. LuLu and I spent most of the time watching television, climbing the seats of dinette chairs onto kitchen counters and standing on tiptoe to reach the hidden snacks, playing jacks on the bathroom floor because it was cool and even. Strangely enough, we got along, LuLu quiet, not doling out her usual teasing and troublemaking. And maybe this is why I remember the rain and the wind and those three days. Because LuLu, for once, was especially nice to me. Maybe this was only so the next time she was mean, it would sting me even more. Still, I held on to the niceness, hoping it would stick.

Her hand in mine, we sat on the couch and shared Fritos, living through another episode of *Lost in Space*. Obviously not interested in our company, Saul disappeared into his room, the strains of his stereo muted, and Minnie read magazines and baked and smoked and occasionally poured herself another glass of wine from a pretty green bottle. I discovered life inside another family, this family, though not my own, one that soon became mine.

Remnants of the rain and wind held on for two more days, and then Mama came back, satisfied and willing to sit a while, her feet up and a glass of wine in hand, like she and Dolly had done what they'd set out to.

I can count the times LuLu was nice to me on one hand: in those days of Hurricane Dolly; when her daddy finally came home and then her mama threw him out; on the bus trip to West Palm when she paid our way and shared her stolen stash, the very same time we met James. But the thing was, we became more like sisters than friends, and that confused the both of us. Over the years, she didn't seem to know how to treat me, and I spent a lot of time ducking her and her mama's moods. And so now in my own house, a year since the last time we've seen each other, she is the bossy little sister again.

Alone for a moment in my bedroom, I stare at the closet door. And as soon as I'm alone, I'm not. LuLu is there beside me, exuberant. She kisses my cheek too hard, her affection pushing me off balance. I want this evening to be fine, this week to go along smoothly. I want to include LuLu in my life now, without the baggage of our lives back then. And though I'm a little afraid to, I ask her if she'd like to see my wedding dress. Instead of saying yes or no, she trips me up, the LuLu who tries to shock me and mostly succeeds.

"You think by marrying someone named James Alan, you can bring Alan back?"

"What?" I can barely breathe.

I think of Alan, in the cemetery with azaleas all around. Of Lillian Walbright, his mother, days after the news of Alan's death, standing in her carport, broken glass around her beautiful bare feet. Of Saul with Lyman, the Walbrights' dog, at his side in the months after Alan's deployment, in the years after his death. Of Minnie in the days of Mrs. B, telling us to mind our own business, as if the death of a friend was something we weren't allowed to grieve.

And then LuLu laughs. "You still can't tell when I'm fooling with you, can you, Rain?"

She slips her fingers into mine and pulls me forward. Like the old days. I'm used to the new days, though, and don't want to end up feeling tormented. Why did I think things might be different? With LuLu, they have always been the same. Her pulling me along into places I don't always want to go, our friendship as intricate and complicated as the antique lacework of my wedding dress.

"No, I can't tell. Not then, not now." I undo my fingers from hers. "And I don't want to have to try. Not anymore."

The dress will stay in my closet, the scents of cedar and lavender settling into its folds. And then tomorrow, a day in late October that James and I will celebrate every year, the brilliant afternoon sun lighting up the bedroom, I'll slip the dress over my head, tie up my hair, let Mama trace the lightest shade of pink over my lips, step into my heels, and gather the calla lilies arranged with roses and ribbon. LuLu will finally see who I am on the day I walk away from her.

But the day doesn't go that way. Very early on, it begins with clouds and builds to rain, and from our back windows I can see the lake is speckled and gray. James has gone for his run, and LuLu is still asleep. The tortoiseshell cat eyes me from her cushion on the porch swing, as I lightly press my fingers against the screen.

Still in my nightgown, I take an umbrella and walk the length of our yard down to the shore in my bare feet. The ground is soft with damp, ashy sand, and I step into the shallows. The water is up to my ankles and warm. I'm not surprised. How many times have I stepped into this lake? Hundreds? Nearly a thousand?

The umbrella shudders with a sudden slight wind, lifting my hands, and I grip the handle more tightly. Is my wedding dress still hanging in my closet, or has LuLu removed it from the satin hanger and crushed it into her suitcase? Is my wedding cake still sitting behind bakery glass, three-tiered and adorned with cream-colored fondant flowers? Is James rounding the north side of the lake, while on the south shore I'm wading barefoot under the shelter of an umbrella? I set it on the ground behind me without even closing it. I don't consider what I do next. I simply slip off the nightgown and drop it next to the umbrella. And then I walk naked into the lake until it's up to my waist, and I swim to the floating dock, still there, turned from brown to silver over years of bleaching sun and persistent rains.

Lillian Walbright is swimming along the opposite shore, her hair slick. She no longer wears the white bathing cap that made her stand out from a distance, even the chin strap bright and obvious. She no longer wears her wedding ring, either, her husband long gone, a black Lab puppy named Alice in his place.

There may be others awake. Hélène Laurent, walking with her black cane through the grove. The littlest Lingstrum girl, a bow in her hair, by now in kindergarten. Saul, sitting in his great-grandfather's lake house, listening to music, reading *Absalom, Absalom!* as much for himself as for his university classes. Minnie, her hair tied back, whipping up eggs in a silver bowl. And Royal, at the house on Sybelia Drive, awake to the smell of coffee and those eggs, by now sizzling in a pan. Everyone awake in my mind, in their houses, on their ways.

And so I don't care about climbing onto the dock in full view, clad only in my own skin on my wedding day. The wind is cool, a breeze from the west, the rain lightening, and I wring out my hair and stand in the center of the dock. It is anchored to a mooring many feet below and bobs gently as I turn and then step to the diving board, which I've avoided until now and surprisingly still has some spring. I stand at the edge and see Lillian Walbright treading water near her own dock. I gather myself, remembering everything Alan taught me all those years ago. Focus on where you want to end up, line up your toes at the edge of the board, bend your knees, gather arms overhead, and then! I stand there and become cold.

Slowly, I raise my arms, hands together, a V toward the sky, bend and spring, and the water glances my hands and arms and body until I'm under the green water, swimming and swimming. I blink and hold my breath, thinking of Alan and Saul, LuLu and Royal, Minnie and Mama, and finally James. The surface seems far away, and I swim farther down, switches of grass and seaweed catching at my hair. Small air bubbles float off above me, my own, and I let myself drift and rise to the surface. And in the wavering glassy light, I remember, as if calling then back to now, as if I were once again ten years old.

Below me, Alan stands looking toward the horizon. The top of his head is dark and sleek, and my feet are on either side of his shoulders, my ankles just below his ears. From this position I mark height and depth, width and what later I understand as arc, getting ready for our very first dives. I can feel him underneath me, relaxed, never tense, and he speaks quietly, instructing me on balance and timing. We are like arrows, attentive and deliberate, our future directions certain. I realize how certain Alan would have been in the moving column of men the night he died. How the dive I made from his shoulders and the one he made after mine would never have saved his life. How staying underwater and not surfacing at all wouldn't ever bring him back.

The lake is dark green with memory, the kind that makes me wonder if I'll ever leave this place. LuLu, Royal, Mama, Alan. They left so easily, each for a distinct reason, all with adventure in mind. I know well how unadventurous I am. Art classes in a college in the same town I've lived in most of my life—that's as daring as it gets. Anna Clara is the haven, Sybelia Drive the sanctuary, the geography of my past. And it's clear to me what happened and how things came to pass, but the future is a hazy thing. Life never turns out how I think it will, and so I don't hope for too much, and then I'm surprised if more comes my way.

Like James and this day. The boy I met aboard a bus on a rainy afternoon, the boy who was spared monsoon season in Vietnam, the boy who'd become a man well before the time he asked me to marry him. And now the rain comes down, harder and harder, just like it did the day we met, and later, the day he proposed. I swim back to the beach behind our house, step onto the sand, and with nightgown and umbrella in hand walk over roots and fallen twigs across the lawn. I recognize this might always be the way. Taking one step at a time.

On the porch LuLu and James stand, drinking mugs of coffee, watching me climb naked up the steps. I give James a kiss on the mouth and my umbrella, and I take LuLu's coffee because I know she makes hers with extra cream. Neither says a word, and then they sweep up the sand I trail across the floors.

I stand in the shower, my head swimming with lost time. LuLu pokes her head into the bathroom and yells something I can't understand. That she's going somewhere.

"Where?" I call.

By the time I pull the curtain back, she's shut the door. The small room is steaming up, and the cat has slipped in. She approaches the swaying curtain, stretching and taking her time. James calls her CoCo, and I haven't asked if he's riffing on the cold drink or the designer. Several weeks ago, the cat wandered out of the grove and invited herself in, her golden eyes oblique and her tortoiseshell pattern mostly black. At first I was charmed. But these days when she perches atop the furniture and curves around my legs, I don't reach down and say her name. Instead, I hear myself nearly shouting "I see you over there" and "Don't even think about it" and "Go away!" Her claws are destined for the vinyl shower curtain, my bare legs, and—the reason the closet door in our bedroom is shut tight—my long, lace wedding dress. As soon as she nears the curtain, though, she turns and lies down on the bath mat. This is always the way. She is lazy and wants nothing to do with my imagination. For that, I'm grateful.

I lean back under the stream of hot water, then twist the porcelain HOT and COLD handles from ON to OFF. The pipes squeak and sigh, the 1930s plumbing challenged but still functioning. I pull the towel down from the curtain rod and curtain rings spin and sing. The air is moist and my mind is saturated with everything to come—the day, the months and years ahead. Ridiculous hopes, incredible fears, and yes, the need for a storybook ending. I laugh at myself. So there's the ending, and what happens then?

In the next room I hear an album placed on the stereo. The dust and crackle against the needle, then Smokey Robinson and the Miracles. I dry off and throw a dress over my head. I'm out of the bathroom and almost at the bedroom door when James intercepts me for a dance in the hallway. He slides his hand down my waist, the other in my wet, tangled hair, and sings "Ooo" in a sweet fake falsetto. I laugh and let him twirl me and kiss me and slowly let me go. The song ends too quickly, our final steps in the living room, and he whispers, "I have a surprise for you." And I say back, "I know."

He keeps disappearing into the garage, where he's set up a darkroom. I can guess what he's doing out there, but I don't even want to try. I don't want to ruin the way his eyes light up every time he says, "I've got a surprise."

He turns up the stereo, opens the window closest to our driveway, though in his closed room of shadows and chemical trays and one little red light, the music is always faint. His coffee in hand, he steps outside. All couples must have, over their long lives together, a tumble of secrets. So many that if housed in the smallest of darkrooms, they'd have to take the form of two-by-threes, tiny and bordered with white, easily hidden away in drawers. I foresee ours over the years: CoCo and her kittens, spilling out into the drive; Mama and Minnie, lost in laughter; Royal and Saul in a two-man canoe on the lake; LuLu and her search for happiness, apparent in postcards from around the world. But those aren't secrets; they are records and predictions caught through a pinhole and saved on shiny, thumb-printed slips of paper.

LuLu has come back. The sound of tires, a door slamming—her ride in a stolen station wagon accomplished. I hear her jangling something, moving things around, and realize she is in James's and my bedroom. When I peer in, she's closing the drawer of the bedside table. Our lack of words is really her lack. What can I say? And then I realize she hasn't seen or heard me, and I shrink back inside the doorway, then into the hallway, and turn for the kitchen so she'll have no idea that I've seen her. There's irony in this decision; I understand this. Then why am I behaving like the one caught, the one who should escape unseen? It's just that I want her act to remain secret until I can be sure of what she's done, and in this, once again, I'm yielding to LuLu, always her accomplice. I'm sure she's taken something: one of the scallop shells from Mama's visit to West Palm, after Hurricane Dolly spilled shells onto the beach; a turquoise barrette LuLu would never clip into her close-cropped hair; a postcard she had sent from the Santa Monica Pier; the silver MIA band to remind me of my daddy.

I stand in the kitchen as if I am the thief, guilty and ashamed. I don't want to storm back in and accuse her. It's too exhausting. And so I wait until I hear the gentle closing of a door and the slight catch and slam of the screen door off the porch. I pad through the house and see LuLu walking toward the lake in her suit, to take the swim I'd taken earlier. It's stopped raining, and the day is still overcast, but brightening.

Alone in the bedroom, I pull the drawer open. The pale pine sticks the tiniest bit, and the lamp tips when I pull harder. I steady the lamp and turn it on. Of the things I placed inside the drawer months before, every single one is still there. And now I am startled. Other things have been added: a small black duck call, its inscription faded; a gold pencil that twists to open; a yellowing seed packet filled with zinnia seeds. I wonder if they will still grow. Things LuLu had stolen years ago, mostly from neighbors along Sybelia Drive. Her treasures. It's clear that she's been snooping, going through our drawers, reaching for the highest shelves, looking under beds. Seeing who we've become. How else would she have known about this bedside drawer and the kinds of things inside?

I reach down for the most surprising treasure of all, the one she didn't steal, the one I gave her. The charm bracelet originally given to me by Mama just before our move to Florida. Each charm carried her guilt, not for my father's absence, but for her own. After years of feeling as though I had to wear it, I'd grown tired of the burden and one day fastened it around LuLu's little wrist. From then on it went back and forth between us, all the way through high school, until eventually LuLu didn't take it off, its sweet shining song her own signature sound. The rose-gold dogs and daisies, the roller skates and stars jingle and chime, as I lift the bracelet from the drawer and slip it around my wrist to the furthest link. Meant for a little girl, it just fits. I hold out my arm to let the ornaments sway and swing, and the cat appears. The bracelet catches her eye and she jumps on the bed and tries for a closer angle, batting at the gold bits and pieces.

I move away from her and remember the open drawer, how she'd love to send the shells flying and take the seed packet in her teeth, the rattle so tempting, chase it around the house, finally shredding the old paper and spilling seeds over the floor. As I reach to push in the drawer, the bright colors of the postcard call to me—the white spokes of the Ferris wheel, the reds and yellows of the gondolas, the background wash of brilliant sky. I turn the card over. It's addressed to Rainey, but no last name, and underneath, Sybelia Drive, but no house number. And in the spot for the message, no words, just a heart filled with Xs and Os. LuLu and her impossible, complicated love. I'm overwhelmed and sad and frightfully happy all at once. And suddenly I want to be with her one more time, just the two of us, before the dizzying reel of wedding-day preparations begins.

I wander through the house, take a half-eaten piece of toast from a plate in the dining room, knowing I should be thinking more about the late afternoon, the flowers and rings and champagne and cake. The toast is loaded with the bittersweet marmalade LuLu loves, and again I feel the sweep of sadness brush against how glad I am. I take the last bite and keep going, on through the living room, push open the screen door and pad barefoot across our yard of wet clover and sparse grass down to the lake. LuLu is lying on the dock and pointing at the mottled white sky like it's a prize just for her, and singing a song that sounds made-up but is some version of "Dead Flowers."

Though I'm terrible at manning a canoe alone, I flip ours over and push the bow into the lake. I step into the stern, oar in hand, another oar on the floor, and balance as I push off from shore. With one leg out of the canoe, one leg in, I hear LuLu yelling in my direction, "I know you think you're the queen of this little town!" Somehow, I manage not to fall into the lake, to find the bench seat and sit on the cool metal, and to slide the oar in and out of the water, bracelet jangling, making my way. At the floating dock LuLu reaches for the painter, loops it around the ladder, a lazy hitch for tying up. She holds the side of the canoe, and when I step out, she whispers in my ear that she'll send me dead flowers at my wedding.

"I know you will," I say, batting my eyes at her. "I'll carry them up the aisle."

"You'd better," she says and laughs.

I don't wait any longer. I'm afraid if I do, I'll lose the chance. "LuLu?"

"What, Rain-Rain?" she says and twists her fingers through the halter straps of her swimsuit. "What, oh-mighty-queen-for-a-day?"

"I want you to know something."

"Are you gonna get all sweet and sad on me? Oh, no..."

"I might." I smile. She knows me so well.

"Well, get on with it then."

"I just wanted to tell you that no matter what, you'll always be my best friend. And I'll miss you when you leave."

"Oh, rain-down-on-my-parade Rainey. You're too funny. You know you've got a new best friend. And you even get to marry him." She screws up her face and punches me softly. Like she always has. "Anyhow, can't marry me, now can you?"

A momentary burst of sun glints off the lake, and I shade my eyes. "That's different. You and me, we've known each other so much longer. Years and years."

"Jesus." She throws out her hands and arms like she's on stage, then sashays across the dock, making it bounce. "Years and fucking years. How did we get so old?"

No matter what, she'll never take me seriously. And then she is the one who gets all serious. She stops her dance and stares out at the island of cypresses.

"Remember Alan and that day he first taught you to dive?"

"'Course I do." After Alan died, I thought of that day all the time, just as I had earlier this morning. The memory of that day has only become clearer, especially since moving into the cottage with James, with our view of the floating dock, of the world so utterly the same and so completely changed from when I first stepped across the Blackwood threshold.

"You were perfect then. The way you knew how to listen, the way you barely touched the water." She looks at me and crosses her eyes. "Of course you're still perfect."

"I'm not." I try my best not to cry. "I'm not at all. And I still miss Alan."

"Me too." She backs up to the diving platform and sits there, facing me. "And I miss Titus and, Jesus, I even miss Lyman. Remember how I didn't cry when James told us Titus was in his squad, that the same fire that wounded James killed Titus?" Her words cluster together like sad children holding hands. "I never ever did cry. I felt hollow and stupid and lonely. And selfish and even mean." She tucks her legs to her chest and hugs her calves. "But when Saul called me and told me Lyman had finally gone, I had to call off from work for two nights. I was a mess. That dog didn't even like me, he liked Saul, and still I couldn't believe it. I cried and cried until my roommates gave up trying to help me feel better. But nothing doing. Nothing helped."

"It's because he was Alan's dog."

"What?"

"When the news came that Alan had been killed, we were little. We didn't know how to be sad about a boy. When we saw Mrs. Walbright breaking all those cups and plates and pretty glass things in her driveway, we still didn't understand he was really gone. It just seemed like he went away and then never came back. And his dog was still around, and as long as Lyman was wandering around Sybelia Drive, then, to us, Alan wasn't really gone."

"Oh. I hadn't ever thought about it that way."

"I hadn't either. Not until James asked me about what it was like to grow up here. And then all these memories came flying back."

"Sounds awful." LuLu smirked.

"Shut up. It was awful and wonderful. And it's my wedding day, so I can be sentimental."

From a section of beach around the bend on the lake, we hear "Hello!" Saul is waving, Hélène Laurent at his side. She, too, is waving her black walking stick. Her white hair is in its typical French twist, and she seems more hearty than frail, standing upright, one hand laced through Saul's arm. Ever since he enrolled in college and then grad school, a way to avoid the draft, though conscription ended well before his number could be called up, they've spent time together. Hélène has adopted Saul as her companion, paying him for the favor in tea and savings. Saul says he initiated the visits, and that she mocks him and he takes it. She tells him every time he comes to her door, her French accent grazing the edges of her words, "You didn't get war, but you got me." Every afternoon they walk partway around the lake, looking for small white Jack-in-the-pulpit flowers and large blue herons, and talk about history. Dynasties and royal elephants, tea imports and the gun trade and government lies, the French, the Vietnamese, the Americans. That's Saul's thing now, what happened and why.

We wave back and LuLu shouts as loud as she can, one hand in mine, raising it to the sky like I'm a featherweight who's just won a fight, the other cupped around her mouth, "Rainey is getting married today, but she's wasting time with me!" And then to the sky: "She swims naked in the lake, and she's my best friend forever and fucking ever."

Saul laughs and Hélène shakes her head, disapproving maybe, most likely just puzzled.

LuLu lowers our hands and notices the bracelet, her fingers glancing the gold links and ornaments. She hugs me hard and again the dock tips and springs, its anchor holding it in place. I hug her back and kiss her cheek, so that she has to push me away. Then she and I climb into the canoe, each taking up an oar, and dip and stroke and glide across the water back to shore.

Beyond the lake house that once belonged to Royal's grandfather, then his father, then Royal, and now where Saul lives, the deep yard is bordered by azalea bushes and birch trees. It's a good place for a man who loves history, its walls and ceilings and views of Lake Sybelia set with the smoke and history of the Blackwood men. Beneath one stand of trees is a row of rabbit hutches, the ones Royal and LuLu built. Inside are the dark brown dwarves and the dusty, lighter brown lops Royal insisted on having once he returned from Vietnam. And in the largest hutch, white and gray and silken, the lone Rex. Every week, especially when James is away on assignment, I walk the short distance between our cottage and the lake house, and I hold one of the rabbits, the smallest dwarf, even though she tends to nip. She settles into the curve of my neck and sleeps while I talk to Saul and, on occasion, to Hélène. She is a fixture in the afternoon shade of the yard, resting after their walk, her black cane leaning against her lawn chair.

On an afternoon in late summer, just a few months back, Hélène closed her eyes and listened, while Saul and I talked. About things we hoped for, about things to come. About what Saul wants to do—teach—and what I'd like in the long run—simple things. A family, to stay in one place, to work in the art gallery, to have all my friends nearby, though

I know how rare this is. How with James's success, a city like New York may be in our future.

"Man-fucking-hattan. You don't want to end up there," Saul said.

"Not end up. Just visit for a while. A Greenwich Village flat, or a big-windowed apartment on the Upper West Side, with a guest room of course." I laughed a little at the thought, yellow taxis and skyscrapers twisting through my mind. "James loves it here, though. We'll see."

"Maybe you do need an adventure." He motioned to the trees, the clouds, the lake, and shook his head. His hair, once shoulder-length, always in his face, was now much longer and tied back, revealing the high forehead, the definite set of his jaw. "Something more than this place has to offer."

"Go to Paris! Go to Saigon! Go to hell!" Hélène offered her advice to the branches above, then closed her eyes again, sighing.

I smiled at Saul, who also looked amused.

"Well, so far," I said, "LuLu is the one who does adventure. I'm surprised you haven't made your way, too. Someplace exotic, faraway, full of ancient ruins."

"I might." And he paused so that the next word seemed a lie. "Eventually."

The sun moved from behind a cloud and pressed its heat onto us. Suddenly awake, the rabbit nudged its face farther into the hollow of my throat and resettled. I felt hot and uncomfortable and knew it wasn't the afternoon, but something in Saul's tone.

"I'd miss you." He laced his fingers together and apart. "I'm sorry, but I would. I already do."

"Oh," I said at first. And then: "I'm here, but—you know." I stopped myself from going on. More wouldn't help.

Hélène, her head angled, feigned sleep. Her fingers tapped against the curve of her cane, perhaps keeping time, perhaps counting the number of times she'd caught me with Saul, years before.

James and I had announced the wedding date a few weeks before. In his honesty, perhaps Saul was just resettling, like the rabbit. Trying to find a way closer, pushing toward the past, the hollowed-out, vulnerable places we once went. Always introspective, he leaned toward melancholy, but also romanticism—college versions of who we'd once been. Before, we were kids, at first cautious, then distrustful, experimental teenagers, looking for love and answers, fumbling in the dark, even in daylight. In confusion, in curiosity, I'd reached beyond Saul to other boys. That I'd met James upended the confusion, set it right, level and clear, like looking into crystal waters through a glass-bottomed boat. Saul, as much as I'd loved him, as much as I still loved him, skirted the dark and mysterious, while James knew of light as well as dark, in photography, in war, in love.

"Saul?"

He seemed to consider his crossed ankles, and I remembered how we first met. Strangers, thrown together—Mrs. B's smoke and laughter, Saul standing in the doorway of his room, LuLu barefoot and chattering, my mother whispering, "Bye-bye, baby. I'll see you in a few days." The Blackwoods like a testing ground.

"I love you and LuLu so much. I always will." And by bundling my love for them, I moved on.

I stood and handed Saul the rabbit, unhappy to be moved from its sleeping spot. That he took the little creature and sat with her a while, looking at me without a smile or a frown, gave me the idea he was fine. Even as I walked away, turning once to see him stroke her russet ears and stare after me.

Strangely, the day doesn't fly by the way I believed it might. From the morning swim to the early lunch with Mama, James, and LuLu, the moments trail past in slow sweeps, each one sweet, sad, amazing, and nearly happy. As if happiness is like the lacework of a wedding dress, that a stitch could come loose in the whole fabric of what up until now is my life, and then everything might unravel. Is it because my daddy won't walk me down the aisle? Or is it the thought that wakes me at night, the idea that James is someone I don't deserve? Or is it that LuLu will surely whoop and holler the minute James and I are pronounced husband and wife, to keep herself the center of attention?

After lunch, I lie down like Mama tells me to. "You need to rest up for later," she says, patting my arm and glancing at James. I wonder if she means for the wedding or later-later. Of course she means both.

I don't sleep, but close my eyes. And in a while, I hear James come in and then feel the mattress shift as he lies down next to me. I blink and look into his eyes, so trusting, so close to mine, and he kisses me. His hand traces the length of my legs and slides inside my dress, and we are warmth and breath in the dim, curtained afternoon, slowly, sweetly in the sooner and then the later-later of lovemaking. Across the valley of James's chest and shoulders are the scars from his wound, the one that brought him home early from Vietnam. I lay my head against a shoulder and sigh, and he tells me he loves me. Then he says, "Open your eyes, pretty Rainey, and see your surprise."

Across the room, on the wall that divides two windows, is a large photograph, black-and-white but also moving with color, the frame wide and expressive and swirled with pattern. I sit up, my hands pressing into the covers, and turn to kiss James one more time before moving to the end of the bed for a closer view.

LuLu and I stand in the center, together yet apart, and we are surrounded by smaller figures. Saul and Royal and Minnie, Mama and Daddy, Alan and Lyman and Titus, even James himself, and all our friends that live around Lake Sybelia. Two girls in that in-between age, still grounded in childhood and wanting so badly to be all grown up. Two girls, best friends, inside the design of a place and its people, a mosaic of red and white swimsuits, the military drab of uniforms, the spinning hues of our mothers' dresses. Two girls, nearly sisters, looking out beyond the mirrored moments—the way to school, the grove at the back of our houses, the winding circle of cypresses and sand beaches and wooden docks that lead around and down to the lake.

I follow the intricate details with my fingers just above the glass of the print. Little pictorial revelations encircle and fold themselves inside even more astonishing images. Minnie and me, tying wine bottles to the oak outside her house, their colors swimming. LuLu sitting in an orange tree, the black duck call in her mouth, her brown eyes keen, her face lifted and laughing. Mama waving at the camera, her red bikini as brilliant as her smile. Royal holding the dwarf rabbit, Titus standing by his truck, Saul lying in glaring sunlight on the floating dock. Hélène Laurent staring straight ahead, a mass of camellias, obscured and out of focus before her. Alan after a hunt, shotgun and a string of ducks in either hand, Lyman at his side. Lillian Walbright, Minnie, Vita, Esther Wild all together, holding tall drinks and looking amused. A field of buttercups, seashells scattered between tree roots, LuLu's swim patches—minnow, dolphin, flying fish.

"How did you do this?" I ask.

"So you like it?" James says. He is leaning against the headboard and watching me.

"I love it! Thank you so much." I turn and jump onto the bed and kiss his forehead, his cheeks, his beautiful lips. "It's incredible. Where in the world did you find all these images?"

He laughs. "From here and there. LuLu helped."

I look back to the collage of photos and realize out loud, "Of course she did."

I envision LuLu stealing pictures from neighbors' deep and shallow drawers, from inside frames propped on bedside tables, from albums in her own parents' house. And then I understand she's asked for them, that everyone who knows us is giving this gift, making it even more astonishing. I curl myself against James, and we look together at the combined patterns and portraits, set in place by the windows on either side like a triptych, a view we'll always have upon waking and before falling asleep.

Late afternoon light falls through the venetian blinds in stripes of sun and shadow across the cottage floors. In my slip, I wander the rooms already chirping with Mama's and Minnie's calls back and forth, soon to be full of voices and high heels, bow ties and laughter. It's decided the outdoor wedding will now be inside, given the unpredictable weather, the yard still damp from the morning rains. My lace dress lies across our bed, the heels Mama brought over at its foot, both safe from the cat. James, at my request, has taken her to Hélène's house, where the stone porch is as familiar as the grove outside.

In the living room, arrangements of white daisies and cream-colored roses offset by bright clusters of small autumn sunflowers are here and there. The cake, three-tiered and covered in marzipan buttercups, sits on a corner table in the dining room. "No tacky bride and groom on this marvel," Mama says, admiring her design.

LuLu is humming loudly in the guest room, and I peer in. She is tucking multitudes of silver bobby pins into her short wet hair, and curious, I approach her and see they are mine. Each one adorned with a tiny yellow flower, the ones that are to be used to pin up my hair.

"You like?" she says, kissing the air between us.

"Aren't those from my dresser?"

"Yep."

She spins a single pin on the surface of the bedside table, and it flies across the room and lands by my bare feet. I bend to pick it up just as she does, and we bump just hard enough. Not enough to see stars, but to wonder why. And then I let go of the question and hold out the bit of silver.

"You want this one, too?"

She takes it from me. "Nice slip," she says, eyeing the ivory satin, and clipping my last bobby into an inch of blond just over her left ear.

Mama calls, "Rainey, where are you, baby?" That it's past time to do up my hair.

LuLu follows me into the hallway, and Mama doesn't see her. Gently, she pulls me by the wrist into the lakeside bedroom and looks around. "Well?" She starts opening drawers. "I thought you'd set them out."

"Mama, stop." I point to LuLu in the doorway, spinning in her saffron dress, its field of white polka dots making us dizzy. "Look in LuLu's hair."

"An innocent accident," LuLu says.

"An act of thievery, you mean." Mama has her hands on her hips.

From her work in the kitchen, Minnie appears, done up in pearls, an apron around her waist. She puts her hands around LuLu's throat and pretends to strangle her. "Get in there, LuLu. You little pincushion!"

LuLu laughs out loud and lowers her head, silver with hairpins, and Mama plucks them out, one by one. "Bring us some champagne, Minnie." And in the mirror, she winks at LuLu and me. "Let's start this party, why don't we?"

One glass later, my hair is arranged, a few tiny daisies slipped in at the last minute by LuLu with no one arguing. I step into my dress, and Mama gathers and loops the sash at the back. In the mirror I check her work, and she notices my jewelry. "Baby girl," she says, touching the bracelet, taking the gold heart between her fingers. By the time I stand in my heels, we hear voices and music in the adjoining rooms.

Minnie unties her apron and says to LuLu, "Your turn next, Miss Lu."

LuLu shakes her head and says to me, "What? Getting hitched? No way, José."

Mama shoos LuLu to one side, and then pulls me forward and kisses my cheeks, one peck on each, which she's always called sophisticated and European. "All grown up and getting married." She smiles and holds my chin like she did when I was little. "Your daddy would be so proud. You know I am, baby, don't you?"

"Yes, Mama."

She turns me in a circle, making sure everything is just so. Then says, "You ready?"

I nod, and she sweeps out of the room, making an entrance into our hall and living room, already crowded with guests. LuLu peeks out and waves to someone to come over. Saul appears in a jacket studded with brass buttons and a patterned tie and, most startling, his hair cut short and combed back. I'm so surprised I cover my mouth so I don't scream, but then I say, "Saul!" And his name flies into the hall like a bird, bright and unbelievable.

"Rainey!" Saul teases me by shouting my name just as loudly.

LuLu is beside herself laughing. "I can't believe you did it!"

"You dared me. That's all it took." Saul straightens his tie, one of the first he's ever worn, and I see it matches LuLu's dress.

"I just said to clean yourself up for James and Rain-Rain's little party. Jeez, Saul."

"Well, I'm so glad you did," I say. I hug Saul, and LuLu squeezes between us.

The stereo goes quiet, Sinatra and the Supremes traded for a surprise. I know for sure it's LuLu's doing when the first notes of "Dead Flowers" come clear into the bedroom. She hands me a bouquet of her making, beach daisies and wild roses, like she's awarding me a gold star.

"Come on, dummies," she says. "Let's do this thing."

With their arms linked through mine, LuLu and Saul march me "down the aisle" into the living room, the sun settling over the heads of the guests, everyone there, everyone smiling, especially James. A hush comes upon the room when the song ends, and there's sadness and peace inside the smiles. For those missing, for new beginnings. And outside as darkness falls, the evening's first fireflies rise and fly, blinking, like wishes and promises, like LuLu's gold stars, heading up and out, circling, coming and going, and tracing their way back again.

ACKNOWLEDGMENTS

The love and gratitude travels far and wide.

Thank you to my agent, Valerie Borchardt of Georges Borchardt Literary Agency, for her sensibility, guidance, wit, and, most of all, for believing. Sincere appreciation to my publishers/editors, Jeffrey Condran and Robert Peluso, at Braddock Avenue Books. My publicist, Lori Hettler, deserves applause for her enthusiasm and juggling acts. Because of her, the book will venture farther. Love and leaps to Annie Russell for the beautiful cover art and interior illustrations and to Savannah Adams for the brightest of book designs.

To my teachers, the utmost appreciation: Michelle Herman, for daring me to write something new all those years ago. Lee Martin, for leading me to understand more about my characters than I thought I could. Laurie Foos, for telling me truthfully that I was writing a novel, not a series of stories. Connie May Fowler, for helping me to understand a way through. Nancy Zafris, for every ounce of your teaching. Tom Jenks, for the wisdom and direction. Jill McCorkle and Steve Yarbough, for the praise and nods that have sent me on my way.

And to the teachers who are no longer with us, but whose influence lives on and on, I'm beyond indebted: Lee K. Abbott, who knew how to keep it real, for "the lady on the bus," and Wayne Brown, for true windward direction.

To my friends, fellow writers, and readers, who all had a hand, and an occasional arm, in this book, wide-open, outrageous thanks: Seth Borgen, seriously, so many thanks for the hours of reading, for the laughter in between. Mark Fabiano, for the unparalleled patience and honesty and heart. Fritz McDonald, for the years of encouragement. Lauren Inness Norton, for another kind of perspective. Mark Edwards, Alicia Hyland, Brian Liddy, Chaney Kwak, and Hilary Zaid—for your friendship and truth.

To the editors who refined and published several chapters of *Sybelia Drive* as stories, sincere and celebratory appreciation: Leslie Jill Patterson of *Iron Horse Literary Review*, Anthony Hagen and Robert Kingsley of *The Rappahannock Review*, Mary Akers of *R.kv.r.y Quarterly Literary Journal*, Cara Blue Adams of *Waccamaw Journal*, Terry Kennedy of *storySouth*, and Stephanie G'Schwind of *Colorado Review*, as well as Lauren Matheny for her beautiful reading of "Rock Salt and Rabbit" and Kylan Rice for his precise, thoughtful interview on the *Colorado Review Podcast*.

To the USMC Combined Action Patrol veterans who provided invaluable information and resources, along with the writers whose books influenced and inspired the language and landscape of much of this novel, profound gratitude: William R. Corson – *The Betrayal*, Al Hemingway – *Our War Was Different*, Al Santoli – *Everything We Had*, Bing West – *The Village*, Gregory R. Clark – *Words of the Vietnam War*, Bernard Edleman, Ed. – *Dear America*, Bill Adler, Ed. – *Letters from Vietnam*, Donna Moreau – *Waiting Wives*, Bobby Ann Mason – *In Country*, Ho Xoan Huang – *Spring*

Essence (trans. John Balaban), Tim O'Brien – *The Things They Carried*, and Yusef Komunyakaa – *Dien Cai Dau*.

To the Ohio Arts Council, The Studios of Key West, the Sewanee Writers' Conference, the Kenyon Review Writers Workshop, and the Vermont College of Fine Arts, my deepest thanks for the awards that allowed the time, space, and freedom to begin and end this novel. And to the Lesley University MFA Program in Creative Writing, unbounded appreciation for the path I'm still following.

To my family—Anne, Barbara, Brad, Catherine, Lacey, Liz, and Lee—and to the poet, film editor, dancer, and soprano in my life—Brad, Tim, Marlene, and Maddie—heaps of love.

To Cecile and Mary Mason, thank you for the sun, lakes, and citrus groves of my childhood, the novel's sense of place.

To Hannah, Zak, and John, straight to the moon and back again, love, love, and more.

Karin Cecile Davidson is originally from the Gulf Coast and now lives in Columbus, Ohio. Her stories have been published in *Five Points*, *The Massachusetts Review*, *Story Magazine*, *Colorado Review*, *The Los Angeles Review*, *Passages North*, and elsewhere. She is the recipient of an Ohio Arts Council Residency at the Fine Arts Work Center in Province-town, an Atlantic Center for the Arts Residency, a Studios of Key West Artist Residency, an Ohio Arts Council Individual Excellence Award, the Orlando Prize for Short Fiction, the Waasmode Short Fiction Prize, and a Peter Taylor Fellow-ship. She has an MFA from Lesley University and is Inter-views Co-Editor for *Newfound Journal*.

Author photo by Angela Liu.

CPSIA information can be obtained
at www.ICGtesting.com
Printed in the USA
FSHW011824150521
81426FS